AFTER THE END

Bonnie Dee

Published 2010

ISBN 978-1-45631-602-0

This is a work of fiction. Names, characters, places, brands, media, and incidents are either the product of the author's imagination or are used fictitiously. The author acknowledges the trademarked status and trademark owners of various products referenced in this work of fiction, which have been used without permission. The publication/use of these trademarks is not authorized, associated with, or sponsored by the trademark owners.

Manufactured in the United States of America

Cover Photograph by
Jinjian Liang

This is a work of fiction. The characters, incidents and dialogues in this book are of the author's imagination and are not to be construed as real. Any resemblance to actual events or persons, living or dead, is completely coincidental.

AFTER THE END

BY

BONNIE DEE

CHAPTER ONE

Through the binoculars, a zombie was even uglier than when seen up close and personal. Of course, when they were near, you didn't generally have time to study them too carefully. There were other things to do—like screaming and running. From a distance it was safe for Ari to let his gaze wander over the creature's rotting skin, its flat, vacant eyes and slack-jawed yokel mouth. Blood stained the lower half of its face, coating cheeks and chin and nearly obliterating the Alpha Kappa Beta logo on the upper half of the thing's sweatshirt.

An "after" then. He could usually tell by the clothes a "before" corpse from one that had been turned after the first wave. Who would bury their beloved Brenda or Beth in a sorority sweatshirt? Most of the first generation zombies wore suits or dresses since they'd come to the banquet from mortuary viewings or funeral services. Or they were naked cadavers straight from the slab at a hospital or city morgue.

The people they'd infected rather than completely devoured tended to wear more casual clothes and generally had a bite or two taken out of them. And wasn't it an amusing sight to see a little girl in shorts and shirt and daisy-decorated sandals munching on an arm held in one hand like a turkey drumstick.

Ari adjusted the binocs, bringing the zombie sorority sister into sharper focus. He immediately wished he hadn't. Her hair remained in patchy, random clumps on her half-scalped head. Bright pink streaks and little sparkling clips decorated some of the long blonde strands. Adorable. She tossed her hair back from her face with a girlish flip and reached for another length of intestine from the body she was eating.

Lucky dead guy wouldn't be staggering to his feet and perpetuating the cycle any time soon.

The zombie's milky gray eyes suddenly turned toward Ari and for a second it was as if she was looking directly at him. His heart stuttered and he nearly dropped the glasses.

"Fuck!" He jerked the binoculars away from his eyes as if not seeing her would hide him, and then he snorted at his stupidity. Of course, she couldn't see him from blocks away. He was well hidden in his perch on the fifth floor of an office building. Even if the thing had glimpsed a flash of light on the glasses, she wouldn't be able to interpret it as a pair of binocs. The creatures weren't that smart.

"Hey, Captain!" The voice coming from behind made him jump and the binoculars slipped from his fingers to clatter on the floor.

"Jesus, don't do that!" He turned to face Derrick. The kid was as jittery as a meth junky without a fix in sight.

"What is it?" Ari dreaded the answer.

"It's Mrs. Scheider. We think it's almost time. Can you come?"

Ari picked up the glasses and took a last glance at the zombie girl and her victim. She was on her hands and knees, head down, burrowing into the man's abdominal cavity like a dog with a particularly good treat. He pulled the binocs from his eyes and packed them into their carrying case before rising. "All right, let's go. And Derrick..."

"Yeah?"

"Quit calling me 'captain'."

"Right."

As Ari followed the younger teenager from the office, a big, drooping, half-dead plant in the corner caught his attention. "Someone's not keeping up on their watering." He tried to put the kid at ease with a little joke—very little—but Derrick didn't crack a smile.

"Dr. Joe doesn't know what to do. Some of the others are saying we should...you know, take care of her right now. But we have to wait and see first, don't we? I mean we can't just kill her, can we?"

If Joe doesn't know, what makes you think I do? It was beyond him how the rest of them kept turning to him for answers and trusting him to make decisions for the group. He still believed it had all started because he was wearing his army uniform and he wished he'd never worn it that day he'd gone to meet Billy, C.C. and the other guys. The goddamn camouflage had somehow convinced everyone he was a man who could take charge and they listened to him as if he had some authority. Stranded souls, they'd been desperate for anyone to tell them what to do and suddenly that had been Ari. But he was only nineteen. The army hadn't said jack shit during basic training about what to do in case of a hostile zombie takeover.

His pulse pounded as he followed Derrick down five flights of stairs to the ground floor where the group was camped. In the conference room, they sat around a big table eating Hostess cakes, chips and slices of an apple they'd foraged from vending machines and desks. The office personnel had squirreled away little nutritious food in their drawers, which was too bad, because a diet of candy bars and soda wasn't helping jittery Derrick any.

Joe crouched beside Mrs. Scheider. The sick woman lay on a pile of folded coats and jackets someone had put together.

"What's up, doc?" Ari stopped himself from mimicking Bugs Bunny. Joking over a dying woman's body was harsh, but when he was keyed up he always made smart ass remarks. "How is she doing?"

Dr. Joseph Morgenstern, who wasn't really an M.D. but a dermatologist, shrugged and scratched at the stubble on his chin. "She regained consciousness for a little bit, but now she's out of it again. From her breathing, I don't think she's got much more time." He lowered his voice. "I'm so out of my element here. I have no idea what else to do for her. If we were in a hospital, I'd give her oxygen, but here..."

Ari nodded. Even if they'd administered oxygen a while ago or had an entire medical team working on Mrs. Scheider, he doubted it would have helped. But they couldn't have gone searching for a tank. It was too dangerous. There was no hospital or medical clinic nearby and even if there were, they'd be hopping with revenants.

"Hey, you're back." Lila's touch on his shoulder brought his head up fast. He looked into her unusual indigo eyes and his stomach gave a little flip. Because she'd taken him by surprise, he told himself, but he knew better. It was the way his body always reacted to seeing Lila, a stomach flip usually followed by a low burn in his groin.

"I see you found brunch for everybody," he said.

She tucked strands of her shoulder length, brown hair behind her ear. "Wasn't much to find. The ground floor had already been picked over. We gathered this stuff from the second floor. We'll have to have to raid a grocery store soon. We can't live on junk food."

He nodded and gazed down at the sick woman's face. She looked old, much older than she'd seemed at the beginning of all this. When was it? Only four days ago? Five? He'd nearly lost track. It seemed this had been their life forever, trekking through a dying city on their way to an uncertain future.

When he'd first seen Mrs. Scheider, she'd been one of those brisk, styled and pressed, white-haired women who could be any age from sixty to eighty. He'd looked right past her on the subway, his attention caught by a sexy, dark-haired chick and her friend sitting farther up the aisle. They were the kind of girls who talked and laughed too loud, enjoying drawing everyone's attention. He'd been happy to oblige because both girls were worth looking at.

The truth was, that day on the subway he'd noticed very few of the people he was traveling with now. He sure as hell wouldn't have struck up a friendship with any of them under normal circumstances. But that day on the subway things had veered far from normal.

Now, Mrs. Scheider looked about a hundred years old, or as if she was already halfway dead. Her skin was paper white, her cheeks sunken and her mouth seemed toothless. The once fluffy white hair was flat and dirty, the designer clothes torn and bloodied. Her chest hitched up and down and her breath rasped between parted lips.

"Too late for oxygen anyway," Dr. Joe said quietly. "We're going to have to be ready."

Meaning Ari was going to have to be ready. No one else would want to do what had to be done here—if it had to be done. Ari wasn't the only one who'd made a kill since this begin. Deb, Derrick, even Sondra had taken out some revenants. But killing one of their own was a different matter. Ari was a soldier so everyone assumed he was equipped to handle anything. He'd have to suck it up and do the job.

"Why don't you clear the room," Ari said.

"I'll do it." Lila squeezed his shoulder lightly and when she took her hand away, he still felt the warmth and pressure of it.

Behind him, he was vaguely aware of Lila talking to the others, chairs moving away from the conference tables, footsteps and voices receding from the room. But most of his attention was focused on the wheezing woman in front of him. He'd admired Mrs. Scheider's sharp tongue and dry humor and he'd miss it.

They'd had been scavenging in a diner, when the zombies came. The ax he'd taken from a store had come in useful in slashing a path through them. The blade cut cleanly through gristle and bone, severing heads like a weed-whacker churning through dandelions. He'd managed to escape along with the people in the front of the diner, while the rest of the crew, who'd been in the kitchen, ran out the back. Only when they came together several blocks away did they realize Mrs. Scheider wasn't with them.

Ari had gone back for her, running harder than he ever had on the obstacle course at Fort Benning. He'd found the woman hiding in a storage room and carried her back to where the others waited. Julie had cleaned the blood from her trembling body. Joe had stitched and bandaged her wound. And Ari had mentally kicked himself for allowing this to happen. He should've kept better watch. He should've kept them all safe. They were his responsibility now whether he liked it or not.

Lila was back now, joining in the vigil over Mrs. Scheider. She crouched beside Ari, her shoulder bumping his. "Do you need me to help?"

Ari looked into her exotic eyes focused on his like searchlights probing his secret thoughts. He shook his head. "No. I'll handle it. Please, just make sure everyone's staying calm and that Deb has set up perimeters. Don't want to get slack with security."

"All right." She rose and walked from the room. His gaze lingered on her backside before the door closed behind her. What kind of a sick perv checked out a girl's ass when a person was dying right in front of him? Especially when it was very likely he'd have to behead the poor old lady soon after she died.

Mrs. Scheider drew in another rattling breath and paused. Ari held his own breath, waiting for her to exhale. His hand tightened on the ax, and then air whistled out between her slack lips. He glanced at Joe. The other man was pale and looked like he'd rather be anywhere but here.

"Isn't there anything else you can do for her?" Ari asked. "I know we don't have morphine or anything, but…"

The dermatologist shook his head, locks of his gray-shot hair tumbling onto his forehead. His beard was growing in and his hair was shaggy. "There's nothing we can do but wait."

Ari sat back on his heels, the ax lying across his legs, and waited.

CHAPTER TWO

Ten days earlier...

Lila had her textbook, *World Religions in Practice: a Comparative Introduction*, propped open on her lap, but hadn't turned a page for the past ten minutes. Alternate scenarios for how last night could have gone kept playing out in her mind. She could've kept her temper. She could've not yelled stupid things she didn't really mean. She could've refrained from crying. She could've been cool and made the breakup as painless for them both as possible.

It wasn't like she hated Doyle or wished him pain. He'd been a good boyfriend, a good friend for two years. But their time was over. Both of them knew it, had known it for months now, but someone had needed to say the words. Since Doyle avoided confrontation of any kind, Lila had finally done it. Badly.

She stared out the window at the lights of the subway station flashing by, the advertisements on the wall and the people waiting on the platform. The train braked and the lights flickered. When the train stopped, the doors slid open and newcomers shuffled into the half-filled compartment. Lila hadn't needed to make room for anyone beside her yet, but probably would before she reached her stop.

She looked at the photograph of a gold-gilded Buddah on the page of her textbook then glanced at the soldier sitting across the aisle from her. He was looking at the two noisy girls a few seats ahead of them. Barbie and Babs, Lila had christened the duo, who talked high, fast and breathlessly. Maybe she was completely stereotyping and the girls were having a profound conversation about art, politics or the meaning of life, but from the snatches she'd overheard, she doubted it.

At any rate, the fembots seemed to have GI Joe captivated. He was a young guy with a compact build beneath his olive green T. His hair was close-shaven brown stubble. She wondered what he'd looked like before Uncle Sam got hold of him. Maybe he'd been the kind who always went for that shaven look. He had a good skull shape for it. Some guys didn't. And why was she staring at him and thinking about his hair, or lack of it?

Before she looked away, she noted the rest of his attire, camouflage pants and shirt with the sleeves rolled up, heavy lace-up boots, dog tags hanging against his chest. Was he expecting a battle right here in the city, or did the army make these guys wear the uniform even when they were off duty? He was probably young and foolish enough to be proud of the fascist military look.

Her gaze slid back to the serene-faced Buddha on the page of her book and she wished she'd remembered her Zen beliefs last night. She'd gone to meet Doyle at his place fully expecting to present the situation calmly and receive an equally peaceful agreement from her boyfriend. *Ex now*, she reminded herself. The man rarely got upset even when he was under a lot of pressure at the hospital where he worked, which from all accounts had been a madhouse recently due to the A7 virus. He was always reasonable. They rarely argued and when they did, their disagreements weren't heated. In fact, even as she'd told Doyle she thought they should break up, for a moment Lila couldn't remember why she was doing it. He really was so easy to get along with.

Then things had taken a strange turn. Even-tempered Doyle had lost it. He'd yelled and cursed and insulted her. Her adrenaline rising, Lila had yelled back. Things she hadn't known bothered her came spewing out. Before it was over, they were both displaying a passion their relationship had been sorely lacking for most of the time they were together.

Now that it was over, she felt a vague anxiety and melancholy and definitely regret for losing her temper, but nothing more powerful than that. She would miss having someone to do things with, a date she could count on, but beyond that she felt fairly confident Doyle would slide quickly and easily into the role of "a guy I used to date back in college." The thought made her sadder than the actual loss of him.

The train pulled out of the station, lights flickering again, and gathered steam as it clattered along the tracks. Lila brought her attention back to the text, which she really needed to read before class that afternoon. She concentrated for the length of a paragraph before looking up again.

A teenage boy and little girl who'd just boarded the train took the last empty seat in the back end of the compartment, the one in front of the soldier. The girl was asking the boy something and he was telling her to shut up. *Brother and sister*, Lila guessed.

Sitting directly in front of her, a fashionable, white-haired lady was focused on her magazine. An African American woman perhaps in her late twenties sat beside her. Lila tried to decide if the woman was wearing extensions in her abundant mass of braids.

She took a sip of her nearly empty coffee and stole another glance at GI Joe. He'd stopped watching the chatty Barbies and was staring out his window, legs sprawled in front of him, a backpack on the seat beside him. Lila smiled at the backpack, nothing military issue about it. The thing must be leftover from his high school days. The blue bag was decorated with signatures scrawled in black marker and a peeling bumper sticker of some local band.

Lila gave up trying to read and closed her book. She shoved it in her backpack, a neutral, unmarred navy, on the floor by her feet. As she leaned over to zip the bag closed, a shudder shook the car. She was thrown forward into the back of the seat in front of her then tossed back into her seat. Her neck snapped at the impact as the train came to an immediate, jolting stop. The lights went out, plunging the compartment into semi-darkness. Emergency light strips down the center of each aisle cast an eerie glow over the chaotic scene.

Cries and shouts resounded through the car. Piercing shrieks and "oh my Gods" came from the Barbie twins. Lila stood and craned her neck trying to see what was going on in the front of the compartment, but everyone else was rising too so she couldn't see anything except other people's backs and bobbing heads. She pressed her cheek close to the window, trying to look down the track, but the subway tunnel was too dark. Was this a collision or a derailment? Lila's heart pounded. She tried to calm down and reminded herself it could be worse. At least no one appeared to be hurt. The train couldn't have crashed into anything too hard. Maybe there'd simply been some massive power outage and they'd be stuck here for a while. She bent to pick up her backpack so she'd be ready if the conductor came to evacuate them.

Just then several loud screams cut across the babble of worried, excited voices. These weren't like the initial yells of surprise, but horrified screams of pain and fear.

"What the hell?" A low voice came from right beside her.

Lila turned to find GI Joe standing in the aisle beside her seat, staring toward the front of the car.

"What is it? What do you see?" she asked, climbing onto her seat to try to get a better view.

"I don't know, but I think we'd better—"

A woman's howling shriek was cut off, ending in a loud gurgle.

"We've gotta go, now!" The soldier grabbed Lila's arm and jerked her into the aisle with him. He shoved her behind him toward the door between compartments. It was closed. Lila's fingers scrabbled against glass and metal as she struggled to open it. As the screaming at the front of the car increased, she jerked the door open. Hands pushed against her back, propelling her into the space between cars. She tripped on the uneven metal floor, stumbled down the steps to the track, banging her knee against the edge of the car before her foot hit pavement. She was spun aside and slammed against the subway car as people shoved her out of the way..

In the dark, a hand grabbed her wrist and pulled. "This way."

"What is it? What's happening?" She didn't know if she'd said it or thought it. Questions repeated in a continuous loop in her head while the horrifying screaming inside the compartment went on and on. It wasn't just one or two voices now, but many as if a massacre were taking place.

"Over here." The soldier sounded confident and his hand was strong. Lila ran with him and so did some others. She could hardly see the other people in the dark, only feel their bodies pressing around her. They were running like a herd of gazelles racing before cheetahs. Jesus, what was happening back there? What was coming after them?

The man running beside her stopped so abruptly he nearly jerked her arm from its socket. He crouched and did something on the ground. Lila stared blindly at his dark shape and realized he was prying open a manhole grate. The crowd divided like water, flowing around them this way and that, but some people became aware of what he was doing and huddled around, waiting.

There was a clang of metal. The soldier rose and spoke quickly. "Whatever's on that train, I don't want to try to run from it straight down a tunnel. If we go into the storm sewer, maybe we'll have a better chance to escape."

The idea of descending into a pitch black abyss didn't seem like much of an alternative to running for the nearest station, but Lila could see his logic. If they couldn't outrun whatever was coming, they should hide. One man was already climbing into the hole. Lila's eyes had adjusted to the very dim light and she could make out the shapes of her fellow travelers enough to see that the next person clambering into the pit was the African American woman with the braids. Following her was her seatmate, the white-haired lady.

Lila turned to the teenage boy and his little sister standing beside her. "You going with them?"

"I guess." He stooped to talk to the girl, who was crying. She shook her head. Her brother grabbed her arms and his cajoling voice grew angry.

Lila looked back at the train, its huge silver body like the carcass of some great beast lying in the tunnel. Adrenaline, sharp as knives, lanced through her veins. Her heart pounded so hard her chest was tight and she could scarcely breathe. More people were spilling out of the subway cars both nearby and farther down the track. More yells and screams, muffled by the closed windows came from inside the compartments. As Lila watched, the silhouette of a person stumbled off the train and dropped to the pavement. The woman crawled across the ground, crying.

Lila took a step toward her to offer help then stopped. Another person was lurching down the steps right behind the woman. There was something wrong with the dark figure and the way it moved with a jerky gait like a marionette. Lila didn't know how she knew the person wasn't a victim. She just felt it.

The hair on Lilas's nape lifted and she backed away. Turning, she grabbed the little girl by one hand and the older boy by the arm. "Move! Now!" She pushed them toward the open manhole, where another man was just disappearing from sight.

"I'll pass your sister down to you," she promised the boy, and he began to climb the ladder. Before he'd gotten very far, Lila lifted the crying girl beneath the armpits and slung her into the pit. She glanced back at the lurching figure—several of them now moving alongside the train. One grabbed a running woman and pulled her close as if in a lover's embrace. Lila didn't see what happened next but screams rang in her ears.

The top of the ladder was clear so she began her own descent, her sandals slipping on the metal rungs. From below came the echoing sound of voices, hands reaching for her and helping her off the ladder.

"Something's coming," she gasped breathlessly. "Something—"

"Is that everyone?" The soldier was beside her. She caught a glimpse of his profile in the darkness as he looked up to the gray circle above.

"Close it! You'd better close it. Hurry!" The whole point of hiding down here would be lost if the—whatever those people were—spotted the open manhole cover.

GI Joe climbed back up the ladder, his body blocking the light overhead. He reached out and pulled the metal cover back into place. The black circle moved across the opening like an eclipse, plunging them into total darkness.

"What now? We can't even see," someone spoke above the little girl's sobbing.

"Anyone have a lighter or matches?" Lila knew the soldier's voice already. How could he sound so calm in the middle of this disaster?

"I do," came a young female voice, followed by the sound of someone scrabbling through a purse. Lila thought of her abandoned backpack, the comparative religions textbook which she knew she'd never see again. She stood in the darkness, listening to the muffled sounds of trauma and running footsteps overhead and felt the warmth of bodies all around her, heard the other people murmuring and moving.

The storm sewer smelled like a monkey house at the zoo, a potent, urine-soaked stench that singed her nostrils. Her body tensed and she fought against the urge to scream. A primitive fear of things that lurked in the dark twisted her gut, but surely nothing down here could be any worse than whatever horrible thing was happening up above.

Several people were whispering about terrorists and the possibility of some kind of massive strike on the city. One man suggested a fast acting, flesh eating virus and someone else told him to shut the hell up. Several people tried to make calls on their cell phones but of course there was no signal down here.

The girl with the lighter located it and struck a flame. In the tiny flickering light, Lila could see little beyond the brown face of the lighter's owner—the woman with the braids. She held the lighter out from her body to try to shed its glow on the space around them. It was less garbage-strewn and rat-infested than Lila had expected, which made sense. This was a storm drain, a run-off for rainwater, not an open sewer despite the smell of piss. Luckily there hadn't been rain in weeks and the concrete floor was pretty dry. The tunnel stretched in both directions like the subway above, disappearing quickly into blackness.

Lila counted ten in their group. In addition to the soldier, the brother and sister, and the two women from the seat in front of her, there was a tall, middle-aged man in a suit and an older Hispanic man wearing a Mets baseball cap. A pretty woman in a tailored blouse and slacks, whose hair straggled from its stylish twist stood with her arms folded protectively over her chest. Beside her was a man with crew cut white hair. The name tag on his gray industrial uniform proclaimed him "Omar Everett."

GI Joe scanned the tunnel in both directions and pointed to the right. "The nearest station would be that way. All we have to do is keep walking straight and we should get there in about ten minutes. We'll conserve the lighter. Only turn it on when necessary."

"No way," Everett said. "I'm not walking blind. We don't know when the next exit will be. We should wait here until whatever's happening quiets down, then go up and check things out."

"He's right," the woman with her pale blond hair in a bun agreed. "We have no idea what we'd be heading into in the dark. Besides, someone in authority will come soon to help. We should be nearby."

"I don't think anyone's coming," Lila said carefully. "At least not for a long time. We're probably on our own. Getting to the next station and then the street is our best bet."

"Look. We can stand here and argue or get moving, but either way, the lighter's going off. We'll need it later." GI Joe managed to sound absolutely confident without coming across as arrogant. The woman with the lighter doused it immediately.

"Maybe we should introduce ourselves." The blonde woman's voice sounded louder when they were all shrouded in darkness. "I'm Ann Hanson."

"I don't think it matters, lady. We can talk later. Right now we should just get the hell out of here!" The Latino accent gave away the speaker as the man in the Mets cap.

"I agree. We should go before someone finds us here," came the voice of the lighter owner.

Or some thing. Lila couldn't shake the image of that lurching shadow grabbing a woman and pulling her close. The shape had been human, but there'd been something very strange about the way it moved.

"Yeah, something seriously messed up is going on up there. No way should we stick around," the teenage boy mumbled.

"I don't want anyone crapping out halfway there. We can take turns carrying the kid. What about the lady with the white hair. Can you make it even if it's a few miles?" The soldier's voice sounded impatient now. Lila could tell he was frustrated and anxious to get moving.

"I'm perfectly capable of walking for ten minutes or ten hours if need be, young man, and you may refer to me as Mrs. Scheider rather than 'the lady with the white hair'." The woman's dry voice made Lila smile.

"All right. Let's move out. Hold hands with the person in front of and behind you." Once more GI Joe grabbed Lila's hand, scaring the crap out of her. Why did she always seem to be standing right next to him?

But Omar Everett wasn't done speaking his piece. "You all do whatever you want, but I'm staying here."

"Your choice," the soldier said, shortly. "Just don't go up until we're long gone. I don't want you giving away our location. Girl with the lighter, want to hand it over?"

"Deb," she said, and moved past Lila to surrender her lighter to the leader before linking hands with Lila. Her fingers were strong and warm. The soldier's hand was even stronger. It tugged insistently on Lila's, pulling her forward.

"Everyone holding onto someone else?"

A ragged chorus of affirmatives came from the group. Even the little girl had stopped sobbing, only an occasional hiccup coming from her.

Lila felt bad leaving Mr. Everett behind, alone in the dark. It didn't seem right. But no one else, including Ann Hanson, seemed inclined to leave the group to stay with him.

Walking forward, Lila instinctively kept her head ducked low. This was like one of those trust games intended to teach you to put your faith in other people, but which usually backfired when you stubbed a toe or barked your shin. She held tight to the soldier's hand and kept herself close behind his broad back. If anyone ran into something it would be him, not her—and wasn't that a selfish thought for someone who considered herself a kind, even spiritual person? When it came down to it, survivalist nature beat out pacifist ideals.

Deb's hand grew sweaty in hers as the group shuffled along holding hands like a chain of elementary schoolchildren on a field trip. Or a barrel of monkeys. Lila smiled at the silly image of red plastic monkeys linked together, and the smile nearly burst into uncontrollable giggles. She was on the edge of losing control and getting hysterical.

"What's your name anyway?" she asked the soldier in an attempt to distract herself from the surrealistic circumstances.

"Ari Brenner."

"What do you think happened? A terrorist attack?" She already knew it was more than an accident. The train hadn't just stopped. Someone had boarded it. *Or some*thing, her inner voice repeated.

"I don't know. No weapons fire so that doesn't seem likely. I wouldn't want to guess right now." He still sounded as calm as if this kind of thing happened every day of the week. Was that part of army training or was he simply the kind of person who kept cool in a crisis?

"A virus, I'm telling you," Mr. Mets Cap called out from behind them. "A flesh eating virus like in the movies. Something like that was killing those people. Could be airborne. We're better off down here."

As if to prove him wrong, the sickly sweet smell of death drifted from the tunnel ahead of them. Lila tensed, terrified of stepping into an animal corpse in the dark. Dead rat? Pigeon? Raccoon? Images of every bloated, fly-ridden creature she'd ever seen by the side of the road filled her mind and she automatically slowed.

Ari squeezed her hand and pulled. "Come on. The faster we get past whatever it is, the sooner we can breathe."

He was right. Without her hands free, Lila couldn't cover her mouth and nose. All she could do was hold her breath, which would ultimately force her to draw in a deeper lungful of the sickly odor if they didn't get past it fast.

"Shine the light. See what it is." Ann Hanson's voice was panicked, as on edge as Lila felt.

"Do you really want to know?" The tall, older man's voice sounded distant and Lila guessed he was at the end of the line.

Ari paused and flicked on the lighter. Its tiny glow was as bright as a flaming torch in the darkness. Lila blinked as her eyes adjusted, then focused on the dirty, damp cement floor. There was a little pile of something furry decomposing only a few yards away. A disgusted shiver rippled through her. Luckily it wasn't directly in front of them so they wouldn't have to navigate around it.

"Keep going," she told Ari.

He let go of her hand to wipe his on the side of his pants, flipped the lighter closed and moved forward. She grabbed hold of his shirt and nudged him in the back. Her fist clenched, bunching up the shirt and she pressed her nose into her arm to shield it from the stench of death.

Ari walked faster. No one complained as he kept up a steady pace until they'd left the eye-watering smell behind.

"Shouldn't we be getting close to the station by now?" Deb asked.

Ari didn't answer. Lila guessed he was as clueless as anyone else about how far they were from the nearest platform—or whether this passage ran parallel with the subway tunnel above. The idea took hold of her that they might not come to another manhole cover, that maybe Everett was right and they should've stayed close to the spot they entered. Her heart beat faster as she imagined being trapped down here forever. A mental image of layers of concrete and dirt between them and the open air made her breathing grow short. She was going to give herself a panic attack if she didn't calm down. In. Out. She breathed, slow and easy. *Let it flow. Deal with whatever happens.*

"Hey, Captain!" The teen yelled. "My sister needs a break. Can we stop for a minute?"

Ari stopped and Lila bumped into him. Deb, in turn, ran into her. She imagined the lot of them tumbling one into another like the Stooges and again crazy laughter threatened to burst from her lips. Lila put both hands to her mouth and leaned against the grimy wall.

"Okay, roll call," their leader commanded. "Say your name so we know everyone's still together."

"Deb Reeves here. Anyone mind if I have a cigarette? I need one bad."

"Patricia Scheider. I'd prefer you didn't. The air down here is foul enough as it is," the white-haired woman's crisp tone allowed for no argument.

Lila pulled her hands away from her face. "Lila Teske still here."

"Derrick and Ronnie Bronson," The boy said.

"I can say my own name! I'm eight. I'm not a baby." The high voice was indignant and petulant. Lila wondered how much longer Ronnie could go before she broke down and threw an all out tantrum. She thought she might join the kid in crying, screaming and kicking her legs. That sounded pretty good right about now.

"Hector Ramirez."

"Ann Hanson."

"Joe Morgenstern."

The names floated through the darkness.

"Do you think we should turn back?" Ann's voice came closer, marking her progress toward the front of the line. "What if we can't find another way out? Or what if we walk right past it in the dark? We should've listened to Mr. Everett and waited for someone to come help us. Wandering around like this is a big mistake." Again her voice sounded as if she was barely holding it together and might fly apart at any second. Ann didn't seem like the kind of person a person wanted to depend on in a crisis.

"Second guessing never accomplishes anything," Mrs. Scheider said briskly. "We're here now. We must move forward."

"I agree." Joe's voice also sounded nearer. Everyone was clustering into a group. "There's bound to be more than one exit and it makes sense there'd be access near a station."

"God knows what we're gonna find up there. Everybody dead or dying," Hector moaned.

"Mr. Ramirez, there's a child here. Mind what you say." Mrs. Scheider reminded him.

"Dude's right though," Derrick chimed in. "Something's going on. The way those people were screaming, maybe it was like nerve gas or something. Or maybe--"

"Shh. Stop it," Lila interrupted. "Let's not conjecture. It's not going to help anything. We'll find out soon enough what happened."

"Jesus, I need a cigarette. Gimme back my lighter."

Ari didn't hand Deb the lighter but did flick it on again. The glow illuminated the faces of the little group making them into eerie yellow masks. "Lila's right. Last thing we need is to start panicking or making up crazy stories. We should think about arming ourselves though. Does anyone have a pocket knife or anything that could be used in self defense?"

"Pepper spray on my key ring," Lila volunteered, then remembered, "which is in my backpack on the train."

Just then a scream echoed through the tunnel from far behind them. Everyone stopped talking and froze. Lila glanced at Ari. His eyes reflected the fire glow and she saw fear in them before he flipped the lighter closed. "Shit!"

She had no doubt Omar Everett had been discovered and attacked. Whatever was up there was now down here, and might have a clue there were more people.

"Gimme the little girl. I'll carry her. We've got to move!" Ari's voice was harsh.

No one argued. Lila seized the hand closest to hers--slender, fine-boned, she thought it might be Ann's—and grabbed the back of Ari's shirt again. Ronnie's leg was around his hip as he carried her. Her knee bumped against Lila's hand.

The group moved forward fast now, marching in silence. And from far away Lila could swear she heard echoing footsteps coming after them.

CHAPTER THREE

The little girl was heavier than Ari had expected, but no more so than the packs they'd had to run with on the obstacle course at boot camp. He wished he'd put her on his back instead of holding her slung around his waist which was an awkward way to carry anything. He also wished to hell he had a weapon. Any weapon. A piece of pipe or a baseball bat would be great, but he'd be happier with an assault rifle. Of course, even an AK-47 wouldn't do much against a flesh-eating virus or nerve gas. He didn't know what had happened on that train, but agreed with the others it was something out of the ordinary.

He listened hard, trying to hear beyond the stumbling feet and harsh breathing of the little group of travelers. The concrete tunnel echoed so it was difficult to tell what he heard, but he thought there were footsteps coming from behind them.

The girl whimpered and gripped his shoulders, her little fingers digging in. She smelled like strawberry gum and sweat. Maybe he was supposed to give her some kind of encouragement or tell her not to worry, but he saved his breath for trotting faster.

"Slow down." The voice sounded like Ann, that woman who'd wanted to stay behind. He wished she had if she was going to hobble the group. He ignored her plea and continued to stride quickly. His palm swept along the wall, keeping them on course and feeling for ladder rungs. He kept his gaze focused toward the ceiling, searching for a break in the blackness, a sign of light to indicate an opening from what felt like an endless coffin. Perhaps he'd been wrong to lead these people down here. Maybe they should've stayed on the track like everyone else and taken their chances that way. Now they were trapped in this tunnel below the tunnel. At least there seemed to be only one possible route. It'd be much worse if there was a maze of choices.

At that moment, as if fate was amused by the idea, the wall vanished from beneath Ari's hand. They'd reached an opening. He turned on the lighter and saw they were at a crossroads. They could continue straight or angle left. Instinct told him to keep going forward, but self-doubt whispered he could be making a big mistake and leading everyone farther away from the station.

He thought about how the train had pulled away from the platform and clicked down the track. Hadn't they veered right? The subway wasn't laid out in a perfect grid. There were twists and turns.

"I think something's coming. We should get moving." Lila's voice behind him was low and tense.

"There's another tunnel. I'm trying to decide which way to go," he whispered back.

People were talking, asking about the hold up, calling out whatever came into their minds.

"Shut up!" he snapped, wishing he could gag every one of them. "All of you shut the hell up." His heart pounded. He shifted the heavy kid in his arms. She tightened her legs around his waist and pressed her head against his chest. Jesus, this kid was depending on him to get them out of here. All of them were depending on him, and he didn't have a clue which way to go.

Lila pressed her hand against his back, her palm warm and reassuring splayed across his spine. "Breathe," she said. "Slow your heart rate, clear your mind, and listen."

Easier said than done, but he obeyed, closing his eyes, which ached from trying to search for any glimmer of light the entire time they'd been hiking through this limbo. He breathed in the dank, oxygen-deprived air and slowly released it. Breathed again and smelled the rotten scent of garbage. Garbage meant people. People meant an access to the tunnel. And wasn't that the faintest whiff of slightly less stale air on his left cheek?

Ari opened his eyes and looked down the branching tunnel. He thought he could see a faint glow. At the same time, he heard footsteps, definite footsteps echoing from far away.

"Move out," he said just loud enough so the group could hear him then plunged into the left hand passage, heading toward the gray light.

The resounding footsteps from behind pattered faster and sounded louder. Whatever was on their trail was trotting now. Ari wrapped his arm around Ronnie and broke into a run, barely touching the wall now to keep his course straight. The dim light became clearer and he headed for it. He stopped when he reached a grate overhead, and the group piled into him. There were no ladder on the wall beneath the grate, no ladder to safety, only the faint light coming through slats half covered by a drift of something, probably litter.

Ari cursed, "God*damn* it!" He peeled Ronnie off him and set her down then moved along the wall, feeling blindly for rungs. There had to be some exit nearby, perhaps a manhole cover he couldn't see because it fit so tightly. If the footsteps behind them weren't growing louder, he wouldn't be panicking, but as it was his heart pounded so hard his chest hurt. They had to find a way out, now.

His knuckles rapped hard against iron. He seized hold of a metal bar and searched for the bottom rung with his foot. Locating it, he climbed quickly to the top of the ladder, reached above his head and felt rough concrete and cool metal. He traced his finger along the lip of a circle before pushing up against it. He held his breath, terrified the cover would be locked from above, but the heavy plate shifted. He grunted as he lifted and shoved it aside.

There was no time to make sure the subway was clear. The danger coming from behind was more urgent. Ari climbed down a couple of rungs before dropping the rest of the way to the ground and landing in a crouch.

"Go!" he ordered Derrick.

Derrick clambered to the top and out the hole. Ari had been

worried Ronnie would freak out about climbing the ladder, but she scurried up it like pirate climbing rigging into her brother's waiting arms. Ann then Deb went, followed by Mrs. Scheider, who climbed slowly but steadily. Joe went behind her to ensure she didn't slip and Hector followed him.

At last only Ari and Lila remained.

"Go ahead," he urged, glancing down the tunnel as he pushed her toward the ladder.

There were moving shapes looming in the dark, coming closer, running fast but with an odd, reeling gait. Were they people or something else? Disbelief flooded through him at what his imagination dared to cobble together from years of watching horror movies. Ridiculous, impossible images of werewolves and monsters flashed through his mind coupled with thoughts of Freddy Krueger or Jason striding along with deadly intent.

But these things weren't striding. They were fucking *running*, and Lila was only halfway up the ladder. The group of people—they *were* people—was briefly illuminated in speckled light and shadow cast by the grate. Ari saw their distorted faces for an instant before he stopped looking and started climbing as fast as he could.

He quickly caught up to Lila as the first of the creatures reached the circle of light coming from the open manhole cover above. Ari glanced down and glimpsed pale skin, a red mouth and black eyes looking back at him. The thing was at the foot of the ladder, climbing up behind him.

"Go, go, go!" he screamed at Lila. He kicked at his pursuer's head, his foot connecting with its face. The creature's head snapped back, but it kept climbing.

Ari kicked again, connecting with its chest and this time he knocked it off the ladder into the darkness below. But there was another coming right behind it. Ari pushed his hands against Lila's ass, boosting her up and out of the hole. He climbed the last few rungs and vaulted through himself, yelling, "Shut it!"

Hector and Joe slid the cover into place and stood on it, their combined weight keeping the hole closed even as something pounded on the metal plate from below. Ari searched frantically for something with which to seal the exit. There was a bench bolted to the floor and a vending machine next to it. He yelled at Derrick to come help him move it. Ari's muscles strained as they wrestled the heavy machine a couple of inches across the floor.

"Hurry," Hector yelled as the pounding from below continued.

Lila and Deb came to lend their strength and the four of them pushed the vending machine across the floor to the manhole cover.

"We'll tip it face down," Ari said. Joe and Hector took the weight as he and Derrick rocked the machine toward them. The two men stepped off the cover, letting go of the machine so it crashed to the ground. From beneath the machine, the pounding noise continued for a moment. Then there was silence.

"*Dios*, what the hell is going on?" Hector voiced everyone's thoughts.

"Whoever they are, there could be more. We should keep moving, but find someplace where we can catch our breath," Joe advised.

Ari rubbed his wrenched shoulder and took a look around the empty platform. Only not so empty. Mingled with the usual trash on the ground were lumps of stuff scattered here and there. It was difficult to make out what they were in the glare of emergency lights that cast everything in sharp relief as if they were living in a black and white movie.

He walked closer to take a look at a pile of shredded rags and red sludge, his stomach tensing as his eyes recognized what they saw before his brain could wrap itself around the concept. Body parts. That's what the lumps were. Limbs, bones and bits of entrails. It looked like a massacre had taken place with very little of the victims left behind.

"My God," Lila's voice came from beside him. "What happened here?"

Ari's gaze flicked to a corpse lying near the wall. He could swear its hand had moved. "I think that one's still alive."

He jogged over and crouched beside the mangled body of a man in an overcoat way too hot for the day. Probably a homeless guy. They always seemed to wear layers of everything they owned, winter or summer. The stench of blood and excrement rose from the sprawled form. Ari held his breath, put a hand on the man's shoulder and gently rolled him over. You weren't supposed to move an injured person, but as bad as this guy looked, it hardly seemed to matter.

The dead man appeared to have been ripped apart by some kind of carnivore. Bites of flesh were ripped from his face, throat and chest. One eyeball still attached to the brain by red tendrils lolled against his cheek. His legs sprawled at impossible angles, a shard of bone protruding through a hole in one of his trouser legs.

The rest of the group had clustered around, except for Ann, who was keeping Ronnie away from the sight. He swallowed the bile rising in his throat. He didn't want to feel for the dead man's pulse, didn't want to touch him again. "Anybody here have any medical experience?"

"I'm..." Joe Morgenstern gave a short, bitter laugh. "I'm a dermatologist."

Ari looked back down at the dead man's ruined face. Macabre jokes about skin conditions fluttered in his mind like bits of litter caught in a whirlwind. "Could you take a look at him?"

Morgenstern crouched and reached for the man's wrist.

"No way that guy's alive," Derrick helpfully pointed out.

"Why don't you go help Ann with your little sister," Lila snapped. "She's scared out of her wits. She needs you."

Dr. Morgenstern laid the man's hand down and shook his head. "No pulse. He's dead."

"Okay." Ari nodded and rose to his feet. "We've should keep moving, get above ground and find out what's happening."

"A virus, I'm telling you. We've probably already been infected." Hector scratched obsessively at his arm.

Joe stood. "Mr. Ramirez, I think we can discount an airborne pathogen or all of us would have been showing symptoms by now. You can relax."

"Werewolves or vampires could rip up people like this." Derrick dared to say aloud what Ari never would have, even though the insane idea of monsters had been whispering in his brain.

Mrs. Scheider shot Derrick a quelling glance. "Don't be ridiculous, young man. This is no time to be inventing nonsense."

"I'm serious. You can't deny *that.*" He pointed at the remains at their feet. "That's real, and no human being did it."

"Come on. Let's go." Ari started to step away, but spared a last glance for Homeless Fred and at that moment the man's single closed eye snapped open. Ari leaped back.

The corpse on the ground began to move, struggling to rise.

"Jesus Christ!" and "Zombie!" Ari and Derrick shouted simultaneously.

Ari seized Lila's hand--she always seemed to be right beside him—and began to run. The whole thing was like a bad drug trip, outrageous and endless. They would spend eternity running through tunnels chased by monsters.

When they reached the stairs, he glanced back at the dead man, still trying to stand on what were probably broken legs. He wasn't making any headway and didn't seem to be much of a threat. Ari scanned the group to make sure everyone was accounted for. Dr. Joe carried Ronnie. Hector held hands with Mrs. Scheider, making sure the older woman kept up. Deb, Ann, Derrick and Lila, whose hand he gripped like a life preserver, were all together.

Ari led them upstairs to the mezzanine level of the terminal where there were a few shops, restrooms, ticket booths and more carnage. Body parts littered the floor near the turnstiles and benches, but there weren't any animated corpses stumbling around. Whatever had gone through here had moved on. Maybe.

The revenants—if that's what they were—that had chased them

through the storm drainage tunnel would have to return to the last open manhole to get out. It would take at least twenty minutes for them to retrace their steps and another twenty to come down the subway tunnel. That should give the group a short time to recover before going up to street level to find God knew what kind of chaos. Before they faced it, they needed to rest and arm themselves.

The power was out in the terminal too and emergency lights cast the area in a gloomy glow. Ari spotted a glass-fronted convenience store and headed toward it, sweeping his gaze from left to right. Nothing appeared to be moving. A glance behind told him the zombie from the lower level had not followed them up the stairs, but it might. He needed to find a weapon to kill the thing if it reared its ugly, eye-lolling head again.

Ari held up a hand to bring the group to a halt while he checked out the shop. Inside, he found magazines, books, DVDs, candy, shelves and coolers full of beverages and snacks—and the unmoving remains of the clerk behind the counter.

He beckoned the rest of the group into the store. "Why don't you pass out bottles of water," he suggested to Ann, who seemed the type who needed a task to perform to keep her focused. She nodded and went to the cooler for some Ice Springs.

"Joe, you watch that door and Hector, the other. If you see anything move, I mean anything, let me know."

"What are you gonna do?" Hector raised his bushy brows.

"Look for weapons. There must be something around here." He sounded self-assured, as if he knew what he was doing, but Ari felt like he was poking his way through a mine field. Somehow he'd taken charge, but he had no business doing it. He was no leader.

Lila and Deb picked up some of the scattered items from the floor to make space to sit, while Mrs. Scheider tried to make a call on her Blackberry. "Still not getting a signal," she announced.

"Me either," Hector said. "No bars."

Ann came from the cooler with arms full of bottled water and headed toward the checkout. Ari stopped her. "Uh, there's nobody to take your money. Why don't you go ahead and pass those out."

"Oh, of course. Yes." Her blue eyes were wide and dilated. Didn't that mean a person was in shock? Well, hell, they all were.

He searched behind the counter, trying to ignore the bits of clerk stuck to everything. It wasn't like he expected to find a gun or bat, this wasn't the kind of convenience store like in his neighborhood, but there was nothing useful for self defense. However, there was a display of flashlights near the register. Ari stepped over a shred of polo shirt with a name tag attached—Maria—and hefted one in his hand. It didn't weigh much and wouldn't be useful as a club, but at least they'd have light if they needed it. He gathered all the flashlights from the display and passed them to the group sitting on the floor.

After another scan of the silent station outside the shop, he continued searching for weapons. Maybe he could pelt the zombies with hard candy or whip CD cases at their heads like Ninja stars. He spun the display rack of sunglasses and decided the center spindle could be detached without too much difficulty. He flipped the rack upside down to dismember the pole from its base and top.

He glanced at the group. Ann offered Ronnie a box of cookies and a stuffed unicorn. She stroked the girl's hair back and offered her a Kleenex to wipe her tear-streaked face. Meanwhile, Derrick was following Ari's lead, searching for something to use as a weapon.

"We've got to find a phone that works and call 911," Joe said, "let them know about the accident and that there's something…strange going on."

"A zombie attack." Derrick casually said the word that made Ari cringe at its absurdity. "You think they'll believe it?"

"Maybe, if it's a widespread phenomenon." Lila picked a tote sack from a hook and began to fill it with snack foods.

"Zombies. Don't be ridiculous." Joe continued to scan the empty station.

"We all saw it," the teen argued. "You said that guy was dead, no pulse, and then he was getting up. Only thing I know that can do that is a zombie. You can call them revenants if it sounds better to you, but they're still the same thing. Animated dead people."

"I must have missed his pulse or his heart temporarily stopped. People have close encounters sometimes," Joe said.

"He was dead, but he was moving. Zombie," Derrick stated flatly.

"Please stop saying that." Mrs. Scheider frowned. "Dr. Morgenstern is right. We need to concentrate on something sensible like finding a working phone so we can call emergency services. Whatever's happening, it *is* an emergency."

Ari thought the network would be overloaded and there was no way they'd get through, but since they didn't have a usable phone anyway, it didn't seem worth bringing up the point.

"I agree about trying to get help, and I'm sure everyone here has family they want to call. But we have to be careful and prepared for whatever we might find up there." Ari freed the center pole of the sunglass rack at last. The long cylinder might be awkward to carry, but it would do for cracking heads. "It could be total chaos and we may need to fight. There might not be cops or anyone else waiting to help us." One look around the bloody subway station should convince them of that.

"Oh, God," Ann moaned softly and rested her forehead on her knees. Hector muttered under his breath and Ari thought he might be praying.

For a moment, they were all silent. He was glad no one was having a major meltdown, making things harder than they already were. Maybe there living in a big city prepared a person for survival, or maybe they were all too shocked to react appropriately. Only Ronnie was smart enough to cry her eyes out.

"With all the emergency preparedness drills we've had since 9-11, I'm sure there'll be military teams on the job soon," Ari continued. "But meanwhile, we have to stay alive. If it is...what Derrick's suggesting, we need to know if the city's been overrun by them and how to protect ourselves." *From zombies.* The ridiculousness hit him and he suppressed a laugh. Probably best if he wasn't the first to break down since he seemed to be the leader.

"I've got to get to my wife and kids." Hector took off his baseball cap and rubbed his forehead. "They're clear out in Brooklyn."

"My sister and me were on our way to our dad's place. He and Mom are going to be freaking out if we don't show up." Following Ari's lead, Derrick had another display rack on its side and was struggling to take it apart.

"My girlfriend's office is near here," Deb said. "If I can't call her, I'm going to go to her."

Everyone splitting up and running off in different directions the moment they hit the street was exactly what Ari wanted to avoid. "We should stick together until we know what's going on. Work as a unit."

Lila looked up from packing water bottles into one of the tote bags. "It sounds like you have a plan. What do you think we should do?"

Ari considered what he'd learned from hours of playing Gears of War 2. "Recon first. A couple of us should go up to the street and report back on what we find."

"While the rest sit here waiting for those things to attack from below? No. You said it yourself. We should stick together, do everything as a group," Lila said.

She had a point. This place was only safe temporarily. But Ari thought whatever was happening above could be even worse. He didn't like the idea of dragging along Ronnie, Mrs. Scheider or anyone else who might be a hindrance, not until they knew what to expect.

The others started weighing in with opinions, giving ideas or suggestions which felt less like group discussion than a situation crumbling into confusion. One of them had to take control and make a final decision. Might as well be him.

"This recon won't take long. Just a quick scan of the area.

Meanwhile, the rest of you gather anything that might be useful to take with us, food and water and anything that could be used as a weapon. For example, lighters and aerosol cans can be makeshift flamethrowers." He wanted to keep them occupied rather than worried and waiting. "Derrick, why don't you come with me? Hector and Joe, guard the others."

"What's with putting the men in charge of the weak womenfolk?" Deb crossed her arms and raised an eyebrow. "We're not useless."

But it was Lila who demanded to go along. She hefted an umbrella in her hand, flourishing it like a fencing sword. "I'm armed. I'm going with you. Mrs. Scheider, lend me your phone, please. I left mine on the train."

"Fine. Let's go." Ari walked from the shop, giving no one else a chance to offer more arguments.

"Aye, aye, captain," Derrick muttered, flanking him on the left and brandishing his metal spindle. Lila fell in on the right with her umbrella-spear clenched in her fist.

Ari motioned them to stay behind him as he went up the stairs toward the street, stepping over mangled body parts that littered the steps. He hugged close to the wall and listened as he neared the entrance. The traffic noise had more than the usual quota of sirens, the wails of emergency vehicles announcing something big was happening.

His pulse raced and his skin was slick with sweat. He gripped his weapon tighter and took another step up just as a fire truck shot past on the street. A few people raced by, their feet pounding the pavement. No one tried to go down the stairs to the subway. Who would want to be underground in the middle of a power outage?

Ari crept up another step then raised his head above the pavement like a small animal poking its head from a burrow to check for predators. The area was complete anarchy and all he could think was "How did things get so fucked up so fast?"

There'd been a car accident on the street. Maybe more than one, it was hard to tell. At least a few cars had collided. Others had been abandoned, their doors left wide open. The one stoplight he could see was dark and there was no cop directing the gridlocked traffic. The flashing lights of the fire truck disappeared around a corner and he realized it had been driving on the sidewalk, plowing past any obstacles that got in the way. People ran in all directions, but not as many as he would have expected. Like in the subway, it seemed the revenants had swept through and moved on, leaving blood, gore and pieces of bodies in their wake.

In the plexi-glass cubicle sheltering the subway entrance only a few feet from Ari lay a face. Not a head, only a face discarded like last year's Halloween mask. After one quick glance, he looked away. He didn't need to see something like that too closely.

"911 has a recorded message about all circuits being busy." Lila reported as she jabbed a number on her phone. "I'm calling my boyfriend—ex-boyfriend. He's an intern at St. Andrews. Maybe he'll know something."

Ari pulled his own phone from his pants pocket and tried to reach his mom, but got her voice mail. Calls to his friends yielded the same results. He felt sick as he imagined why they might not be answering their phones.

Now what? He tried to imagine what his drill sergeant, Vogt would command. Climb a wall, do a few sets of pushups. Nothing in the book about responding to a full scale zombie attack.

"What's going on?" Derrick moved past Ari to take a turn looking at the carnage outside their foxhole. He pulled back, pale as a corpse, hugging his skinny arms around his body. "What are we gonna do?"

"Get someplace safe. Find a battery powered radio so we can learn what's going on and what's being done about it. Get better weapons" Ari took another look at the street, ignoring the confusion and concentrating on the layout. There was a large sporting goods store within sight, the perfect place for guns, blades, bats, bows, and other supplies. It should be as safe a place as any to squat while they took stock, and maybe they'd find other people there. Preferably living ones.

The sound of shattering glass and screams came from farther down the street. Ari's gaze swept to the source of the noise. A storefront window had burst out about a block away. He couldn't see what had broken through it until the people scattered to reveal a blood-streaked man staggering to his feet while a revenant lurched disjointedly after him. Running people blocked Ari's view, but he saw the moment when the predator caught her prey and bit down on his shoulder. Her teeth ripped right through the fabric of his shirt. Ari hadn't known blunt human teeth could do that.

He dropped down into the relative safety of the subway entrance, breathing as if he'd run five miles and pressing his body tight against the wall. "We'd better go back down."

Lila held up her hand and continued talking. "Doyle. Doyle! I can't hear you. You're breaking up. Hello? Doyle?" She flipped the phone shut with a curse and handed it back to Ari. "The connection was terrible and Doyle was…in shock I guess, like he'd checked out."

Ari understood that. He felt light-headed and disconnected himself, observing everything as if from a distance.

"He and some others are trapped in a wing of the hospital. He kept saying, 'They're coming. I can hear them coming.'" Lila's voice broke. Ari prayed she wouldn't start crying, he couldn't deal with that. He needed her to keep being strong.

"My mom works at St. Andrews, too." He thought about her bending over the steam press in the laundry and a shambling creature coming up behind her, but slammed his mind shut when the image of gnashing teeth and clawing hands got too graphic.

"The hospital is across town so these attacks must be going on all over the city," Lila said.

Derrick jabbed his finger on the keypad of his cell phone, his acne-sprinkled face contorted in a scowl. "My mom's not there. I'll try my dad."

Ari was nervous. They should go back to the group and get them moving to the new location before the zombies from below made it to the terminal. But first he took one more look at the street, carefully avoiding glimpsing the disembodied face to his left. People still ran in all directions, a few zombies among them, snatching, grabbing and biting. Cars attempted to make it around the jam in the street by driving onto the sidewalk. A cop car crawled through the stalled traffic and finally came to a halt.

Two officers piled out, guns drawn, shouted something then began shooting into the crowd. Ari jerked as the shots popped. A man reeled backward, fell to the sidewalk, then climbed back to his feet. Zombie. The word was becoming less ridiculous now. The man stumbled toward the police like a drunk. Each fired several more rounds but still the thing kept coming.

"Head shot!" Ari muttered. "Has to be a head shot."

His hypothesis was proved wrong as the female cop shot the creature point blank in the forehead. The impact made it teeter backward before resuming its steady course toward the police cruiser. The other cop continued to shoot as he backed toward the car and got in the driver's side. His partner ran toward the other side of the cruiser, but the zombie caught hold of her Kevlar vest and pulled her to him before chomping into her throat. Blood gushed in a fountain as the creature severed an artery, spraying them both in red.

This entire scenario played out within seconds, so fast Ari could hardly process it. Instead his mind focused on the details. *Cop wearing a flak jacket? They at least know there's rioting going on but probably not much else.* If he'd learned one thing during his short stint in the military, it was that people in charge were often as ignorant as everyone else about what was actually happening during a crisis, especially in a bizarre situation like this. These weren't terrorists with guns, but reanimated dead people. When a point black shot to the head didn't take them down, what was a cop to do? Apparently drive away, because that was what the policeman did. The stupid metal pole in Ari's hand seemed more useless than ever.

"Did you see that? Did you fricking *see* that?" Lila was beside him, staring at the chaos.

He grasped her arm and pulled. "Come on. Let's go."

Ari started downstairs, tugging Lila along with him. Derrick followed with the cell phone still clutched in his hand. "Why won't anybody answer?"

Ari's foot skidded on a slick of red goo. He half fell down a couple of steps, dropping his makeshift weapon. The pole rolled down the rest of the stairs with a loud clanging.

Lila grabbed his arm and hauled him up off his ass. "Are you okay?"

"Yeah." He rubbed his elbow which had whacked the concrete steps sharply and continued on his way. He picked up his club at the bottom of the steps and jogged down the short hallway toward the terminal with Derrick and Lila on either side of him.

Deb waited there, smoking a cigarette. "What took you guys so long? What's happening?"

Ari glanced at his watch. They'd been gone less than five minutes. "Chaos. The cops don't have any control. People are running all over the place and there are more"—he forced out the word—"zombies."

Deb exhaled a puff of smoke. "Jesus Christ. I've got to get to Julie."

"I know you're worried," Lila said. "We're all worried about someone, but going off alone is a bad idea."

"There's a sporting goods store nearby. We should try to get there, gather some gear and arm ourselves," Ari added. "After that we'll discuss where to go next, and if anyone wants to split, they can."

Just then a little girl's piercing shriek echoed through the corridor. The wail made the hair rise on Ari's neck. He hefted his metal pole in one hand like a javelin and raced toward the sound. With the others pounding behind him.

CHAPTER FOUR

Lila's heart nearly stopped at Ronnie's horrifying wail coming from the station. Ari took off like a shot with Derrick right behind him. Deb cursed and tossed her cigarette to the floor. Lila gripped her ridiculous umbrella and followed, mentally preparing for the slaughterhouse they might find.

As she raced over the cement, her breath hitched in and out as if she'd run a few miles instead of several yards. Her mind felt disconnected from her body and from this never-ending nightmare. There was no way to comprehend what was happening. The best a person could do was react to it with at least a little courage and common sense.

They rounded the corner to the platform. Lila couldn't see anything wrong—other than the bits of carrion which had already been there. There were no zombies and after one piercing shriek, Ronnie hadn't screamed again. The group was clustered inside the shop, people Lila already felt strangely bonded with although they'd only just met. Joe argued with Hector, while Ann and Mrs. Scheider crouched on the floor beside Ronnie.

Derrick barreled past the others. "What happened? Is she all right?"

Ronnie's arms were wrapped tight around Ann's neck and the woman held her close, rubbing her back and murmuring something.

"She saw something that frightened her," Mrs. Scheider said.

Hardly surprising given the circumstances, Lila thought as she crowded into the store along with Ari and Deb.

"Damn it, Ronnie! You scared the crap out of us." Derrick knelt by her.

The girl lifted her blotchy, tear-streaked face from the blond woman's shoulder. "I couldn't help it. I saw a spider, a big one. It was huge! I had to scream." She glared at the two older men. "And then *he* yelled at me. He shook me."

"I didn't," Joe said. "I grabbed her arm and told her to be quiet. I didn't mean to frighten her."

"You don't yell at scared little kids. That's no way to calm them down." Hector glared then spoke soothingly to Ronnie. "It's okay, *hija*."

"God, Ronnie. You're such a big baby." Derrick shook his head and set his weapon on the floor.

"We're all in danger. We can't have kids screaming. That's all I'm saying," Joe muttered.

"He's right. It's bad up there and we sure as hell don't want to draw any attention down here. Seems the whole city's in crisis that's not likely to break any time soon, but we can't stay here either." Ari jerked a thumb toward the subway tunnel. "Not with what's still down there."

He described what they'd witnessed and told about the sporting goods shop. "I think we can make it there, and I'll feel a lot better after we're armed."

"What good does it do when a shot to the head doesn't even kill them?" Hector asked.

"Do you have a better idea, Mr. Rodriguez?" Mrs. Scheider sounded cool and composed even if her coiffure and couture were considerably less crisp than they'd been on the train. "Taking any action is better than taking none at all."

"Medulla oblongata!" Derrick suddenly whirled around from studying a rack of chips. "That's why the shot to the forehead didn't work. It doesn't matter if their brains are damaged. In some zombie lore the heads must be completely severed. Cutting through the nervous system at the base of the neck stops them from functioning."

"You're saying they have to be beheaded," Ari said.

"That's my guess."

They all stared at Derrick. He sounded so certain and they were so desperate to believe in anything, Lila thought, even the guess of a kid raised on too many horror movies. Well, why not? Would a scientist have a better idea of what stopped a revenant?

Just then, a movement in the terminal caught her attention. Lila turned toward it. Something was moving in the shadow of the stairs to the lower level. She squinted and touched Ari's arm. "Hey, what's that."

He turned to look. They both stared at the thing crawling out of the darkness of the stairwell. It was the dead man from downstairs. Lila recognized the trench coat. They hadn't worried about the revenant pursuing them since his legs were broken. But apparently the creature's will was stronger than its physical disabilities, because the zombie was crawling relentlessly toward them.

Ari took a step forward. "God*damn* it." He picked up the pole he'd leaned against the counter and strode toward the creeping menace. Lila trailed after him, unable to look away from the abomination making its painstaking way across the floor. The thing's shoulders hitched and its hands braced against the cement as it hauled its broken body forward like a wounded soldier trying to escape a battlefield. Behind her, the others continued talking. Then one by one their voices fell silent as they saw the crawling zombie.

Ari jabbed the man in the side with his pole. Lila reached out a hand and whispered "no" to herself. It seemed so wrong to poke at the pitiful creature. But in an instant the zombie turned from pitiful to dangerously feral. It whipped a hand out lightning fast and gripped the pole, almost pulling it from Ari's hands. The creature looked up and bared its teeth, the dangling eye on its cheek bouncing jauntily at the sudden movement.

Ari jerked the pole from the creature's grip, raised it and brought it down on the zombie with an audible thump. Again and again he hit the undead thing, but still it wouldn't stop crawling. The zombie reached for Ari's foot. He leaped aside and smashed its hand with his boot. He slammed the pole across the back of the creature's neck several times.

"Find me something sharp to cut its neck with," he called out.

"Use the pole like a spear. Jab into the hollow at the base of its skull. That should impale the medulla." Joe went toward him, but didn't rush to help.

His suggestion was easier said than done. Ari tried to impale the zombie but it twisted away from his stabbing blows. The broken body thrashed like a landed fish, making it nearly impossible for him to hit the right spot. When at last he drove the pole into the creature's flesh, blood gushed from the wound. The heart must still be pumping. Lila watched in horror as the thing spasmed.

Ari's arm muscles strained as he pushed against the pole, keeping the dead man pinned to the floor. "Not working. Somebody get a knife."

Lila dashed back into the store, searching frantically for anything sharp enough to cut through flesh, gristle and bone. There was nothing. She could think of nothing to help. *Blind panic. This is what blind panic feels like.*

"One of these shelves," Hector yelled. He swept the items off a metal display shelf and Deb helped him pull the shelf from the frame. Hector ran with the shelf toward Ari and the struggling zombie.

Joe and Hector's bodies blocked Lila's view. But she didn't want to see any more. She waited beside Mrs. Scheider, her body tense as she caught glimpses of Ari wielding the sharp edge of the shelf over the prone zombie. He grunted as he bore down, driving metal through flesh. The thing that had once been a man made a gurgling noise and lashed out with its arms and legs once more before going still.

"It worked," Derrick whispered.

She glanced at the white-faced boy beside her. Although his makeshift weapon was clenched in his hands, he hadn't gone to help.

Neither had Joe or Hector. They'd stood nearby, letting Ari do the job alone. Lila realized with a flush of shame she'd done the same.

Hector moved, affording her a glimpse of Ari standing over the finally dead zombie. He dropped the metal shelf with a clatter and stooped to grab the pole he'd tossed aside. Straightening, Ari walked toward the shop. His expression was grim and his hands blood-spattered. He stopped and looked around at the rest of the group.

"More of those things may be coming. We've rested long enough."

No one argued as they gathered the things they'd commandeered from the store. Lila shouldered two totes full of water, juice, and food, their combined weight pulling on her shoulders. She gripped the red umbrella, which seemed totally useless now, but acted as a sort of security blanket for her psyche—something to hold onto.

When they were all ready, Ari led them upstairs to the street, going first to check that the way was clear. He called back over his shoulder. "I don't think it's going to get any better than this, very few people on the street and no undead that I can see. The way to the store looks clear."

Lila glanced at Ann Hanson beside her. The woman's expression was calm to the point of blankness. She held Ronnie's hand and bent to whisper to the whimpering child. Lila could see that Ronnie was Ann's red umbrella, something to cling to and take care of while the world fell apart.

"Move out," Ari called.

The group climbed the stairs as a tight unit, emerging from the shelter of the underground to the danger of the streets. Ari kept them moving at a fast clip, down littered sidewalk and around abandoned cars as they crossed the street.

Lila looked at buildings around them, so familiar and normal. This was her city, but eerily empty, as if it was early morning instead of the middle of a busy weekday. Had the people all run for shelter, clearing the streets, or had the government given some evacuation procedure to follow? Maybe there was some location they should be heading. Although they'd only been underground for a short time, she felt like she'd missed an important inter-office memo instructing them on how to respond to a zombie attack.

The trek from the subway entrance to Superior Sporting Supplies was surprisingly uneventful. Other than having to step around gore, there was nothing to impede their progress. Within minutes all nine of them were safely inside the building. The scent of leather and plastic from shoes, bags, jackets and other gear pervaded the store. It was a clean odor of new things at odds with the primal smells of blood, bodily waste and sweat she'd been inhaling. Lila wished she could scrub herself as clean and new as the store smelled, and scour her mind of all the horrific images that polluted it.

Power was out here, too. Light flooded in from the front windows, while a few emergency lights illuminated the back part of the store. Rows of display racks made dark tunnels down which anything might hide, but they didn't find another living soul in the store. No dead ones either or signs of death. Perhaps the people who worked here had stepped outside to see what was happening and had gotten carried away in the madness.

"We'll sweep the entire store and make sure it's safe," Ari said. "Lila, wait by the front door and lock it when I give the all clear."

He put down his makeshift weapon and took something more lethal from the hunting and fishing area, a knife with an eight inch blade. Ari, Hector and Joe went toward the back of the store to secure the storeroom, while Deb and Derrick checked out every aisle in the store. Everyone returned to report the building was deserted and Lila locked the door.

At the gun counter, Ari chose rifles and ammo from the gun cabinet after he'd found the keys. "That cop's gun might not have stopped that zombie, but if we blow the whole head off, they aren't going to keep going."

He handed out weapons to everyone except Ann and Ronnie.

Ann was helping the little pick out a pair of tennis shoes to replace her sandals. Lila glanced at her own sandals and decided she'd better get better footwear for walking, too. But first Ari gave them all a tutorial on how to use the guns.

Lila held one called a CVA Buckhorn 290 Magnum. It was heavy. She breathed in the sharp tang of gun oil and metal as she rested the stock against her shoulder. She never would've imagined when she got up this morning with her mind twisted in knots over Doyle that she'd find herself several hours later with a rifle in her hands, learning how to squeeze the trigger. Lila shook off the foggy feeling of disconnect and brought her attention back to what Ari was saying. If she concentrated on the motions of what she was doing, she could keep her panic at bay.

"We don't want to draw attention with random gunfire. Don't shoot unless you have to and make every shot count. Aim for their heads and don't think of them as people, only targets. They aren't people anymore."

"What if the guns don't work?" Hector, always the pessimist, sighted down his unloaded rifle and squeezed the trigger.

Ari smiled grimly. "Run like hell." It was the first time Lila had seen him smile and even though his smirk was ironic, it looked good on him.

He suggested they each find a knife, baseball bat or other weapon. Some did that, while others took the opportunity to make calls on the three available cell phones. The store phone was down because of the power outage apparently of this entire section of the city.

Lila put down her new rifle and borrowed Ari's phone to call her parents. They were hundreds of miles away in Ohio and hopefully safe if this situation only affected the New York area. She was desperate to believe it was true, although there was nothing to give her any such hope. With something so crazy, what was the likelihood this wasn't a wider phenomenon?

The phone rang five times, each ring ratcheting her tension up another notch, before her mother picked up. "Hello, Lila?"

"Yeah, it's me, Mom. Is everything all right there?"

"Your dad and I are okay. What about you? We've been watching the news. It's terrible! How are you? Are you safe?"

"A store. I was on the subway with these other people when it was attacked and we escaped. We haven't seen any news yet. We don't know what's going on. The city's a mess. These things are killing people."

"Oh, sweetheart, we've been so worried about you. I called your cell over and over."

"I left it on the train with all my stuff when we ran." Hearing her mom's concerned voice made her eyes sting and she blinked away tears. "What's happening, Mom? What are they saying on TV."

"These attacks are happening all over the country. Stories are coming in, but no one really knows anything. You know the media. If they don't have any idea, they bring on experts who make up theories. The general consensus seems to be this is some kind of virus. But you tell me how a virus can make dead bodies rise and walk." She drew a deep, audible breath and her voice was steadier when she continued. "You know I'm not the most religious person, but if this isn't the damn apocalypse, I don't know what is."

There was a noise in the background and a "give me that" before her dad's voice thundered into the phone as if he was trying to yell all the way from Ohio. "Lila, listen to me. Are you someplace safe? You need to get someplace safe, lock the door and ride this out. That's what your mom and I are doing. Whatever's happening, the army will get it under control soon. You just have to protect yourself until then."

Lila looked at the rifle and ammo, the scope and night vision goggles lying on the counter beside her. "I'm trying, Daddy. I'm with some people from the subway and this one guy has had some military training. He's kind of our leader. I'm not at my apartment and I can't get there. It's blocks away, all the public transport systems are shut down and the streets are jammed with abandoned cars. We haven't decided what our next move should be yet."

"Let me talk to this guy."

Lila glanced at Ari, selecting vests and boots, holsters for the knives and other gear. "He's kind of busy right now. Has the President or someone made a statement yet? Is there something we're supposed to do or something the military is planning on doing? And are you sure you and mom are okay?"

"We're fine. Don't you worry about us. Our house is so far out of town, we're not in the thick of things. Wouldn't even have known anything was going on if I hadn't happened to turn on the TV."

"Dad, arm yourself. I know you don't have a gun but you need to get an ax or butcher knife. Anything sharp. We think you have to behead these things in order to stop them. Ari killed one that way, and one of the people here thinks it's about severing the spinal column."

Ann came up beside her, clearly wanting to use the phone. "I've got to go now. The phones are down here. We only have a few working cells and no way to recharge them. Take care of yourself, Dad. Tell Mom I love her. I love you both."

"Love you, too. Call again as soon as you can. Let us know what's happening."

"I will." She hung up and surrendered the phone to Ann, the weight in her chest nearly choking her. She ached to be with her parents right now, secure, loved and safely out of this nightmare city.

She walked back toward the front of the store. Ari beckoned her to join him. "Try this. See if it fits." He held out a hunting vest, and she slipped her arms into it. He zipped up the front. "It's no Kevlar, but might protect you a little and there are lots of pockets for carrying things."

Lila looked down at the heavy brown camouflage vest looking ludicrous over her short skirt and wedge-heeled sandals. "I need some pants and shoes, too."

Ari scanned her bare legs. "I don't know. That's kind of a good look for you."

Was he flirting? Here, now, in the middle of an end-of-the-world disaster? Her legs burned as if his assessing glance carried the heat of a torch. He met her gaze, brown eyes sparkling, and her stomach gave a little flutter.

She smiled. "Okay, player. I'm going over there now." She pointed to the shoe aisle, where Deb and Mrs. Scheider were finding good walking shoes to replace their high heels. Her smile disappeared as she reported to Ari what she'd learned on the phone. "By the way, my mom and dad in Ohio say this attack is happening there, too. There haven't been announcements on the news, just conjecture, and the government isn't giving and information."

Ari frowned. "There must be a battery powered radio somewhere in the building. I'll look for one."

Lila removed the hunting vest as she passed Hector, speaking in rapid Spanish into his cell phone. She tried to catch the gist of the conversation from his expression. With his thick brows knitted it was hard to tell if he was upset or relieved.

She reached the shoe aisle where Deb reached to the top shelf for a box. Several other shoe boxes littered the ground around her feet.

"How's it going?" Lila offered a little smile.

Deb shook her head. "Great. Not enough to be in the middle of a disaster, but I can't find a pair of shoes that fit." She lifted a white, gray and orange patterned tennis shoe from the tissue in the box and stared at it. "Did you talk to your family?"

Lila reiterated what she'd told Ari about the situation extending nationwide. "What about you? Did you reach your girlfriend?"

Deb's expression was as grim as Hector's. "No, but sometimes she turns her cell off when she's at work."

"God, this is a nightmare." Lila moved down to the six and half section and grabbed a pair of tennis shoes at random. "I keep thinking I'll wake up, that it couldn't possibly be real."

"Or we're being punked on a grand scale," Deb said dryly.

Mrs. Scheider came around the corner of the shelving unit

wearing a pair of pristine white nurse shoes with her tan pant suit and pearls.

"Were you able to reach anyone, Mrs. Scheider?" Lila asked.

"My daughter in Connecticut. She and the children are all right. They've got some kind of shelter set up in the town hall, where everyone is gathering. Soldiers evacuated the houses and are on guard at the shelter. But Christine's husband is in the city and she can't reach him. The connection was terrible and part way through our conversation her phone went dead." Mrs. Scheider's mouth was tight, but her calm voice betrayed none of her worry. Cool under pressure. Lila admired that.

Deb sat on the floor to pull on the pair of shoes she'd selected. "My girlfriend, Julie works in a research and development lab. It's not far from here. I was going to meet her for lunch today." Her voice grew thick and she swallowed hard.

Lila knelt beside her and patted her back. "She's probably all right. Try not to worry." Her words were as useless as condolences to the bereaved, but she had to say something.

"I've got to get to her. I don't care what any of you say. I'm going." Deb tied her shoes with emphatic tugs of the laces.

"Putting yourself at risk won't help your friend," Mrs. Scheider said. "We must work from logic not emotion if we're going to get through this."

Lila frowned at her. Wise counsel wasn't what Deb needed at the moment. She settled onto the floor beside Deb to try on her own pair of shoes and changed the subject. "How long have you and Julie been together?"

"Five years. We had a commitment ceremony last fall. We're thinking about adopting."

"That's nice." Lila searched for something else to say. Small talk was beyond her at the moment, but she knew Deb needed the distraction. "A baby or an older child?"

Deb propped her arms on her knees and looked at Lila, her eyes bright with unshed tears. "Maybe a little girl about five or six. There are so many older children who need homes, but they come with a lot of baggage. I don't know if I'm ready to deal with that."

"Do you work?" Lila continued to ask questions, trying to ease Deb's tension and maybe her own.

"I have a small, home-based business so I could continue to work but be with the kid when she gets home from school."

Static blasted from a radio at the front checkout counter. Lila and Deb scrambled to their feet and went to join the others. Ari had found an old boombox and put in fresh batteries. He turned the dial slowly but nothing except crackling fuzz came through the speakers.

"The main power grid must've been destroyed by something." Joe rested his folded arms on the counter and cocked his head toward the radio.

The rest of them clustered shoulder to shoulder, concentrating on the slender thread that would connect them to the world outside. At last a broken transmission came from the speaker, a man's voice in short bursts interspersed with snow.

"Go back, go back! You got it." Hector waved his hand.

Ari fiddled with the tuner and the antenna sticking up from the boombox until the voice came in clearer, then he turned up the volume. The smooth delivery of a professional reporter was replaced by the shock of a terrified man.

"Reports coming out of Washington are conflicting. No official explanation for the phenomenon has been given. Indications are that events occurring throughout the United States may be facets of a widespread terrorist attack. Power outages, violent assaults and accounts of...cannibalism have been reported in all major cities. People are encouraged to stay indoors or find safe shelter until the crisis has been resolved. Military troops and transports are deployed nationwide. From Denver comes an unsubstantiated report of a skirmish between National Guardsmen and possibly unarmed civilians causing an unconfirmed number of casualties."

The reporter's voice was obliterated by static. Ari rotated the antenna, searching for the signal and caught more fragments of the news bulletin. "...at least fifty confirmed dead...witnesses described the attackers as 'zombies'...scientists claim the phenomenon might be... We interrupt this broadcast for a press briefing from the White House..."

"There! You got it. Stop moving the damn thing," Hector shouted.

But the announcer's voice almost immediately broke up again. Ari tried for several minutes to get the station back then stepped away from the radio with a curse. Joe took his place, scanning up and down the dial for another signal, but only static came from the radio.

"If we could find a battery-powered laptop with an air card for satellite reception, we'd have the whole internet for information," Derrick said. "All this stupid store's got is a couple of desktops in the offices in back. I checked. We need to get to an electronic store."

"No. I need to go find my girlfriend. I'm not waiting anymore." Deb shouldered the rifle Ari had assigned her. In the camo-vest and pants she wore, she looked like an entirely different woman than the one Lila had first seen on the train. Her dark face was fierce, her jaw set and her eyes narrowed. She looked like a warrior ready for battle.

The others tried to convince her of the wisdom of staying with the group.

"I've got my family in Queens, my wife and my little girls. You think I don't want to get to them? But there ain't no way," Hector said.

"Because it's clear across the city and over the bridge. But Julie's only a few blocks away," Deb argued.

"We should find someone in authority. There must be patrolling police or even soldiers," Ann said. "There's probably someplace they're sending everyone to keep them safe."

"Like the Astrodome after Katrina? What a great idea," Deb scoffed.

Derrick loudly pressed for a trip to Best Buy, while Ronnie

whined about wanting her mommy, the poor kid. The clamor of voices grew as everyone expressed an opinion about what they should do, where they should go or told about the loved ones they needed to reach. Their bickering voices rose above the continuing static of the radio.

Lila wanted to retreat someplace absolutely silent, wrap her arms around herself and rock until this bad dream was over. She looked at Ari, who'd walked away from the group to sit on the floor and lean against a shelving unit displaying fishing rods. Resting his arms on his knees, he closed his eyes. She studied his strong jaw, his full lips pressed grimly tight and the spatters of blood on his olive drab T-shirt. God, what he'd had to do to that thing in the subway and no one had even remembered to thank him for it.

She went over and sat beside him, offering a bottle of water from her tote bag. "Here."

He opened his eyes and accepted the bottle. "Thanks." He uncapped and drank deeply, his Adam's apple bobbing with each swallow.

A little flutter of heat in her belly made Lila look away. It was so wrong to be attracted to a stranger while her loved ones and maybe the entire world was in jeopardy. She gazed at the industrial green carpet on the floor. "So, how are you doing?"

"Fine. You?"

"Holding up." Unable to think of anything to say, she was glad to sit in silence for a few minutes. Finally, she spoke again. "Hey, thanks for what you did, killing that thing. It must've been hard."

He shrugged. "Had to be done."

"No one else was brave enough to do it. How long have you been in the army?"

His smile was a tight grimace. "Three months. I'm home on leave from BCT. I'm supposed to leave for Arizona next week for AIT."

Lila wrinkled her nose at all the military acronyms. "Why does all that mean?"

"Basic combat training is the same for everyone," he explained.

"After that you go for advanced training in different places. At Fort Huachuca I'd be learning intelligence gathering techniques."

Torture training? Lila wondered but didn't ask.

Ari gave back the nearly empty bottle. "What about you? Where were you going when this happened?"

"Classes at NYU." She thought of her professors and other students and wondered what they were all doing. Had anyone made it to class today?

"What's your major?" he asked the obligatory question as if they were making small talk at some party.

"Undeclared. I'm in the Liberal Studies course at the College of Arts and Sciences. Pretty soon I'll have to decide on a field of study." Two years into the program and she still wasn't certain what that field would be.

Then she realized it probably didn't matter any more. Here she spoke of the future as if everything was normal, but they now lived in a world overrun by zombies. In a few brief moments, between taking a ride to school and the train coming to an abrupt halt, the world had changed, and along with it, her perception of how the universe worked. She'd believed life was life and death was death with little overlap besides an occasional near death experience. Now she would never be the same. None of them would be.

Lila looked at Ari and lowered her voice. "Are you scared? Cause you don't act scared."

A real smile flashed across his mouth and he gave a sharp bark of a laugh. "Am I scared? Good question."

CHAPTER FIVE

He was numb and his stomach felt sour and sick like the morning after a night of partying but without any of the fun of getting drunk. Was he scared? He was beyond it, running on pure adrenalin and instinct. Even as he'd demonstrated how to load and fire a rifle or searched for a radio or gathered supplies his brain had replayed killing the zombie over and over. He felt the jolt of the pole in his hands as it hit the thing's body, the yielding flesh when he tried to impale the neck and, worst of all, the sensation of sawing through flesh and bone with the too blunt edge of the metal shelf. Beyond afraid, beyond horrified, he was fucking traumatized.

"I've had better days," he said dryly.

Lila smiled, a little quirk of her lips that brought out a dimple in one cheek. "Yeah, me too. If you'd asked me earlier in the day, I would've said last night was about the worst experience I'd gone through in my life. This kind of puts it in perspective."

"Why, what happened last night?"

"I broke up with my boyfriend of two years, and I thought it would go better than it did. He's usually a calm guy, but he was upset to say the least." She shook her head and her bangs fell over her eyes. She absently pushed them back, a gesture he was becoming familiar with. Ari wanted offer her a barrette or something.

"Anyway, it was an ugly scene," she continued. "I was feeling pretty crappy about it on the train right before all hell broke loose."

"Hell on earth," he murmured, leaning his head back against the cool metal display rack and watching the others' faces as they argued. "Have to say, it's more fun fighting zombies in a video game than in real life."

"What you had to do must've been awful." A frown puckered her brows, and the strands of hair she'd pushed back fell forward again. He longed to brush them out of her eyes that were a deep shade of blue that almost bordered on purple.

"Yeah, well, we all might have to be ready to kill the way things are shaping up," he answered gruffly.

"I don't even squash bugs when I find them indoors. I take them outside and let them go."

"These aren't bugs. They're not even really alive. I think you can feel justified in putting them out of their misery. If those bodies' real owners were still alive, they'd thank you for it."

"I suppose you're right." Lila smiled briefly and the dimple in her cheek flashed again. "Some brave new world, huh?"

She rested her chin on her drawn up knees, silent for a moment before she added, "I'm worried about my ex. It sounded like the hospital is overrun."

"My mom works there, too and I haven't been able to reach her. I know how Deb feels. I want to go to her, but I guess we're all stuck with each other for a while." Ari thought he could probably make it on his own if they all split up, but some of the others would be helpless. It wouldn't be right to ditch them.

"Guess so." Lila exhaled and started to climb to her feet. "And I guess we need to be a part of this." She nodded toward the escalating argument. "We're going to have to make some decisions and it's probably better if everyone's not yelling at each other—especially since they're all armed."

What he wouldn't give to be back at training camp with someone barking out orders all he had to do was follow. He followed Lila back toward the others.

"Hey," he said, and when everyone continued to loudly promote his or her own agenda, he repeated more sharply, "Hey! Listen."

They all fell silent and looked toward him. Joe turned down the volume on the static-filled radio.

"No one has to stay here against their will so if you want to go so badly, Deb, you should, but I believe we're safer staying together. We can find a way to accommodate what everybody wants to do. Derrick, you want a laptop? That's a good idea and we'll try to get one and food, too. Many of you are anxious to get home to your families. Let's talk about the geography of that, keeping in mind you'll probably have to walk all the way. Then there's the idea of trying to find some military personnel to evacuate us from the city."

He drew a breath, hoping he'd covered all their concerns and made them feel "heard" because now he was about to shoot them down. "The problem is it's dangerous out there and we're on foot. Some of us might not be able to run fast enough if we had to, especially after what we've already been through." He indicated Ronnie with a flick of his gaze. "To me, it makes the most sense to spend the night here where we're fairly safe. In the morning, after we've all had a chance to rest, we can reassess the situation. Meanwhile, we'll send out a party for supplies, but the majority of the group should wait here."

There were murmurs of agreement and he felt a surge of relief that there wasn't going to be any contention, then Deb spoke up.

"I hear what you're saying and I appreciate the logic, but I'm going." She slung a rifle onto her shoulder. "I'm going now. If I can, I'll come back here with Julie and whatever news I find out."

No one tried to persuade her anymore. Her determined face stopped their attempts. Lila said, "good luck" and Ann murmured, "be careful" as they watched Deb walk to the front of the store and check the street through the display window. She let herself out the front door, and Lila went to lock it behind her then stood, watching her disappear down the street.

Ari felt like he'd lost one. At the same time he wished he could take off like that, too, but a glance around at the faces of the remaining members of their group reminded him why he couldn't. He didn't know quite why he felt a sense of personal responsibility for their wellbeing, but he couldn't seem to shrug it off much as he'd like to.

Lila came back over from the door. "What now?"

Ari thought about a course of action. "There should be a guard at the window, keeping watch. We'll take turns. There's no way to recharge our cell phones so we shouldn't use them except to periodically try to reach 911. Derrick, you and I will go for supplies. I saw a grocery store farther down the block, and a rent-to-own place where you can get computer supplies." He wanted Derrick along because the kid knew what he needed. Ari wasn't computer ignorant, but knew more about cruising the internet than actually setting up systems.

"If you meet other people, you could bring them back here. There's safety in numbers." Ann's long fingers fiddled nervously with her bracelet. "Maybe you'll even find a policeman who can tell us what to do?"

"Maybe," Ari agreed, but he thought the cops were as clueless as anyone else, and he hesitated to expand their group by too many. The smaller the team the better the organization. Right now, despite the fact they were practically strangers, Ari felt he had a handle on who everyone was and what to expect from them. So far, no one had lost their cool too badly. Add in a wild card, someone unstable or abrasive and the group dynamic would shift.

"They say the first stage of a crisis is the most dangerous," he continued. "After things settle down is the time to make a move."

"There should be enough camp beds and sleeping bags for all of us here. We'll set up camp while you're gone." Lila supported him and he was grateful for it.

"I'll keep first watch," Joe volunteered.

"I want to go with you," Hector announced. "I'm a good shot and I can't stand waiting around any more. I wanna see what's happening out there."

Ari thought he could move faster with only him and Derrick, but Hector might prove useful. At least the guy could shoot. Likely the only shooting Derrick had done was with an X-box controller. "Okay," he agreed.

They checked their gear. With a rifle strapped to his back, a skinning knife in a holster by his side and another semi-automatic in hand, Ari figured he was as ready as he'd ever be. Hector also had his rifle held ready for use and Derrick held several empty backpacks to carry their loot.

Joe opened the door and locked it behind them after they'd stepped out onto the sidewalk. Even with sunglasses on, the outdoors seemed bright after the dimness of the store. Ari squinted down the street with its jumbled cars and nearly empty sidewalks. Such quiet stillness in the middle of the day on a city street was weird and unsettling. There were sirens in the distance and some traffic noise, also a helicopter off to the south, but overall the impression of desertion and silence rested like a muffling quilt over the city.

Pieces of the man who'd broken through the window earlier lay among the shattered glass in front of that building. There were other broken bodies here and there, but no living people in sight. Then in the distance, several blocks away, Ari saw people moving. He raised his binoculars to see if they were living or zombie. Several figures darted quickly down the sidewalk and around the corner. They were living humans. He'd already become familiar with the jerky gait of zombies, like marionettes operated by an amateur puppeteer. That should make them easy to outrun, yet the creatures seemed to be doing a pretty good job of attacking and killing people. They weren't slow, merely awkward

"This is freaky." Hector, walking on Ari's left, echoed his thought. The man's white knuckle grip on his rifle and his darting gaze made Ari a little nervous. It was good to be alert and vigilant, but not so good if the guy snapped and started shooting randomly.

They reached a mom & pop grocery which had caught Ari's eye earlier. Iron grates covered the display windows. The door was locked.

Frustrated, Ari jerked on the door for a few seconds then began to beat at the lock with the butt of his rifle. A flurry of movement inside the store stopped his assault and a moment later the door opened a few inches. Dark eyes peered through the gap. "What do you want?"

"Groceries," Ari kept the *duh* to himself. He held his rifle in one hand and held up his free hand, palm open to show his harmless intent. "Just groceries. That's all. There's a group of us. We need supplies."

A woman's voice speaking in Korean came from behind the man in the doorway, a rapid-fire patter of either fear or anger. The storekeeper muttered a sharp comment and opened the door a little farther. "Hurry up. Come in."

Derrick and Hector entered first while Ari scanned the street one last time, then he followed them into the store. With its shuttered windows, the interior was even darker than the sporting goods store. But Ari noted the hum of a small generator which was keeping the refrigerated cases cool. A woman with her black hair in a loose ponytail stood behind the counter, staring at them. Beside her was an older man with white shot hair pointing a pistol at them.

The younger man who'd answered the door also had a hand gun. He let them see it, but didn't hold it on them. He bobbed his head in greeting. "Any news about what's going on?"

"Zombies," Derrick piped up and Ari cringed at the word, which still sounded preposterous. "They've overrun the city, and from what we heard on the radio, the rest of the country is under attack, too."

One dark eyebrow shot up. "Zombies?"

"Take a look around, man. Do you have a better explanation?"

"A virus or some other disease infecting people. Maybe a terrorist chemical attack that hits the nervous system and makes people go crazy. But zombies? Come on." The man holstered his gun. Ari noticed the old man behind the counter didn't.

"That's what I said," Hector added. "A virus."

The store owner nodded toward the shelves. "Go ahead and get what you need, but we're accepting cash only today."

"Are you kidding me?" Hector's voice rose. "We're in a crisis and you're worried about money?"

The man exchanged glances with his family members behind the counter. The old man rattled off some more Korean. The muzzle of his gun never faltered, remaining trained on the customers.

The younger guy frowned. "I don't want trouble, but we can't just give stuff away."

"I've only got about twenty bucks." Ari cursed himself for not collecting cash from the others. It hadn't even occurred to him.

"I don't have anything," Derrick said. "I left my wallet in my jacket pocket and my jacket's with my sister."

Grumbling in Spanish, Hector fished in his pocket and pulled out a few crumpled bills. "I was going to cash my paycheck at the bank so all I've got is this."

Ari mentally added up all the food they'd need to feed the group, not only for tonight but possibly for several meals more. A little over twenty bucks wasn't going to cut it. "I'll make you a deal." He set his rifle down, leaning it against a shelving unit, and took the spare rifle off his back. "A trade. You give us supplies. We give you this rifle. Trust me, you're gonna need more protection than a couple of handguns can provide."

"You have to sever the heads from the spinal cord," Derrick added a helpful tip, "either cut them off or shoot through the back of the neck. Head shots don't work. They'll just keep coming."

The store owner accepted the weapon, examined it, and nodded without conferring with his father this time. "All right. Take what you need."

Ari collected perishables from the coolers first. He had a feeling before this was over they'd be eating a lot of canned foods. As he packed the items into one of the knapsacks, Ari asked, "How long ago did this start happening?" He wanted to know if the timing coincided with the attack on the subway.

"A few hours, I heard a car crash outside and my wife called

911," the man said. "It didn't take long to figure out there was something more than an accident happening. The power went out and people were running and screaming. I locked down the shop right away and we've been in here ever since."

"Mama!" a child's voice called from the back room. The woman murmured something to her husband in Korean and left through the door behind the counter.

"Where's the rest of your group?" the shopkeeper asked.

"Down the street in the sporting goods shop. We were on the subway when it was attacked." Ari shoved a bag of apples into the nearly full knapsack.

The man nodded. "The national guard or somebody has to come soon."

"I don't know. Could be awhile." Ari zipped the bag and hefted the heavy weight onto his shoulders,. It was just as well he'd traded the extra rifle. He couldn't have carried it anyway. Also a good thing he'd spent hours training with a pack on his back during the past weeks.

The man unlocked the door and Hector poked his head out. "Looks okay."

He stepped outside and Derrick and Ari followed him.

"Good luck," the store owner said as they walked past.

The sound of the door locking behind them reminded Ari of his stint in juvie, only now he was being locked into an outside world that was far more dangerous than detention.

They moved quickly past debris, abandoned cars and body parts, to the Rent-A-World across the street. This door was also locked, but the display window was smashed so they stepped right it through into the store.

Bits of safety glass crunched under Ari's boots as he led the way inside. He paused, waiting for his eyes to adjust from sunlight to the dark interior of the building. No working generator here—ironic considering they sold electronics. Or maybe they had one but no one had lived long enough to turn it on. He held his rifle ready to pop any shambling thing that raised its ugly head, but the place seemed empty.

Derrick beelined straight to the computer department, listing aloud all the things he wanted, as he searched the shelves.

"You lost me after 'computer'," Ari said. He followed Derrick, keeping alert for any surprises coming from the dark shadows. The encounter with the Korean storekeepers had reminded him it wasn't only zombies they needed to look out for. Frightened humans with guns could be just as lethal.

Derrick studied the packaging of an air card. "We won't be able to activate this, and with the power down there's no way besides satellite to get on the internet."

"Just grab anything you might need and we'll find out if it works later." Ari was anxious to get back to the group. He kept running scenarios in which they returned to find the rest of their posse torn to pieces. Images of Ronnie's blood-streaked face or Lila's body sprawled on the floor haunted him. He scanned the back of the store where the shadows were deepest and Hector did the same, keeping his eyes on the street outside.

At last, Ari couldn't take any more of Derrick's farting around. He stood over him as the kid shoved a package of cable and other electronic paraphernalia in his pack.

"Come on. Get moving," Ari prodded. "We've gotta go."

"Aye-aye, Captain." Derrick snapped a salute.

Ari felt like kicking the boy. The smart-ass attitude wouldn't normally have bothered him, but he was exhausted and dangling by his last nerve. He wanted to close his eyes and not open them again until all this was over.

Derrick zipped the bag closed, heaved it onto his thin shoulders and followed Ari to the front where Hector stood sentry.

They crunched through the window glass back into the bright sunlight. Ari flipped his sunglasses down over his eyes and marched double time toward the sporting goods store. He was almost there when Hector called out, "Hey, wait up."

Ari stopped and turned toward him. The older man lifted his Mets cap and ran a hand through his short, dark hair. "Listen, I can't go back with you guys. I know what we said about sticking together, but I've gotta try to get to my wife and kids. My mind's not going to change by morning. I need to get started now."

Ari felt like someone had added another stone to the heavy pile in his gut, but he nodded. "I get it, man, but we could really use you. Other than me, you're the only one who knows how to shoot."

"You're crazy! No way you're going to make it all the way across the bridge," Derrick said.

Hector shrugged. "I've been thinking about this 'stick with the group' thing. What's out there—" he pointed down the street "—ain't going to be stopped by a half dozen people with rifles. One guy's might have a better chance to get where he's going, sneaking and hiding. Don't matter anyway. I've got to try, for my kids." He paused then added, "Good luck."

That was it. He turned and walked away, his leaving as abrupt as Deb's had been. What could a person really say after goodbye?

"Shit," Ari muttered under his breath. He believed Hector was right; a guy alone with no one depending on him could probably survive longer. Ari should take his cue and cut out, go to the hospital and see if he could find his mom. But as he watched Hector's short, stocky frame grow smaller then turn a corner, Ari knew he couldn't abandon the people waiting for supplies and protection. Whether he liked it or not, they'd somehow become his responsibility.

Derrick pounded on the door. A second later it opened and Derrick slipped inside. With a last glance at the deserted streets, Ari followed.

CHAPTER SIX

The hours since the attack seemed like months. Lila was bone-tired but too jittery to sit down and relax for a few minutes. She felt as charged up as if she'd drunk a six-pack of Red Bulls. To keep her mind from spinning out of control, she concentrated on setting up bedrolls. There were only a couple of camp beds, but plenty of air mattresses and sleeping bags. She located a kerosene stove and camping cookware to heat water, and hoped Ari would think to bring back coffee and tea bags. It was a foolish little desire when the world was coming to an end, but focusing on unimportant details was the only thing keeping her sane.

"We should hang tarp over the windows," she suggested to Ann. "When night comes, we'll want to have a little light in here but don't want to draw attention."

Ann went to get a couple of packages of tarp and hooks to hang it on. "Orange, green or blue?" she asked, fanning the squares of brightly colored plastic.

"What do you think, Ronnie?" Lila turned to the little girl, who was gripping the stuffed unicorn she'd picked up at the subway store and staring vacantly at nothing. "Do you want to choose a color?"

The little girl's gaze cleared and focused slowly as if she was coming back from a long way. "Um, blue's the prettiest."

And probably the most opaque for concealing light, Lila thought. "Blue it is."

She searched for a stepladder in the back room and then screwed hooks into the wooden frame around the window. Outside, Joe pulled the metal grill across the windows for an added safety measure, while Mrs. Scheider covered him with a rifle. The elegant elderly woman in pearls toting an assault rifle may have been one of the most bizarre sights Lila had seen all day.

When he came back inside, Joe took over the job of inserting hooks while Lila threaded thin rope through the eyes of the tarp and tied it in place with Ann and Mrs. Scheider supporting the weight of the tarp. It was good to be busy, to feel a little useful instead of totally helpless and vulnerable. Lila wasn't a fan of surrendering control of her life and these preparations gave her back a margin of power.

She began to worry about how much time had passed since Ari, Derrick and Hector had left. How long did it take to gather a few groceries and a computer? Lila slammed the door shut on the images of death and dismemberment that bombarded her and focused on tying knots. Worrying wouldn't bring them back any sooner.

The already dimly-lit store was plunged into twilight blue as the tarp blocked the afternoon sunlight. Lila left an edge open so they could look out, and she'd just climbed off the stepladder when someone pounded on the door. Derrick's voice was muffled on the other side. Joe unlocked the door and let him and Ari inside.

"Where's Hector? What happened?" Ann asked.

"He left for home." Ari's curt tone conveyed his feelings about it.

So now there were six of them. Lila hadn't even known Deb or Hector until a few hours ago, and yet she felt abandoned. The others in their group had every right to do whatever they wanted, but each loss felt like a cut, another wound in an already painful day.

Derrick settled down with his computer and accessories and Joe squatted next to him to offer any help he could. Lila and Ann worked on putting a meal together, while Mrs. Scheider sat with Ronnie, talking quietly. Lila overheard her inventing a story about the unicorn.

As she opened a can of beans—*staple of the survivalist*, Lila watched Ari standing by edge of the tarp looking out the window. Sunlight streamed through the glass, casting him in a halo that contrasted with the darkness around him. Appropriate since he was the nearest thing they had to a savior at the moment.

She turned her attention to scooping beans from the can into a pan and wished Deb was still with them. She'd have some feminist comment to make about gender roles rearing their ugly heads in a crisis—the women cooking, the men protecting and providing. Lila missed her caustic remarks and sarcastic attitude.

She glanced at Ann, who was making sandwiches with cheese and lunchmeat. The woman had fine, pale hair that hinted at Nordic heritage. Her face was slender, her nose narrow and slightly upturned, her complexion poreless. She looked like fragile porcelain and Lila imagined she had the delicate temperament to match. Ann wasn't the type of woman one would expect to hold up under pressure, but Lila must be stereotyping, because Ann hadn't fallen apart yet. Not any more than the rest of them had.

"Tell me about yourself," Lila said. "What do you do? Where do you live? Do you have family nearby?"

Ann paused from smearing mustard on bread and glanced up. "I'm from Minnesota originally. I work as a curator at a small art gallery." A sharp laugh that sounded more like a sob burst from her. "Maybe I should say 'worked'. Nothing is ever going to be the same again, is it?"

A world where people bought art to hang on their walls did seem light years away from hunkering in a sporting goods store, cooking over a camp stove.

"The military will get things under control," Lila promised, adding dryly, "if there are enough soldiers left who aren't overseas." She wondered if this phenomenon was limited to the U.S. or if it was happening worldwide. She'd give anything for some news right now.

"How about you?" Ann asked, plopping slices of bread on top of the row of sandwiches.

"I attend N.Y.U. No major yet. My parents aren't too happy about that." A wave of homesickness washed over her as she pictured her mom and dad sitting in their living room watching TV. She ached to be with them.

"What do you think caused this?" Ann murmured as if they might be overheard, or as if the enormous thing happening all around them was some kind of secret.

It was Lila's turn to give a humorless laugh. "In the movies isn't it usually some ray from outer space that activates zombies?"

"I don't know. I never watch that kind of movie."

The simple picnic supper of sandwiches, potato salad, baked beans, veggies and dip was ready. Ann set out plates, napkins and plastic cutlery in a neat circle and Lila called the others to come and eat. How civilized. How normal.

She didn't think she was hungry, doubted she could swallow a bite, but surprisingly, once she picked up her fork, she devoured her plate full of food in minutes. The others ate with equal ferocity, Derrick downing several servings before returning to cursing at the computer and his inability to get the air card functional.

Ari still stood sentry at the window. Lila took him a plate of food and a juice box.

"Thanks." He glanced at her and she was struck again by the warm brown eyes and ridiculous length of his lashes. Then her attention was caught by the dried blood spattering his shirt and pants. He hadn't taken the time to change into something clean. She should go pick out a shirt and pants for him.

"How are you doing?" She rested a hand on his arm, thinking about him sawing through that zombie's neck, the sheer savagery of it—and how she'd been cheering him on inside. Apparently her belief in non-violence fell by the wayside in the midst of a zombie attack.

He glanced at her hand. "I'm okay. There was a family holed up at the grocery store. It made me think of how many thousands of people must be all over this city, keeping hidden, waiting it out. They're sure as hell not out on the streets. But other than hearing one chopper and a few sirens, it seems like nothing's happening. I don't think the military knows how to deal with this, and if it's happening everywhere, maybe the entire infrastructure of the country is down. Help might not come for a long time. We're going to have to rely on ourselves to stay alive."

The flat way he said it was chilling. Lila had clung to the idea that someone in authority would fix things soon. Rescue would come. But what if there were no police, no soldiers, tanks or helicopters, no Red Cross volunteers with care packages—just more zombies and more dismembered corpses piling up? And what if there was no safe place to escape to? Only more danger beyond the city, and a world that would never go back to normal just like Ann had said.

She squeezed Ari's arm. "Hey, let me watch for a while. Eat your food and get washed up and changed."

Ari hesitated and looked out the window. He seemed like the kind of guy who wouldn't trust someone else to do a job right. As egotistical as that seemed, Lila did feel more secure knowing he was keeping watch.

At last he nodded. "Okay. Call if you see anything happening out there."

"I think I can handle it. Don't worry," she assured him.

"Sorry. I'm not usually bossy."

"You're not being bossy. You're leading. Somebody has to. Go on now." She gave him a little push. "Take a break. You'll feel better."

"Somehow I doubt that." But he strode away toward the back of the store and the restroom. Joe had moved a water cooler bottle near the sink so they could wash up. Not having running water was a pain, no doubt one of many inconveniences they'd soon get used to.

Lila peered through the crack between the tarp and the window frame at the street outside. It was astonishing that a city of thousands of people could go dead—pun intended—so quickly. The area was deserted, the abandoned vehicles giving an eerie sense that their drivers and passengers had vanished en masse, zapped away by a space ship or sucked into the afterlife like in some movie about the biblical end times.

A flicker of movement at the corner of her eye caught Lila's attention. A woman was running down the street. No, not running, shambling in that jerky fashion that proclaimed she wasn't normal. Whatever activated zombies' bodies, electrifying neural pathways to allow the muscles to function, didn't do a very good job of it.

Lila opened her mouth to warn the others, but the creature turned a corner and disappeared. They were still out there, as if there'd been any doubt. Lila released a shaky breath and scanned the neighborhood with diligence. She watched as the sky went from gold to pink to gray, and then the sun set and the city was plunged into darkness.

Joe came to relieve her and Lila went over to where the other refugees were arranged in a rough circle around a single kerosene lamp.

Derrick had dragged over an inflatable raft and covered it with sleeping bags for him and Ronnie. He and his sister lay on its cushioned surface. Mrs. Scheider sat in a folding camp chair with a book in her hand and a battery powered reading light clipped to the book. *Survivalist's Medicine Chest* was the title. The woman sipped from a cup as she read, as relaxed as if she was cozied up at home with a cup of tea and a mystery novel.

Ann stared morosely at the kerosene flame. She was red-eyed and her face puffy. She must have spent some time in the back room crying. Lila didn't blame her. She wouldn't mind a good long cry herself, but hadn't really had an opportunity. Besides, she felt more numb than despairing. She must be in shock.

Ari sat cleaning a gun. No surprise there. How could a brand new weapon that had never been used need a cleaning? But he evidently needed something to do with his hands to keep him distracted. Everyone had their own way of coping. Lila dropped onto the air mattress and sleeping bag set up beside Ari's.

She looked around at the glum faces and decided to try to lighten the mood. "Is it time to break out the S'mores do you think? Maybe sing some campfire songs?"

Ronnie's head popped up from her pillow and she sat up, crossing her legs. "I went to camp last summer. I know some songs." Her chipmunk voice warbled surprisingly tunefully, "Make new friends, but keep the old, one is silver and the other gold."

Lila joined her on the familiar song. "A circle's round, it has no end. That's how long I want to be your friend."

She glanced at Ari to find him grinning at her. "Girl Scouts?"

"Eight years." She turned back to Ronnie. "Do you know any more?"

"Yeah, but everybody's got to sing it this time. It's easy." The little girl's face glowed in the yellow light as she began, "This is the song that never ends. Yes it goes on and on my friends…"

"Some people started singing it not knowing what it was," Lila came in on the cheerful nonsense song and Ann surprised her by joining in, "And they'll continue singing it forever just because, this is the song that never ends…"

They went around again and again until Ronnie broke down giggling and rolling back and forth on the raft. She bumped into her brother and Derrick impatiently pushed her away.

Lila smiled, pleased to see the little girl happy however temporarily.

Ari looked at her with raised brows. "Really? This is what girls do at camp?"

"Boys too. Didn't you ever go to camp?" she teased.

"No. I went to juvie for a while but I don't think that counts."

"My mom made me go to band camp one summer," Derrick chimed in, "and we *never* sang weird songs."

"How about you, Mrs. Scheider." Lila tried to include the older woman in their conversation. "Did you go to camp growing up?"

"We had a house in the Hamptons so I went there every

summer, but there were plenty of bonfires on the beach. However, I'm afraid I've never heard that song. Do you know 'Alice the Camel'?"

"Oh my God. Things are surreal enough without the singing. Please no more," Derrick begged as Mrs. Scheider started singing.

But the three women and Ronnie carried on until they reached the "boom, boom, boom" part of the song.

"Hey," Joe called from by the window. "Keep it a little quieter, okay?"

Awareness of the danger they were in washed over them like a bucket of water putting out their campfire. Their laughter died and they fell silent. Lila could see Ronnie crumbling, her little face scrunched up as if she might cry again.

"Hey, Ronnie. What grade are you in?" Lila tried to distract her.

"Third."

"What's your teacher's name? Do you like her?"

"Ms. Tanoff. She's okay." The girl put her chin in her hands and stared at the lantern, her chin trembling.

"I remember third grade. Mrs. Baumbottom. We used to call her Big Bottom." Lila dredged up a story from her childhood to entertain the girl. "Once I drew a cartoon of her with her big bottom sticking out behind her. The kids were passing it around. Can you guess what happened?"

Ronnie's eyes widened. "She got it."

"That's right. One kid was passing it to another when she intercepted it. The picture didn't seem so funny anymore. I was scared to get in trouble, but also felt really bad about hurting her feelings."

"What happened?" Ronnie gasped, caught up in the dramatic tension as only a young child could be. "Did you get detention?"

"Well, she'd taken the drawing from Brian Stevens and at first I thought she was going to blame him. I'd have to tell the truth so he wouldn't get into trouble. But Mrs. Baumbottom looked at that picture and then straight at me. She knew my drawing from art work I'd done. Since my name wasn't on it, there was no proof it was mine. I kept my mouth shut and looked away."

"What'd she do then?"

"She had the whole class write a page about how they felt when someone made fun of them."

"You got off lucky." Derrick toyed with the zipper of his sleeping bag, drawing it up and down. "Bet the other kids were pissed at you for making them extra work."

"I don't know if I'd call it lucky. I felt almost sick with guilt while I was writing my paper. Later I went to the bathroom and cried my eyes out."

"Soft heart." Ari lay on his stomach on his bedroll with his head propped on one hand. "I did a helluva lot worse things when I was a kid, and I didn't feel sorry about them. I would've been the kid putting a tack on Big Bottom's chair for her to sit on. Me and my boys were kind of rough."

Lila could picture a gang of pint size thugs running around terrorizing the schoolyard and the neighborhood. It sounded like Ari's life had been a world away from her peaceful suburban childhood. She smiled at him. "So tell us something you did."

"I did a lot of dumb shit. Got in a lot of trouble. But a story the kid can hear? Let me think." He considered for a moment. "How about an embarrassing story? Once when I was in fifth grade I wanted to impress this girl at a party so I ate a whole can of Cheez Whiz, straight from the can down the gullet. Why I thought she'd think that was cool, I have no idea. I was ten. Chased it with a full can of Mountain Dew. After that I felt like I needed to burp, but when I did..."

"Oh no, man!" Derrick hooted. "No way."

"Yeah. Not only did I puke in front of everybody but it splashed on the girl I had the crush on. I impressed her all right."

"Sick." Derrick rolled on the raft, laughing.

"Boys are a whole different species from girls, aren't they?" Lila asked Ann. "And they don't get much better when they're older from what I can tell."

"They try to impress you with money instead of Cheez Whiz," Mrs. Scheider said dryly. "And the result is a great deal messier than a little vomit. My late husband splashed plenty of the fallout from his failed financial schemes on me."

All eyes turned to her as everyone waited for more explanation, but she refocused her attention on her book.

Lila prompted Ann. "We haven't heard from you. What childhood story do you have to share?"

Ann pushed strands of her blonde hair back from her face. "Nothing to top that, but there was a time I was embarrassed--not by something I did to myself but by something that happened to me. The summer before freshmen year our family suffered some…setbacks and my mom had to give up the lease on her car. She bought an old minivan to replace it, saying it was a better way to transport kids anyway. I was humiliated when she insisted on dropping me off at school in the thing. I wanted her to let me out a block away, but she wouldn't. She had to park right in front where everyone could see us."

Derrick grunted in agreement about how embarrassing parents could be.

"So there I was, a brand new freshman, terrified about fitting in at high school and forced to ride in my mom's ghetto van. One morning I got out and slid the door back and it just kept going, right off the track. The door literally fell off the van. Everybody waiting to go into school looked and laughed. I thought I'd sink into the earth I was so humiliated. It was the perfect way to start high school."

"Damn, I thought I'd done some embarrassing things," Derrick said. "You people are like the masters of making asses of yourselves."

"That van was not my fault," Ann protested in an almost serious tone that made Lila smile. Ghosts of embarrassments past were hard to kill. "How about you, Derrick? What's your worst moment?"

The boy flushed bright red. "Nothing. I don't have one."

"Yes you do," Ronnie shoved him in the shoulder. "What about the time Grandma came to visit and walked into your bedroom and caught you--"

"Shut UP!" He punched her shoulder much harder than she'd hit him and the girl let out a piercing shriek.

"Children, behave," Mrs. Scheider said.

"Quiet!" Joe strode over from his lookout by the window to glare at them all. "This isn't a pajama party. The last thing we want to do is draw attention. In fact, you should probably douse the light and get some sleep. Ari, I'll take first watch and I'll wake you later."

It was the most Lila had heard from Dr. Morgenstern since their ordeal began. His fatherly tone served to quell both Ronnie and Derrick. The girl flounced onto her side, dragging the covers over her head. Sounds of sniffling came from beneath the butterfly patterned sleeping bag. Derrick muttered under his breath but settled down.

Mrs. Scheider turned off her reading light and marked her place in her book then went to her cot. Lila's mind was buzzing and she was sure she wouldn't be able to sleep. Ari seemed relieved to take orders for a change. He turned the lamp as low as it would go then stretched out on top of his sleeping bag cushioned by an air mattress.

Lila felt him breathing in the dark beside her. She glanced over, but it was too shadowy to make out more than his general shape. Still she was very aware of his presence. Her body responded to it with a primitive pull. Their two bedrolls were side by side and she longed to shift closer until they were touching. She wouldn't mind if he rolled over and put his arms around her in his sleep. Wasn't that the way every road trip romantic comedy went? But this was hardly a comedy and in horror movies usually one of the protagonists ended up dead.

All the horrific images of the day tumbled through her mind as she lay alone in the dark, adrenaline still zinging through her veins. Tears spilled from her eyes, trickling down her cheeks and into her ears. She impatiently rubbed her face dry. She didn't want to disturb the others by sniffling like Ronnie, and she was too tired to drag herself to the back room of the store for some privacy.

"Are you okay?" Ari's voice floated through the air.

"Yeah," she croaked. "I'm fine."

"We'll find a way out of the city tomorrow somehow," he promised.

"Sure." But she didn't feel confident things would be any better in the outside world. She wondered how her parents were doing, and her friends and Doyle. He'd sounded terrified when she'd talked to him on the phone. Was he even still alive? She'd give anything to be with people she loved instead of this group of strangers. But on the other hand, she felt safer with Ari than she would have with Doyle, who tended to talk all around a decision before finally making it. The situation they were in didn't leave room for second guessing or wavering. She felt surprisingly close to Ari even though she didn't know much about him at all.

"Before we go to the marina I want to stop by St. Andrews and try to find my mom," Ari said.

She didn't know how to respond. Everyone wanted to locate their relatives, but the hospital seemed like the last place they should go after what Doyle had described. "I don't think that's such a good idea," she said gently. "From what my ex said, it's zombie central there. As harsh as it seems, I don't believe we can run around the city checking on everyone's family. We need to get our group someplace safe."

Ari didn't say anything for a few minutes and she was afraid she'd pissed him off. Lila reached out and touched his arm. "I'm sorry, but that's what I think. All we can do is pray and hope our loved ones make it someplace safe, too."

He exhaled. "You're right. My mom might not even be at the hospital anymore. She could be anywhere. But to cut her loose like that feels so wrong. It's been the two of us ever since my dad left years ago. I've always looked out for her."

Lila slid her hand down his arm to hold his hand. "I get it."

His voice lowered to a whisper so soft she could scarcely hear it. "I wish I could go where I want and didn't have to worry about all these people, you know? I don't know how they got to be my responsibility.

I'm no leader."

Lila turned to stare at his profile in the dark. Was he kidding? "Yes you are."

He shook his head. "I don't know what to do any more than anyone else does. Why do you all even keep listening to me?"

She smiled. "Because what you suggest makes sense and we all want to stay alive. But more than that. You *seem* confident and in this situation that's as important as knowing exactly what to do. Your confidence helps keep the rest of us from panicking."

He snorted. "I could be confidently leading you right over the edge of a cliff. Would that make me a good leader?"

"Sorry, Ari, you'd still be a leader—just not a smart one. You can't deny your nature. There are those who lead and those who follow and you're the former."

"That's a lot of insight coming from someone who doesn't even know me," he muttered.

They fell silent then, lying with their hands linked in the darkness. Lila stared at the shadows cast by sporting goods displays, the cardboard cutout of a grinning fisherman with a custom grip pole, shelving full of soccer and running shoes, baseball cleats and ski boots. What kid didn't fantasize about getting locked into a store and having the run of the place for a night? If this were some kid's movie, they'd be skateboarding up and down the aisles and shooting paintball guns at each other, having the time of their lives set against a pop soundtrack. She choked back her laughter with a snort.

"What?" Ari's sexy, low voice floated to her again.

"Nothing. Nerves. I'm just getting a little giddy."

"You should sleep. We all need to sleep—put this out of our heads for a while."

"It would be easier to fall asleep if you two would be quiet," Mrs. Scheider's crisp tone cut across their whispering.

"Night, Mrs. Scheider," Lila chanted like a Walton child, laughter still trembling in her voice.

Ari chuckled, the sound as warm and comforting as a cup of hot cocoa heating her insides. Lila crushed the attraction that had been nibbling at the edge of her consciousness all day. She was sure it had more to do with their extreme situation than actual feelings. A person would cling to any flotsam after a shipwreck.

"Good night," she murmured to Ari, then pulled her hand from his and turned over on her side. She had barely enough time to think that she'd never be able to fall asleep before oblivion claimed her.

Someone pounding on the door of the store, snapped her awake. Lila sat bolt upright, head whirling, heart pumping and legs ready to run. She blinked away her disorientation and focused on Joe going to open the door. Her first irrational thought was that he'd gone crazy and was about to let the zombies in to feast on them. Ari jumped up from his sleeping bag and ran toward the door. Lila scrambled to her feet and the others did the same. Ronnie whimpered and Derrick shushed her. Lila bent to search for her weapon by her bedding.

Joe opened the door and several people hurried into the store, all of them dark, featureless shapes.

"They're everywhere out there. Jesus Christ! We were lucky to make it here alive." Lila recognized Deb's smoke-roughened voice and relief rushed through her.

"Did any zombies see you?" Ari locked the door behind the newcomers, while Joe peered out the window to make sure they hadn't been followed.

"No. I don't think so, or they would've been on us." Deb leaned her rifle against the wall. "I'm sorry. I didn't know where else to go."

Lila turned up the kerosene lamp then joined the group at the door, grabbing Deb and giving her a hug. "I'm so glad to see you. This must be Julie."

"Pleased to meet you," the redhead greeted her and indicated the man with them. "This is Carl. He works with me at Quantus."

Carl was a tall, thin, dark skinned man with slightly bulging eyes and a receding hairline. He nodded. "Hi."

"It's getting worse out there," Deb said. "It's almost like a second wave is going through. The things are everywhere."

Lila shivered. She'd begun to feel a false sense of security here in this place they'd claimed as their own. It had been too easy to convince themselves the zombies had passed on to another part of the city, leaving a ghost town behind. But Deb was trembling and the others looked equally shell-shocked.

"Come and sit down." She led them to the camp site.

Ann went to heat water on the camp stove. Mrs. Scheider set up more chairs for the newcomers and the three sank gratefully onto them. Deb launched into the tale of how she'd hooked up with Julie and Carl.

"There's usually a receptionist at the front desk and you can't gain access to the offices or labs without a pass, but when I went into the building there was no one there. The door to the offices was torn off its hinges, blood and bodies everywhere." Deb sipped from a bottle of water Lila gave her, her hand shaking. "I went in back and searched until I found Julie and Carl."

"I was at my desk when we were attacked," Julie added her part of the story. "People burst into the room, and I thought they were junkies or something until one of them grabbed Abbie Woolsey and bit her neck. I jumped up from my chair. I didn't even try to help her. I just ran."

Deb grasped her hand. "You couldn't have done anything, babe. You know that."

"But I didn't try. None of us did. We all ran like rats." Julie pressed her lips tight together and stifled a sob.

"You did what you had to in order to survive," Lila said softly. "We all ran yesterday. We all left people behind." There were murmurs of agreement from some of the others.

Deb resumed her story. "By the time I got to Quantus, the zombies had moved on--mostly. When I was searching for Julie, one came around the corner straight at me." Her rough voice wavered a little and she swallowed. "I, uh, used my knife like you showed me, Ari."

"It all happened so fast," Carl spoke up at last. "One minute I was working on my computer and the next I heard screaming, people running, things smashing. The things burst into the room where I was working and I ran out of it. I heard them coming from both directions down the hall so I ducked into a supply closet to hide. Julie was already in there. We blocked the door. We didn't see what happened but we could hear it."

"We waited a long time, long after things got quiet," Julie added. "And then I heard Deb's voice calling my name so we came out."

"I think I might know what caused this," Carl said. "I believe it might be the result of a virus."

"No shit," Derrick said. "That's zombies one-oh-one. It's always in the blood."

Carl frowned. "No, I mean a specific virus—the A7. Quantus Labs has been working on an antidote for it. You may have heard about the new drug on the news."

"What does that have to do with the zombies?" Lila asked.

"It's possible..." Carl cleared his throat. "The work we've been doing may have been flawed."

"Flawed how?" Dr. Morgenstern left his lookout post to listen to his explanation.

"You have to understand, I'm a lab tech with fairly low level clearance. I see parts of the whole. I do the testing I'm asked to do and work on certain aspects of a project. So it's not my business to know how Quantus research is funded or what pharmaceutical company will ultimately manufacture the drug we design."

"Your point?" Ari asked impatiently.

"Rats treated with the antidote were initially healed but it altered their blood structure in minute ways. Still, the results were positive so we administered to test patients. All symptoms connected to A7 disappeared. That drug should never have been cleared without much more rigorous testing, but people were clamoring for a cure. So it was released without sufficient clinical trials either due to government intervention or because a pharmaceutical company was eager to make a fast buck." Carl exhaled a deep breath.

"And you believe people who took the drug, eventually died and then reanimated." Mrs. Scheider made the preposterous claim sound plausible.

"Yes. That's exactly what I fear."

"But why all at once? How could it have been so widespread?" Ari asked. "The logistics don't add up."

Carl shook his head. "You don't understand. This snowballed very quickly. The drug—A7 Counter, we named it—was manufactured on a massive scale and shipped to hospitals from coast to coast. Hospital staff countrywide began administering it almost simultaneously. The first wave of deaths might have taken place within days, but no one was in a hurry to panic the public with a possible connection to the antidote. After death there was likely a delay before the post-mortem results—i.e. zombieism—became apparent. By then more people were dead or dying.

"The very first attacks may have gone unreported, bodies in hospital morgues or mortuaries rising to devour or kill attendants or undertakers, spreading their altered blood to others. By this morning, on my way to work, I heard a radio news report of bizarre assaults at several area hospitals. The information was sketchy and quickly suppressed."

"What about those initial test patients?" Lila asked.

"I recognized a couple of them among the zombies that stormed our office," Carl said. "I hadn't known they died. That information was not something I was privy to. I can't give you an exact timeline of how all this played out, only my best guess. But apparently, some of these reanimates came directly from our own on-site morgue, where the bodies had been awaiting dissection. I believe the mutated blood causes a neurological jumpstart after death. The process expends a lot of energy giving the reanimates a ferocious appetite for living tissue."

"It seems like it's more than mingling blood that spreads the mutation." Ari strode nervously back and forth, his brows knitted in a frown. "Their bites, their saliva, must carry something for it to spread so fast. And that guy in the subway didn't take long to rise either."

"Like maybe the pace is accelerating." Lila offered Julie a bandage for a gash on her forehead. "Fast enough that it spread like wildfire, beyond the ability of the authorities to get a handle on it. Now what can they do? Say 'screw civilian casualties' and start bombing infected areas?"

Carl accepted the cup of tea Ann offered him and sipped it before speaking again. "I've been going over all the research in my mind and I think I see the flaw in the formula. Given a working lab with proper equipment, I believe I could find a solution to stop the mutated blood from causing reanimation." He gestured with his hand, sloshing tea over the rim of his cup. "Obviously it's too late for those already dead, but it could be administered to the newly infected to curtail the effect."

Deb snorted. "But meanwhile we have zombies running around eating people and infecting others."

"I believe I could find a solution for that as well," Carl said. "Darts filled with a solution that would stop the reanimates' neural systems. Better than bullets for bringing them down. Of course it would take time to develop these remedies and produce them in the necessary quantities."

"But you think you could do it?" Joe said. "Find a cure?"

Carl nodded. "There are files on my hard drive at work with formulas and data that I'd absolutely have to have as a starting point." He turned to Ari, instinctively recognizing him as the leader of the group. "I have to go back. I need to get that research."

"The zombies are thicker than ever out there. We're really going to have to run a gauntlet to get anywhere." Deb nodded toward Ronnie and Mrs. Scheider. "We can't drag everyone along. I vote a team goes for the hard drive and the rest stay here."

"No." Mrs. Scheider was as decisive as always. "Once you have what you need, you'll want to keep going out of the city. It would be a waste of time to come back for us, and we don't deserve to be abandoned because some of us are a little slow."

"I'm not talking about abandoning anyone," Deb argued.

"A strike team," Derrick chimed in. "That makes sense."

Ronnie clung to her brother's hand, whining. "Don't leave me. I don't want to get ate up by zombies."

"That won't happen, honey," Ann comforted her. "We'll be safer here. In fact we should all stay here until rescue comes."

"What rescue?" Deb snapped. "Get it through your head, no one's coming. But that's fine. You stay behind. You'd be useless in a fight anyway."

Tempers and voices rose as everyone argued and offered an opinion. Suddenly Ari's voice cut across the din like a knife. "No one's leaving anyone. We move as a team. We'll find a safe place for the group to stay nearby while a few go into the lab and retrieve the data. Then we'll head to the waterfront, find a boat and get the hell off this island."

Complete silence followed his pronouncement. It was a reasonable plan. Even Deb couldn't argue.

"Look," Lila said, "Everyone's exhausted. Our nerves are fried so let's get some sleep and talk more in the morning."

Wired from the influx of new people and information, it took some time for everyone to settle down to sleep. Lila lay awake on her pallet beside Julie rather than Ari and wished he was still by her even if they didn't touch. Just having him next to her had helped her to relax. She watched him standing guard near the window and listened to sounds of occasional screams and gunfire outside. Zombies were on the prowl. Lila expected any minute the door would rattle or the window shatter as they stormed the building, searching for fresh meat inside.

She prayed to the Organizer of the Universe to please put the world back in order and restore her to the life in which her biggest worry was passing a test or breaking up with a boyfriend. She begged for an end to this nightmare and fell asleep, still praying.

CHAPTER SEVEN

"No more arguing. This is the way we're going to do it." Ari clenched his jaw in an effort not to add a curse to the statement. He'd learned a lot from observing his sergeant at basic training. The man hadn't been a screamer, not at all like the "tear 'em down to build 'em up", frothing at the mouth sergeant he'd expected from watching too many movies. When Sergeant Vogt called out a command, he expected it to be obeyed so it was. He was a quiet yet masterful disciplinarian and his unit had responded to it by being consistently at the top of the boards.

Now Ari appreciated how difficult the sergeant's job was. Getting a group of mismatched characters to work as a team was not easy. Running away from the zombies in the subway, the group had deferred to his lead, glad to follow anyone who they thought could get them out alive. But now their individual personalities and agendas were emerging. Everyone had a different idea about what they should do, the route they should take or what items were indispensible to bring along.

"Everyone carries something, even Ronnie. We go out the back exit and move through the alleys as much as possible. Quantus Labs is seven blocks from here. That doesn't sound like much, but we may have to fight our way through those seven blocks." *And that's just the beginning. How the hell am I going to get all these people to the river alive?*

He'd considered his plan for most of last night. He'd already established that the main thoroughfares out of New York, the bridges and tunnels were too dangerous to travel. It would be too easy to get trapped by the flesh-eaters. But they should be able to snag a boat from the 79th Street Boat Basin marina. Unfortunately they wouldn't have keys so he hoped boats were as easy to hotwire as cars. He'd had plenty of practice on those.

Ari asked Deb to take point. She was sharp-eyed, fearless and knew the way. She'd had at least one kill now so he felt confident she wouldn't hesitate if she needed to fight. He and Joe flanked the group on either side and Derrick and Lila brought up the rear. The weaker members of the group were clustered in the middle. And he placed Carl dead center, a commodity to be protected at all costs. Ari was well aware this had gone far past mere survival of their group. They now harbored a man who might have the solution to humanity's downfall in his brain and on his hard drive.

Each member of the group wore a hunting vest. The padding might protect them from tearing teeth. Everyone except Ronnie was armed with knives and a pistol. The group in the center carried backpacks crammed with goods, while the "soldiers" on the perimeter were armed with assault rifles. Their job was to protect. They couldn't be hampered by heavy knapsacks.

After they were ready to go, with Deb poised to take that first step out the door—a critical moment for it was impossible to tell what they might encounter in the alley, Ann Hanson suddenly decided to melt down at last. To be honest, Ari was surprised she hadn't folded before. She'd raised questions, but for the most part had gone along with whatever the group decided. Now she dug in her heels and refused to budge.

"I don't want to go. We're safe in here. We should stay and wait for help." Her face was ashen, nearly matching her white-blond hair. Her eyes were huge and Ari could see she'd checked out. She didn't want to see reason or deal with the world they were facing. She wanted to continue believing in cavalry who would ride in and save the day.

"Ann, you can't stay here alone," Lila slipped an arm around the trembling woman's shoulders and hugged her.

"I can't go out there. I can't!" Ann protested, her voice rising. Tears trickled down her cheeks. She let her backpack drop to the floor and covered her face with her hands.

"Snap out of it," Deb ordered. "We're all scared but we have no choice. Now get a grip."

Ari could see neither Lila's gentle coaxing nor Deb's gruff commands were reaching Ann. She had turned in the blink of an eye from a functioning member of the team to a nervous wreck. He had a decision to make and his stomach rolled as he realized he'd already made it. He couldn't put the whole group in jeopardy by dragging along a basket case. They couldn't hang around here waiting for her to snap out of it. The truth was that despite what people believed, in the military sometimes you did leave a man behind if he was going to jeopardize the mission.

He stood in front of Ann, took her by the shoulders and stared into her unfocused eyes. "Listen to me." He kept his voice calm and level. "If you truly want to stay here, nobody's going to force you to go with us. But you have to understand you're in far more danger alone here than you are with a group. The zombies will be searching for fresh meat. They're smart enough to realize people are hiding indoors and they'll go through the buildings hunting them. Are you willing to risk that?"

Ann swallowed and wiped away the mucus running from her red nose. "I'll be quiet, and I'll find a hiding place in case they do get in. Just leave me some food and water. I can wait here until things get better. It has to happen soon. The army will storm the city. They'll rescue us."

"Jesus. You're crazy!" Deb said.

Ari held up a hand to silence her. "It's up to Ann. If she's really that terrified or if she's going to freak out once we get outside, then she should stay behind."

"No!" Ronnie shrieked and threw her arms around Ann's waist, burying her face against her. "I want to stay with Ann."

Things were rapidly spinning out of his control. Ari felt sick. As if there wasn't enough stress having to face zombies, now he had to deal with a little rebellion of two.

Derrick grabbed his sister's arm, pulling her away from Ann. For a moment, Ari thought he'd shake her, but he squatted beside Veronica and looked into her face. "Monkey, you want to try to find mom, don't you? We can't stay here. You've got to be brave and go out there no matter what we have to face. I'll protect you. I won't let any zombies come near you."

Mrs. Scheider stooped to talk to her, too. "And I'll hold your hand the whole time. We're only going to walk a few blocks. You can do that, can't you?"

Ronnie sniffled and whimpered, but nodded.

Ari leaned to whisper to Ann. "Are you coming or not? No one's going to make you, but don't undermine the kid's confidence. If you're staying, say goodbye to her with a smile then go in the other room, wait for us to leave and lock up behind us. But if you're going, pull it together and pick up that fucking backpack right now."

Ann looked into his eyes, her own red-rimmed from crying. She shook her head and muttered, "I can't do it and none of you should either. You'll be ripped apart out there."

She seemed to have forgotten that he, Derrick and Hector had had a successful foraging trip yesterday. But maybe hearing zombies running past last night, and the distant screams of victims and gunfire had unhinged her.

"All right." He stooped to pick up her pack and took out some cans of food and bottles of water. "Here's your share of the provisions. Good luck."

Lila and Mrs. Scheider each hugged Ann, then Lila whispered to her for a minute, clearly taking one last shot at convincing her it was suicide to stay.

Ann knelt and hugged Ronnie. "Be good. Take care of Bright."

She indicated the stuffed unicorn she'd given the girl in the subway store.

Ronnie nodded and clutched the rainbow colored animal. "You should come with us."

"I'm sorry. I can't. Good luck, Ronnie." Ann rose and said goodbye to the others before leaving the back room. The door to the storage room shut behind her with a soft whoosh of air.

"All right. Anyone else having second thoughts?" Ari slipped his arms through Ann's abandoned knapsack and hoisted it up. He didn't give them much time to consider before giving the order to move out.

Deb took her place in front, her gun drawn and opened the exit door. She stepped from the storage room into the alley. Ari doubted this way was any safer than the street out front. Their adversaries could pop up anywhere, but psychologically it might give the team more confidence to imagine they were slipping away unnoticed out the back door.

The alley was deserted except for dumpsters and litter. They took their positions with the stronger people encircling the weak and started down the narrow passage. Ari's gaze swept around them and up at the windows of the buildings. The sense of being watched was palpable. He hadn't felt nearly this much paranoia on their expedition yesterday. His nerves prickled almost painfully. His skin felt too tight and he was distracted by the sound of his own uneven breathing.

Steady, he warned himself, *before you have a goddamn panic attack.* Sergeant Vogt had instructed his men in how to deal with the tension of battlefield conditions. He'd advised focusing outside of oneself and becoming completely aware of the environment. "A good soldier is an antenna, eyes and ears taking in information and reacting to it in an appropriate manner. Concentrate on the job and your fears will stay under control."

That meant no second guessing or feeling guilty about leaving Ann Hanson, either. Ari relaxed his grip on his rifle and kept his body loose yet poised as they emerged from the alley onto an empty side street. Cars were abandoned here, too, although not as many as on the main thoroughfares. Human remains littered the sidewalk. After awhile they stopped trying to step over or around them. There were too many bits and it was impossible to avoid them all. The smell of decay rose in a choking pall from the rotting meat, and Ari imagined how much worse it would be after several more days had passed. They had to get out of the city as soon as possible.

Ronnie started to whimper again and Mrs. Scheider told her to stop looking down. "Keep your eyes up, honey. Focus on Deb's back or the buildings or the sky. Don't think about where you are. Picture where you want to be."

Sage advice, except right now Ari needed to mentally be exactly where he was, paying attention to the moment he was in. A sound caught his attention and he looked back over his shoulder. Lila and Derrick, the rear contingent of their cadre, were on guard, scanning the deserted area through which they walked while keeping their weapons ready. Lila caught Ari's look and glanced behind her so they both spotted their followers at almost the same time.

Coming up the street about two blocks behind them were several stumbling, blood-streaked figures. The things were as deadly as sharks silently swimming up behind their quarry. These creatures had that same dead-eyed stare but considerably less grace in their movements.

"Zombies sighted," he barked at the rest of the group. "Move double time."

They'd discussed what to do in case of an attack. In the time it took the group to accelerate from a brisk walk to a trot, the zombies sighted them and began to move faster, too.

"We've been spotted." As the group began to run, Ari fell to the back, ready to protect the rear. He ran alongside Lila, who muttered underneath her breath "Omigod, Omigod, Omigod."

The zombies raced after them with a stiff-legged gait. Any second they'd catch up. Ari went to phase two. "Go!" he ordered. Joe scooped up Ronnie, Julie grabbed Mrs. Scheider's hand and they raced after Deb and Carl. The group would head for a specified meeting point. Meanwhile, Ari, Lila and Derrick whirled around, ready to fight.

Time seemed to stand still like in a car spinning out on an icy road. Ari noted details with detached calmness. There were three men, two women and a young child of uncertain gender racing toward them. One man was balding and paunchy and looked as normal as if he'd just gotten up from his La-z-boy to get another beer from the fridge. Another seemed to be missing his jawbone. A pair of glasses hung askew from an ear of the third. One of the women wore a dress he thought was rust brown until he realized it was simply blood-soaked. He took in these images with one assessing glance.

Ari pointed his rifle and was a hair away from shooting when suddenly Ann burst out of the alley in front of the zombies. She didn't see them, wasn't even looking their way as she ran toward Ari.

"Wait. I changed my mind. I want to go with you," she called. "Wait!" And then she became aware of the sound of running feet behind her. Her head snapped around and she screamed.

"God*damn* it!" Ari growled. He couldn't shoot with Ann between him and their pursuers. A second later it didn't matter because the creatures were on her. They grabbed her and dragged her down like cheetahs on a gazelle. Ann's screaming was abruptly cut short. So was the momentum of the zombies as they fought over the struggling woman.

Lila screamed. Derrick shouted, "Fuck!" and Ari unleashed a round from his rifle at the feeding zombies. The bullets tore through them, knocking them around a little, but not stopping them.

Ari grabbed Lila's arm. "Run. We can't help her." He glanced back one last time, long enough to take a mental snapshot of Ann's foot clad in a brand new tennis shoe. The zombies were on top of her like a football pileup. One of them tore at her leg and that pristine, white sneaker beat erratically against the pavement. Ari checked to make sure Derrick was with them, then faced forward and ran like hell. Lila did her best to keep up, but soon he was dragging her with him. They soon caught up with the rest of the group, who'd turned a corner headed north.

Julie caught sight of them first. "You made it! What happened?"

Ari scanned the way ahead of them, well aware the danger at their back wasn't the only one they might face. "Turn left here," he called to Deb. "We need to get inside somewhere and take a breather."

She nodded and pointed to a McDonald's. "In there." There were several entrances and plenty of windows from which to keep a lookout. She led the way inside where the stink of fry grease and overheated corpses hit them like a wall. Ari took shallow breaths as he looked around the restaurant for any movement. It seemed to be deserted, at least of the living. He didn't think the zombies were bright enough to lie in wait for victims, but underestimating them might cost their lives so he sent Joe and Carl to do a quick walk through of the building. Meanwhile, the rest of them collapsed in seats or on the floor, gasping for breath.

Lila bent over in a corner and heaved. The sound of her vomiting started Ari's own stomach churning and bile rose in his throat. He couldn't get the sight of Ann's jerking foot out of his mind. They couldn't have saved her and had to take advantage of the opportunity to escape, but he'd felt like shit leaving her to those monsters. He swallowed hard and closed his eyes.

"Only four more blocks to go," Deb's smoky voice floated to him. "We can do it. We have to do it."

God bless the cheerleader. He needed that right now when the situation seemed hopeless. He rubbed his hand over his eyes and opened them. "Okay. Let's see that map again."

Deb produced a hand drawn map she'd sketched before they started out. "We got off track, but we can cut over here."

Ari nodded. "And here's where you want to camp out." He indicated an X marking a hotel.

She nodded. "I think it's the best location; many ways in and out and places to hide if things go bad, plenty of beds for everyone and food in the kitchen. I'm guessing we'll find a lot of people camping out there. Hooking up with some more able bodies could be useful." She jerked her head at Mrs. Scheider, who was nearly passed out in her seat with Ronnie, slumped across her lap. Ari didn't like the way she kept referring to those two as dead wood, but she was right. They were weak links and the group needed to be at its strongest in order to survive.

"What happened?" Julie asked again. "How did you get away?"

"Ann," Lila spoke up. "Ann happened. She changed her mind and tried to come after us. Those things caught her and took her down which gave us time to escape."

"She was a stupid lady," Derrick practically shouted. He pushed away from the table where he was leaning and stalked over to the soda machine. His shoulders were shaking and he kept his back turned to them as he filled paper cups with the tepid, sugar-water.

"My God," Julie murmured. "I'm so sorry."

What are you sorry for? You didn't know her any more than we did. And you sure as hell didn't eat her," Ari wanted to say. He glanced down to find his legs trembling. Derrick wasn't the only one shaken by the loss.

Joe and Carl returned from the kitchen bringing food with them, not burgers and fries, but limp salad from the warm cooler and packaged, uncrisp apple pies.

"Nothing back there," Joe reported. "Just more of the same." He nodded at the decimated bodies around them. ""What do you suppose happens when the zombies run out of food sources? Can they feed on any kind of meat or does it have to be living? What keeps them from eating each other?"

"Just a guess, but I'd say they need the electrolytes in energized, living blood and tissue. Dead meat wouldn't satisfy them," Carl said. "And it's a very good question—what *would* happen if they were imprisoned without fresh food. I suppose eventually the bodies would shut down and return to their natural state. Only a guess, of course."

Ari drew as deep a breath of the foul air as he dared. "We shouldn't stay here long. We'll bring the food along. The sooner we get where we're going, the better."

He doubted anyone was hungry anyway. He certainly wasn't. Nothing like adrenalin and endorphins to keep you flying and the scent of decay to put you off eating. He reached across the table and touched Mrs. Scheider's arm. "Hey, are you going to be all right."

She opened one eye and looked back at him. "I'm not unconscious, young man. I'm resting. That's what we're supposed to be doing. I'm in excellent physical shape and I'd be perfectly fine if we had to walk another five miles."

"What about her?" Ari nodded at Ronnie. Derrick had crouched beside his sister to offer her a drink.

"I'll carry the little girl for a while," Carl volunteered. "The least I can do since you're protecting me like I was made of glass. I feel so useless."

"You're too important to risk," Ari said. "What's in your head is as important as what's on your hard drive. You'll stay back with the others while Deb, Joe and I go for the computer."

"I should go with you instead of Joe. It makes the most sense." Derrick stood up, sloshing soda over the edge of his cup as he set it on the table. "I can take the hard drive out of the tower. You probably don't even know what one looks like."

"Fine," Ari agreed, glad Derrick had made the offer. "We three will go."

"I should go, too," Julie said. "I work there. I know the layout of the place and which terminal is Carl's. You'll need me to be your map."

"Babe, no!" Deb protested, shaking her head. "I'm not taking you along. As soon as we find someplace safe, I plan to park your sweet ass there. Carl can draw us a map."

"*Babe,*" Julie stressed the word hard. "I think you know how well I respond to being told what to do. I'm going with. End of discussion."

"Whatever," Ari said. "We can figure out who does what later. Right now let's just concentrate on getting all our sweet asses to the hotel without any bites taken out of them." Not at all funny under the circumstances, but sometimes black humor was the only way to keep your sanity.

It was hard to get moving and head back outside. Shelter was deceiving. A person could start to think he was safe just because he was indoors. Important to remember there wasn't safety anywhere and to stay alert all the time. Ari dragged himself to his feet. "Let's move out."

"Yes sir, Captain," Derrick said. Sometimes Ari couldn't decide if he liked or hated the kid, but he did trust he could depend on him and that was pretty much all that mattered right now.

"Everybody get down!" Joe's sharp whisper cut across the murmur of small talk. "Look outside."

A large group of zombies, different from the ones who'd attacked Ann, was moving past practically right outside the window. And here they were in plain view, chatting. Ari cursed his carelessness. Thank God, Joe at least was paying attention.

Everyone dropped down behind tables and chairs and watched the shuffling herd move past. Naked and clothed corpses mingled in *We Are the World* harmony, all economic brackets, races, and genders joined together at last with one common goal—eating the living. Several lifted their heads to sniff the air but none of them looked through the glass windows as they went past to search for potential victims. From their behavior he guessed they were attracted by smells and their vision probably wasn't too keen. They were merely mindless nervous systems seeking sustenance to keep functioning.

Ari glanced at Lila beside him and flashed on last night and her hand in his as they'd lain in the dark. He would've liked to hold more than her hand and might've tried, if they weren't sleeping with a group of people. He thought she would've let him, too. But then she'd pulled away and turned her back on him so maybe she wasn't that interested.

Maybe she'd simply needed comfort and would have held Mrs. Scheider's hand if the old lady had happened to be lying next to her.

Anyway this was no time to think about Lila and his attraction to her. There were plenty more important things to occupy his mind besides fantasies of kissing some chick he'd just met, who wasn't even his type. Lila wasn't all that built, her hair was kind of mousy and she was way too educated. Yet he couldn't deny that her unearthly blue eyes seemed to see straight inside him and the low tone of her voice made his skin prickle. And he liked the way she expressed herself, calm, intelligent and ironic, a far cry from the girls he'd grown up with.

Ari shook off his thoughts, and watched the last of the zombies disappear from sight. At last he rose. "I guess it's as safe as it's ever going to be out there. We should get moving."

They checked their weapons and headed back outside. The day was overcast and breezy; the air promised rain. Ari took point this time, leading them along the new route Deb had set. He resisted the urge to continually glance behind him. He'd delegated Joe to bring up the rear this time and must trust him to keep watch. Ari had learned quickly that giving orders wasn't so hard, but having faith in others to follow through was difficult, especially when your life and others depended on them. He understood now why men in combat units developed utter trust in one another.

The city was still unearthly quiet. For Ari, who'd been raised on the music of traffic and sirens, the utter silence except for the calls of birds flying overhead was disconcerting. Even worse was when an occasional distant scream ripped through the air. Each time it sent a fresh shot of adrenaline through him and set his pulse racing even faster. The only comfort was that the zombie's attention was focused on someone other than them—which was no comfort at all.

New York rats were always bold, but with no people around to deter them, they were out in broad daylight feasting on the carnage. Crows and seagulls also tore at the carrion with their beaks and didn't fly away even when the group walked right past them. Ari tried not to see exactly what body parts the scavengers were enjoying and kept his attention focused on anything moving in the perimeter of his gaze.

"Over there," he alerted the group, pointing to a group of people a few intersections away. He wasn't sure if they were alive or not and didn't want to wait to find out. "We'd better cut this way." He led the group down a side street and continued the zigzag path toward the Albermarle Hotel. They didn't encounter any more zombies although they did spot them, always at a distance and often occupied with eating.

Funny how fast a person could adjust to the new order of things in order to cope. Ari had stopped thinking of what the zombies ate as people. Now when he glimpsed the flesh-eaters feeding, he only prayed they devoured their victims completely so new zombies wouldn't swell the numbers of the undead.

At last their destination was in sight only blocks away. Ari's spirits lifted as if they were assured of a complimentary suite with pillow mints, fresh towels and hot running water in the shower. He knew better. Reaching the hotel didn't guarantee relief. Perhaps they'd all built it up in their minds as some safe, zombie-free zone, a haven in the midst of chaos.

A few blocks away from the hotel he could see the reality didn't match his fantasy. The front was swarming with zombies, going inside and coming out with bloody limbs and entrails like diners at an all-you-can-eat buffet. The sidewalk beneath the decorative awning was gore-spattered. The revenants milled around, some of them standing and staring vacantly into space. Evidently it *was* possible for them to eat their fill and what they did in their down time was absolutely nothing.

Ari motioned his followers off the street. "We're going to have to find someplace else. Is there anywhere closer to Quantus where we could park for a while?"

"There's a theater," Julie said. "Stage shows not movies. It should be deserted. There wouldn't have been anyone in there during the day, so no reason for zombies to go inside and no dead bodies. I think it would be a good camping spot."

"How do we get there?"

Julie and Deb led the way. Ari dropped back to the rear flank, keeping a close eye on the mass of zombies overrunning the Albermarle. The group trudged a block east before heading north again, walking in a tight unit. Carl carried Ronnie and Julie helped Mrs. Scheider, who, despite her vow that she could walk miles if need be, was beginning to limp.

At last Ari sighted the marquee of a small theater up ahead. He nearly shit when he read the title of the play that was currently running, "Zombie Prom".

"You've gotta be fucking kidding me," he muttered.

"It's a musical," Julie said. "They say it's very funny."

Joe hooted then clapped a hand over his mouth. Tears welled in his eyes as he suppressed his laughter. "I'm sorry. It's too ironic. I can't..." He broke off, chuckling and wiping tears from his eyes.

His hysterics were contagious. Lila started to giggle and Deb chuckled. Even Mrs. Scheider snorted once before regaining her composure.

"Don't lose it now. You guys have to keep it together a little longer," Ari warned, but he was fighting back his own bout of hysteria. He sobered instantly when he saw a movement from the corner of his eye. When he glanced that way, it was only a stray cat poking through garbage.

They marched at a fast clip the last few blocks to the theater and pressed flat against the wall while Ari picked the lock on the double doors. He didn't want to smash his way in. After they were inside they could lock up, keeping the building zombie-proof. It'd been a while since he'd picked a lock and he'd lost his touch, but at last he got the door opened.

He went in first to check the place out, but didn't expect to find anything since the building had been locked tight. The lobby was clear and so was the theater. Emergency lights faintly illuminated the rows of chairs and the stage, ready for a performance with a high school cafeteria set. Ari went back to the lobby and the others were already inside.

Carl and Joe moved a candy counter in front of the doors to fortify the glass. The others collapsed on benches or on the worn red carpet. Derrick stood staring at the pulp magazine style poster for "Zombie Prom: A Musical Comedy" which hung on one wall. He shook his head and cursed under his breath.

Ari checked his watch. It felt like they'd been out on the streets for an entire day. Actually, it was still early. There was plenty of time to take a rest then go for the data at the lab, but all he wanted to do was curl up in a corner somewhere and sleep. He shook off the paralyzing fatigue. "Derrick, Lila, you two want to help me check out the rest of building? There's a whole backstage area. We can't be too careful."

Lila pushed herself up off the floor without a word. When Derrick continued to gaze blankly at the poster, she nudged his arm. "Come on."

He blinked and looked at her as if coming back to earth. "This is beyond surreal. I don't know how much more of this I can take."

"I know." She put an arm around his shoulders and hugged him. The normally prickly kid didn't pull away. Ari felt a rush of longing to have Lila's arm around his shoulders like that. Her comforting hug would feel so good.

"Let's go." He led the way into the theater. They searched the rows, the stage, the dressing area, wardrobe and prop rooms. Ari even checked the light booth at the back of the theater. There were several exit doors, all of them sturdy metal with solid locks. This place was as tight and safe as a bank vault. He felt confident about leaving the main group here while the strike team went on their mission.

"All clear," Derrick reported as he came from the restrooms, swinging his knife around his head like a Samurai sword.

"Thanks. Do you want to go tell the others it's safe to come back here?" Ari asked.

Derrick gave another one of his mocking salutes and marched

off to do his bidding.

"That kid drives me nuts," Ari said to Lila after the door closed behind him.

"He lives to bait you. I can tell you don't have a younger brother," she said. "Neither do I, but I've worked at an outreach program for a few years and trust me, that's normal teenage boy asshattedness. I'm sure you were like that a few years ago."

Ari smiled. "Never."

Lila slipped her arm through his. "Come sit for a minute." She led him to a row of seats and they dropped onto the faded, flattened cushions. She looked up at the pressed tin ceiling way overhead and the elaborate proscenium framing the stage. "I bet this theater was really gorgeous back in its day."

"Mm," he murmured, hardly hearing her words as he was concentrating on the pressure of her hand on his arm. What a pussy he was turning into, excited by her least little touch.

"I thought, before the others get here, we might want to talk about what happened out there…to Ann."

"Why? It happened. We can't change it. There's nothing to say. We have to keep moving forward."

"I know, but I thought it might help if we discussed how we feel about it."

He shook his head, snorting. "Women. How in the hell does talking about feelings fix anything. I fucked up by leaving her behind. She died because of it. End of story."

Lila's eyes burned into him. "Is that what you think? Really? Ann's death wasn't your fault. She chose to stay and then she chose to follow us. Those were her decisions."

Ari shrugged. "I shouldn't have left her. It was the wrong move. If I'd given her just a few more minutes, given you time to work your magic, she would've listened to you and come with us. She wouldn't have been…" He couldn't say 'eaten'. The word brought back that image of Ann's sneakered foot shaking as a zombie tore a chunk out of her leg.

Lila stayed silent so long he thought she agreed with him that he'd made a terrible call. But her next words took him by surprise.

"I feel horrible saying this, but if Ann hadn't stayed behind and come out when she did you know what would have happened to the rest of us." Lila's voice was small but steady. "She saved us. Maybe that was her destiny, while our path is to get Carl someplace where he can maybe fix all this. I believe in free will, but I also believe in pre-ordained patterns. Sometimes you can't see how the means justify the end until you reach the end."

"Wow, that's…really Zen," he said a bit sourly. "I'm glad you can find comfort in that."

She smiled, not getting pissed off at his sarcasm and snapping back like most girls he knew would have. "That's what beliefs are for, to give comfort. It doesn't mean I really know what the hell I'm talking about." Her smile widened and he had to smile back.

Their gazes locked for a powerful moment and he wanted to lean in and kiss her. Just once, quickly, before the rest of the group broke in on their quiet moment. But it was already too late. The door at the back of the theater opened and everyone came trooping in.

"The big dressing room in the back is a good place to camp," Derrick said. "It's got an exit door so if anything goes down we can get out fast. I'll show you." He led the way onto the stage and behind the scenery with the others straggling behind like refugees bearing backpacks and bundles.

Ari sighed and rose, his muscles aching as if he'd run a marathon rather than walked a few city blocks. Knowing he had to go out there again was what made him so weary. He could understand Ann's desire to hibernate and wait for everything to blow past. But Lila was right, if not about cosmic design then at least about the part where they had to get Carl someplace where he could work his magic and save the day. And the next step was to get the critical data from Quantus Laboratories.

CHAPTER EIGHT

It was a lot easier moving with four people than with a group. Ari, Deb, Derrick and Julie scurried along the walls of the buildings like rats, dodging from doorway to alley to dumpster or whatever other protection they could find. Within minutes, they'd covered the short distance to Quantus.

The building was a generic metal and glass structure. The single word "Quantus" was etched in white script across the glass doors with no indicator of "laboratories" or "research and development". These people were drawing no attention to what their work was about. From the outside it appeared like all the other office buildings in the area.

They squatted beside a parked truck. Ari was about to lead them to the door, when a group of people came from around a corner on the opposite side of the street. The first living people outside of their group he'd seen close up since the Korean family yesterday. The urge to connect with other survivors was strong and he wanted to call out to them, but felt in his gut it wasn't safe. Not here. Not now. Their mission was the prime imperative; retrieving the data and returning safely to their own group. Taking the time to explain their agenda to strangers and discuss their plans wasn't practical.

The others seemed to understand this as well. They huddled close together, watching silently as six men and two women, one with a baby in her arms, ran down the street in the same erratic pattern as themselves—like wild animals running from cover to cover. How many others were out there? There couldn't possibly have been enough zombies to take down the majority of the living—not in one thirty-hour period. Impossible to believe only a little over a day had passed since this thing had begun. It seemed like a lifetime ago.

At last the people disappeared around another corner. Ari waited only a few minutes longer then led the way into the laboratory. The reception area was a shambles and, as Deb had said, the door to the area beyond was torn half off its hinges. Ari realized with a jolt that it was broken as if something had burst through it coming *out*, rather than going in. He remembered what Carl had said about recognizing a couple of the human test subjects among the zombies.

With all the personnel devoured, the creatures were probably long gone now.

Probably.

Julie led them down the silent, stifling corridor to the office where Carl's computer was. The hallway was lit by eerie emergency lights that frosted everything in white and turned the red bloodstains on the carpet and walls to black. Julie turned on her flashlight and the beam played over all sorts of things they'd rather have not seen. The farther they moved into the building, the more the sense of oppression grew. Ari hated being this far from an easy exit, not knowing what might loom around the next corner. He held his rifle ready and his knife was at easy access by his side.

"In here." Julie reached for the knob of a door.

"Wait!" Ari stopped her with a hand to her wrist. "Let me open it."

She moved back and let Ari go first. He turned the knob and pushed the door open with his rifle. The room was darker than the hallway, one light serving to illuminate the room in case of power outage. There was only one way in and the room was strewn with body parts.

"Deb, watch the hallway," Ari ordered. He stepped over a lab-coated torso—headless and limbless—and entered the room.

Julie gulped and put a hand to her mouth as she fought to

suppress her retching. Ari took her arm and led her around the corpse, glancing back to make sure Derrick was still with them. The boy kept his gaze raised, refusing to look at the mess on the floor that slid beneath his feet. Smart boy.

"Over here," Julie whispered, gesturing to the right with her flashlight. "The cubicle with the fractal art. Carl loves fractals."

All the cubicles made Ari nervous. He felt certain any minute something would pop out from one of them, but forced his paranoia down and concentrated on reaching Carl's office space. It was an eight by eight foot square, but what it lacked in space it made up for in technology. Carl's monitor was huge. Derrick practically wet himself when he saw the set up.

"Sweet!" He dove to his knees and popped the top off the tower. "Can you hold that light down here?" he asked Julie. She shone the beam while he unscrewed the hard drive.

Ari let Derrick do his thing with the computer and stood at the entrance of the cubicle. After a glance at the colorful pictures of fractals decorating Carl's space, Ari scanned the room, trying to figure out how Carl had escaped alive. The zombies would have entered by the same door they did. There was no other way out. Ari noticed a pile of corpse pieces in a back corner of the room and thought he understood. The flesh-eaters had chased most of the personnel there and feasted. Carl must have taken one look at them when they'd entered and dove underneath his desk. Only after they'd passed by him, had he slipped out and escaped, leaving his co-workers to their fate.

Ari didn't fault him for it, nor for blurring facts to make himself feel better about what he'd done. It was hard to be heroic in a situation in which you were weaponless, helpless and terrified. Maybe Carl could've tried to fight the zombies and help his friends, but then he'd be part of that pile in the corner instead of alive and with a plan in his mind that might save the world.

"Almost finished?" Ari asked.

"Working on it," came Derrick's muffled reply, and a moment

later, "Got it."

Ari opened Mrs. Scheider's purse, which she'd emptied it of all her contents. The purse was hard-sided so it would protect the drive which had no case. Derrick wrapped the memory storage unit in a clean piece of fabric and laid it in the purse as gently as if it were a newborn.

"Hey," Deb called softly from the doorway. "I hear something coming. Hurry up."

Ari's stomach dropped. His worst nightmare had featured being interrupted in the middle of their retrieval operation by a zombie attack. He gave Julie the bag to carry and the three of them moved quickly from the room.

Deb's gaze was riveted on the corridor leading toward the back of the building. She gave a terse report. "Footsteps coming from that way. Let's go."

They ran toward the front of the building as the distant sound of footsteps grew louder. Around a corner and through the clerical offices and they'd be back to the reception area. At the corner, Ari motioned the others back and flattened himself against the wall. He peered around the corner to check that the way was clear and his blood turned to ice. Three zombies loitered in by the water cooler like office drones.

He drew back. "Three of them."

"We can't go back. More are coming," Deb whispered.

"We're going to have to kill these three. Are you ready?" He looked into all their terrified eyes, but there was no time to wait for answers. They would have to be ready. "Knives only so we don't alert the ones behind us. Slash at the face and when they're blinded, pull your target around and chop through the back of the neck."

Ari plunged around the corner, blood roaring through his veins like a freight train. He went for the largest of the zombies—a big black man wearing a blue suit and a paisley tie. His dress shirt was stained dark red with blood. One of the original zombies must have taken a lethal bite from his throat before he'd gotten away. Ari wondered how the man had escaped being eaten to crawl off, die and resurrect. Then

Ari spared no more thought for his opponent's history as he flew at the man and slashed his blade across the blank eyes.

The zombie bellowed, so maybe they could feel pain or at least surprise, but he didn't respond with the normal human reaction of putting his hands to his face. Instead, the creature immediately reached for Ari, grabbing his shoulders in two big fists with a grip like a vise. Ari struggled to pull free. The revenant opened his mouth and the rancid smell of rotten meat wafted toward Ari. Then the zombie lunged for his face and Ari actually heard the thing's teeth click as it just missed him.

Over the creature's shoulder, he saw Derrick's wild-eyed face. The boy raised his skinning knife and brought it down on the back of the zombie's neck just above his shirt collar. Derrick grunted as he hit the solid bone of the spinal column and tried to slice through it.

The zombie's grip on Ari loosened. Ari jerked away, then spun around to check on the others.

Deb had a man in a coverall pinned to the floor. She'd straddled him and was swearing as she tried to avoid the zombie's clawing hands while cutting his throat. Meanwhile, Julie was backed against a desk, using a chair on casters as a barrier. She rolled it this way and that to keep her opponent at bay. Instead of simply tearing the chair out of her hands, the zombie kept trying to go around the obstacle like a windup toy bumping against a wall.

Ari attacked the zombie from behind, grabbed her and sliced hard across the back of her neck. Blood gushed in a warm fountain that blinded his eyes. He wiped them clear, momentarily panicked that infected blood may have entered him through his tear ducts. The fact Carl didn't believe it worked that way didn't comfort him right now.

In the seconds it took for him to clear his eyes, the zombie woman turned on him and attacked. She clawed at him with press-on nails that broke off as she tried to tear through his shirt. Ari wrestled her to the ground and sawed at her neck. This time the big blade shredded her spinal column, ending the flow of energy through her nervous system. She switched off like a robot and lay on the floor, truly dead at last.

Ari gasped for air as he scrambled to his feet and looked around.

Derrick had finished off his zombie and stood over the body with his chest heaving, too. He met Ari's eyes, his expression grim but triumphant.

"Die, damn you, just fucking die!" Deb yelled as she sawed away at her opponent. She'd taken the harder route of cutting all the way through the neck from the throat. She couldn't quite get through the last bit of bone, though her knife was buried deep in the thing.

The creature hit a hard blow to the side of Deb's head, knocking her off him. He twisted out from under her and went after her, his head lolling on the stalk of a neck like a broken flower. His head was literally falling off, hanging down his back and still he grasped for Deb.

Before Ari or Derrick could help, Julie stepped in. She'd set down the purse with the hard drive in it, and hefted her knife. While the injured zombie flailed around, blindly, mindlessly seeking his adversary, she moved in close and sliced at the last bit of bone and tendon protecting the fragile bundle of nerves. She severed it and the flesh-eater dropped like a stone.

There was no time to rest or recover as the footsteps of more zombies echoed from down the hall. Ari grabbed the precious bag with the data and ran past the desks and through the door to the reception area with Deb, Derrick and Julie right behind him. They raced through reception heading for the outdoors. Ari opened the front door and ushered each of them through; Derrick first, then Julie, but he thrust the purse at Deb. "Take this. Get them back safely."

Deb looked hard into his eyes and nodded, understanding what he was saying and accepting the responsibility. "Good luck." Then she was gone, out the door after the others.

Derrick turned to face the incoming zombies, raising his rifle. He'd mow them down with a few rounds to buy some time for the others. If he aimed at their throats, the bullets might tear right through the critical spot and take some of them out. He felt like a block of ice, like steel, beyond fear, running completely on adrenalin and nerves. He'd fight until the others had a good head start, then slam out that door and lead the zombies in the opposite direction. If he was smart and lucky, he'd be able to get away and double back to the theater.

He listened to the approaching footsteps, wondering how many there were. And then there was no more wondering as his pursuers stormed into the room.

CHAPTER NINE

Lila paced the lobby. She'd volunteered to take first watch because there was no way she could relax right now, not with Ari and the others out there. At first Joe had been reluctant to let her. What was it about men thinking only they could keep watch? But he'd finally surrendered the position to her and gone in back to take a much needed rest. He'd gotten less sleep than any of them, since he'd been up most of last night.

So, while the others rested, Lila restlessly wandered the lobby of the theater until she felt she knew every square inch of carpet, had memorized every line of the Zombie Prom poster, and even knew the precise location of each crack in the ceiling plaster. She knew the color, make and model of all the vehicles in the street outside, and the number of windows in the building across the street. She'd seen a flicker of movement in one of the upstairs windows and had continued to stare at it for five minutes straight, but the curtain never moved again. How many people were waiting out the storm behind windows like that one? How many survivors throughout the city and beyond?

She didn't even want to think of the larger scale of this thing. Escaping Manhattan was all she could wrap her mind around. Worrying about the rest of the country, especially her parents in Ohio, was too much. And she *really* didn't want to consider why there'd been little military presence in the city. It spoke volumes about how bad things had gotten in the outside world.

Her anxiety climbed. Ari, Deb Julie and Derrick had been gone too long. They weren't ever coming back. They were all dead. She checked her watch and two more minutes had slipped past. The strike team had only been gone about an hour. It was far too soon to start writing them off.

Lila forced herself to count the diamond shapes on the carpet and breathe in and out to the count of twenty. In a little bit, she felt her heart rate slow and her mind clear of some of her fears. She scanned outside again. No sign of death on this quiet, tree-shaded side street. Except for the lack of cars going past it could be a normal day.

And then she saw a darting movement from the corner of her eye. She looked up sharply and caught another glimpse of a moving figure—three. They were far down the street. Lila stared harder. They ran and paused, ran and paused, and she could definitely tell they were living human beings. A few yards closer and she could make out their shapes and the color of their clothing, hunter camouflage which they'd all picked up at the sport shop. It was Deb, Derrick and Julie, but where was Ari? Her stomach did a roller coaster drop.

Lila hurried to the theater to call for help in moving the concession stand away from the door. Carl and Joe moved it, while the others clustered in the lobby. Seconds later, the returning strike force came in the door, breathless from running and red-faced.

Lila grabbed Deb's arm. "Where's Ari?"

Deb shook her head. "Don't know," she panted. "Out there. He may be all right." But the look in her eyes expressed her doubts.

Lila's gut churned. "What happened? How did you get separated?" She couldn't curb her accusatory tone.

"We got the hard drive." Derrick held up Mrs. Scheider's beige leather purse. Carl took the purse from his blood-stained hand, while Mrs. Scheider offered water bottles and rags to the three so they could wash off the blood.

Derrick took a deep drink of water, dampened the cloth and wiped off his face before continuing. "There were zombies. We had to fight our way out of the building. We heard more coming and Ari stayed to give us time to get away."

"I knew them," Julie said softly. "The ones we killed. Carol Stokes' desk was right by mine. I talked to her every day. There was our office manager, Sam Masters, and the janitor. I can't remember his name, but I knew him."

Deb pulled her girlfriend into her arms and held her tight. "It's okay. We're safe now."

Julie broke down then, sobbing into Deb's shoulder. The rest of them turned away, giving the women their privacy. But Lila wasn't finished questioning Derrick. "So what exactly happened? What was Ari doing when you left?"

"I don't know. I was first out the door. I didn't even know he'd stayed behind until after we were a block away. Deb said he was going to hold them off. That's all I know."

Lila bit her tongue. Derrick sounded upset and she could only imagine what horror he'd been through. Bombarding him with more questions to which he had no answers wasn't fair. It wasn't his fault Ari had decided to try to be a hero. If he was here now, she'd shake him until his teeth rattled then kiss him until their mouths fused together from the heat of it. But more than likely he was gone, just gone and she'd never see him again even to say goodbye. She felt sick.

"We shouldn't linger here in the lobby," Joe pointed out. "There are too many windows. We might be spotted." He and Carl blocked the door again, then ushered everyone into the theater.

"I'll stay here and continue my watch," Lila insisted. "You can spell me in a couple of hours." But she knew she'd stay here for the rest of the afternoon and all night, waiting for Ari to return.

The lobby was quiet once more after the door closed behind the others. Lila exhaled a shaky breath and breathed in slowly, but this time her anxiety wouldn't alleviate. She exhaled again and sobs came from her in staccato bursts. She put her hands to her mouth trying to hold them back, but now the dam had finally broken she could no more hold back her tears than stop a river from flowing. Her shoulders shook as sobs wracked her body. Her knees gave way and she sank down onto the floor, covering her face with her hands. She cried for the loss of Ari but also for the loss of an entire world, swept away in the blink of an eye.

She huddled on the floor by the candy counter and cried until her eyes and her head ached. Afterward, she wiped away her tears and sat staring at the colorful candy bar wrappers, granola bars for the more health conscious, displayed in the case. There was a prominent sign on the door "No food or beverages in theater please" and she imagined the patrons between acts, milling around the lobby having their snacks or going outside to smoke a cigarette. The familiar patterns of life—a Saturday evening out for dinner and a movie, or dinner and a stage show, club hopping, dancing, drinking, bowling, shooting pool, shopping, hanging out with friends—all gone forever.

Lila shook off her incapacitating sorrow, grabbed hold of the candy counter and dragged herself to her feet. This was why she hadn't allowed herself to cry before now. She'd known if it took hold of her, if she allowed herself to experience the full impact of loss, she might not be able to do what needed to be done. Right now that was standing watch. She'd assured Joe he could trust her to keep a sharp lookout, and all she'd done for the last ten minutes was cry like a baby.

Blinking away the last of her tears, she scanned the street, shaded by the buildings across the way. It was late afternoon, edging toward evening, and with every second that ticked past it seemed less likely Ari would return. Lila looked down the street in the direction from which Deb and the others had come. There was no movement, and then, suddenly, there was—right next to her, coming from the opposite direction. She whirled around to see Ari and a few other people running past the window toward the front door. He banged on the glass, demanding entrance. Lila didn't take the time to call for Joe to come and help. She pushed the candy display with all her strength, nudging the cabinet away from the door a few feet then she unlocked the door and stood back.

One by one the newcomers slipped through the narrow opening. There was a plump woman, perhaps in her thirties, carrying a blanket-wrapped infant in her arms. She was followed by a heavyset man of about the same age. Her husband? The pair squeezed with difficulty past the display. Behind them came a young Asian woman who appeared to be in her twenties. Her hand was wrapped in a bloodstained cloth.

Ari entered behind them and locked the door. He and Lila heaved the display case back into its fortifying position then he turned to her and offered a Schwarzenegger impression. "I'm back."

She pounded a fist against his chest before throwing her arms around him and hugging him fiercely. "Where were you? What happened?"

"Let's get these people in back first." He gently extricated himself from her fierce hug. Together they led their guests into the theater.

The camp site was set up in the dressing room, but the group was currently gathered in the theater seats. Ronnie sat at one of the cafeteria tables of the stage set, coloring, while Mrs. Scheider sat beside her, reading her survivalist guide.

At their arrival, everyone jumped up from their seats, clamoring questions.

Ari introduced the strangers. "This is Doug and Gloria Patton and their baby, Ian." He pointed to the dark-haired woman, who was unwinding the bandage from her hand. "And Sondra Chin." The newcomers murmured a ragged chorus of "heys" and "hellos".

Ari perched on the edge of the stage and drank an entire bottle of water before telling his story. "I thought I'd buy some time for the others, slow down the zombies by shooting them up and then run like hell. I nearly shot these guys."

Doug interrupted. "When we heard people moving around in the building, we thought it was the monsters at first, but then we heard y'all whispering. I wasn't sure yet whether we wanted to get too friendly so we followed you. Then we heard the sounds of a fight, a woman cussin' a blue streak and knew for sure you were human." He shook his head. "I shoulda called out right then, but I was still being careful. Lucky I did finally shout a 'howdy' as we came through the door or your boy here woulda blown my head off.

"By the time we talked a while and exchanged stories, it was too late to catch up with the rest of you," Ari continued. "And then we had to take a couple of detours on our way back so it took a while." He looked at Deb. "You made it back with the hard drive though, right?"

Carl held up the purse. "Right here."

Lila busied herself with passing out water bottles to their guests. She noted the supply was getting low, but they should have enough to make it through the night and tomorrow they'd be on their way out of town. They could pick up more supplies then. She stooped to check out Sondra's damaged hand. Jagged red marks scored her palm and the flesh around them was an angry red. "What happened?"

"Cut it on the edge of a piece of metal just before I met the Pattons." Sondra tipped the bottle, spilling water onto her hand. "I was shopping when the attack happened. Trying on clothes in a dressing room. Do you like this top? I never even had to pay for it." She glanced down at the splashy flowers on her blouse and shook her head. "It does nothing for me."

Lila appreciated her dry humor. Then she glimpsed Sondra's expression and realized the woman wasn't joking. She was actually thinking about fashion in the middle of all this.

"When the screaming started, I stayed right where I was and waited until it died down. Then I came out and saw…everything. I made it back to my street only to find my apartment building on fire and the street in front of it full of zombies killing people as they came out. I met the Pattons when we all spent the night in the same empty warehouse." She held up her hand. "That's where I got this cut."

"I can take care of that." Mrs. Scheider produced the first aid kit she'd taken from the employees' restroom at the sport shop and knelt beside Sondra to treat her hand.

"We're tourists, just in New York for a couple of days," Doug took up the story. "We were sightseeing, pushing Ian in a stroller, when we saw this gang of...well, I thought they were addicts or thugs. I knew something was wrong with 'em so we headed the other direction." Doug put an arm around his wife, who remained quiet, focused on rocking her baby. "And then things started happening all around us. I grabbed Ian from his stroller and we ran for the nearest building. Nearly run straight into one of the things and that's when I realized they weren't human. We barely got away."

"How'd you end up at the lab of all places?" Deb asked.

"We spent yesterday running and hiding, not knowing where to go or what to do," Doug said. "Saw some grisly sights I can tell you. Saw some helicopters too, flying low and shooting at anything that moved, living or undead. Saw some soldiers come barreling out of the back of a troop truck and fanning out over a city block. I was going to go to them for help, till I saw them shoot a few unarmed civilians. They weren't taking any chances and weren't too particular on whether they were killing zombies or people.

"I figured we'd better get out of the city so we headed for the waterfront. Spent the night in a warehouse where we met Miss Chin. The next day we were walking down an alley when we got chased by zombies. The exit door to a building was hanging open. We ducked in, pulled the door shut and barricaded it." He nodded at Ari. "And then we met your friend, here."

"What about you folks?" Doug asked. "Ari says you were all on the subway together, and he explained about the lab and the anti-virus, but we didn't have time to talk much."

Derrick answered for everyone, succinctly explaining about the A7 antidote with its disastrous consequences according to Carl's theory. Then he proceeded to give thumbnail sketches of each of them that made Lila smile.

"This is my sister, Ronnie. She's eight. Over there is Mrs.

Scheider. She's rich and smart and doesn't put up with bullshit. Dr. Joe is a dermatologist not a real doctor so he can't fix anything. Ari's in the army and always acts like he knows what to do. Deb is kind of bitchy but she's cool, and that's her girlfriend, Julie. She's a secretary at the lab with Carl, who's kind of a scientist." Derrick concluded with. "Lila goes to college. She's pretty nice."

"Pretty nice? That's all I get?" Lila asked.

"Better than being the designated bitch," Deb said.

"There used to be more of us," Derrick added. "Ann worked at a museum, but she…died. And Hector was a cool old dude who left to go find his family."

Lila was concerned by how silent and withdrawn Gloria Patton was acting. The woman sat in one of the plush theater seats beside her husband and patted the blanket-wrapped bundle in her arms. Little Ian had been so quiet since they'd arrived Lila began to have the horrible suspicion Mrs. Patton was carrying around a dead child. She went over and offered the woman a packet of trail mix and peered into the blanket at the sleeping baby's face, round-cheeked and rosy. He was snoring slightly and the tightness in her chest eased.

"Does your baby need anything? We don't have much an infant can eat. How old is he?"

Gloria looked up at her with a blank gaze. Doug rubbed her back. "Honey, Lila's talkin' to you. Tell her about Ian."

"He's six months. He's on breast milk and cereal now, too."

Lila glanced at Doug. "I suppose you'll need diapers and stuff."

He indicated the bag he wore over one shoulder. "We have a few left, but we'll need supplies tomorrow." He paused then added, "So, do you people have a plan in mind?"

"Like you said, to the waterfront to get a boat," Ari said. "We'll head to the mainland and try to find out more about what emergency plans are in place, and get Carl to the authorities so he can share what he knows."

"Wish I could see the data right now," Carl complained.

"You can," Derrick said. "I've got the laptop and cables. I can connect the hard drive if you give me a few minutes." He set to work with Carl leaning over and giving him suggestions that made Derrick's shoulders grow tenser by the second.

"I think Carl's going to get his head bit off in about a second." Lila sat down beside Ari. The rest of the group had broken off into side conversations and at last she had a moment to talk to him privately.

He looked over at Derrick. "He was amazing today. Saved my ass. I had a zombie at my throat and he finished it off."

"Really? I didn't hear about that." She studied Derrick. "It looks like he's dealing with it all right. That had to be tough." Then she turned her attention to Ari and realized he was as blood-splattered as the rest of the strike team had been when they returned. "You should clean up and get some rest."

She rose and held out her hand to him. Ari took it and she pulled him to his feet and led him back to the dressing room. There was a sink with no running water, but also a cooler to draw water from.

"I'll find you something clean to wear," Lila promised as filled a basin with water for him to clean up with. She glanced over to find Ari shirtless, and her stomach did an acrobatic series of somersaults. For a moment, her gaze was glued to his chiseled pecs and abs and, oh God, those powerful shoulders. She swallowed and looked away.

Lila carried the basin over to where Ari leaned against the counter while he unlaced his shoes. She set the water down, keeping her eyes averted, but couldn't help inhaling his scent—male sweat that wasn't at all unpleasant but tugged on a spot deep in her belly. Heat blossomed through her and her body tensed with want.

"I'll, uh, get you some clothes," she repeated lamely, and hurried off to the wardrobe room. Everyone was wearing clean clothes, courtesy of the theater. Racks of costumes from a wide variety of productions made for some interesting outfit choices. Lila's favorite was Joe's circa 1970's powder blue leisure suit. It had been the only garment large enough to fit his lanky frame and it gave the reserved man an amusing flair.

For Ari she found a vaguely Robin Hood looking costume. She passed on the tights, but thought the collarless, long sleeved shirt with a tunic style vest over it actually looked comfortable. She also grabbed a couple of pairs of pants for him to try on. They all needed to stop by a store tomorrow for a fresh change of underwear. Not that it was a top priority by any means, but if they had to get other supplies, they might as well be clean and comfortable.

When Lila returned to the dressing room, Ari was finger combing his damp hair back from his face. He'd stripped down to his undershorts so Lila got another pleasing eyeful of male flesh—good, strong thigh and calf muscles and a pair of oversized feet.

"Here you go," she said overly brightly as she handed him the pile of clothes. "There's kind of a bizarre assortment of stuff back there."

He held up the shirt and vest and looked at them doubtfully. "No kidding."

"Look at it this way. Who've you got to impress? We could all wear clown suits or muumuus every day and it wouldn't matter any more. There've gotta be some perks to an apocalypse," Lila teased.

She was rewarded with a smile, a big beautiful smile that lit his shadowed eyes and made them sparkle. Her heart flipped like a landed fish. She hated the way her body betrayed her, suffering all the pangs of a childish crush, her hormones rampaging beyond her control.

"How do you like my outfit?" She strutted an imaginary catwalk and posed, hoping to earn a full fledged laugh from him.

"Very sexy. I especially like the sparkly unicorn." He indicated the image on the front of the T-shirt Ronnie had picked out for her to wear. His words were joking, but his eyes lingered on her rainbow and unicorn emblazoned chest a few beats longer than necessary, checking out her attributes as she had his.

"Wonder what play this was used in." Lila picked at the rhinestones studding the unicorn's horn and made small talk to quiet the rapid beating of her heart. But though she tried to pretend everything was normal, the air between them was charged with enough electricity to light the building.

Ari moved closer, filling her vision although she didn't look up. She felt him there and it was almost as if he'd already touched her. "I thought you weren't coming back," she said softly. "You scared the hell out of me. Don't do that again."

"I don't plan to." He reached out and picked a loose piece of glitter glue from the unicorn's tail. His fingers happened to graze her breast in a completely accidental way.

Lila's lips twitched in amusement. She looked up at Ari and all the oxygen was sucked from her body at the searing heat in his gaze. What the hell? This had escalated so fast and so unexpectedly she felt like she was sliding inevitably down a mudslide into a yawning pit from which there was no escape. But it was a tumble she wanted to take.

She licked her lips and his attention dropped to her mouth. She leaned toward him and his hands slid around her waist. And then their faces were inches apart and Lila's eyes began to close.

The door slammed open and footsteps entered the room. "Ari, are you here? Oh!"

Lila opened her eyes and stepped back, blood rushing to her cheeks. She ducked her head. "Yeah. So, I'll, uh, do that." She looked over at Sondra as if only just realizing she was there. "Oh. Hi."

Transparent, stupid charade. As if anyone looking at them couldn't tell they were about to kiss. Why was she covering anyway? It wasn't anyone's business what they chose to do. But she certainly wasn't going to kiss in front of a complete stranger and didn't really want to have the entire group gossiping about them.

"I'm sorry." Sondra smiled. "I just wanted to ask Ari about the plans for tomorrow. I need some things from a store and wondered where exactly we'll be shopping."

Lila stared at her. Shopping? Was this girl serious? She acted as if they were going on a spree rather than foraging for necessary supplies. It was a wonder she was still alive.

"I don't know. It depends on what happens on the way. We'll make it up as we go along." Ari sounded impatient. He wasn't any happier than she was about being interrupted.

"Because I was thinking," Sondra continued, "We're fairly close to Humboldt's and that would be—"

"I'll keep that in mind." He cut her off. "Look, it's been a really long day. If you don't mind, we can discuss it tomorrow. I'm exhausted."

Sondra's perfectly shaped brows drew together in a petulant frown. "Sure. I understand. I just thought we could all use new clothes." She nodded at Ari's odd attire and laughed. "I mean, *really* use new clothes. Is that all you could find?"

Her brilliant thoughts were interrupted as the door opened and more members of the group trooped into the room. Disappointment and the remnants of desire swirled through Lila. She and Ari were clearly not going to get a chance to pick up where they'd left off.

"Carl's taking first watch," Derrick reported. "Doug's next, then Joe. The Pattons say they'll sleep in the theater, because their baby wakes up at night. Ronnie's staying with them. She likes the baby, and that Gloria has a real 'mom' vibe even if she is a little out of it."

"Sounds good." Ari accepted his report. As Derrick turned to prepare his bedroll for the night, he added, "By the way, thanks for today, man. You saved my ass."

"No problem." Derrick tried to sound casual, but Lila could tell he was pleased Ari had recognized him.

Her moment with Ari was past. With people milling all around there was no more time to talk, let alone do anything else. Perhaps she could've given him a nod and gotten him to go someplace else with her. It was a big theater with lots of private spaces. But Ari was practically swaying on his feet with exhaustion. He needed to sack out not make out.

Lila turned her attention to redistributing bedding so the

newcomers would have places to sleep. She carried the blankets she'd gathered into the other room where Gloria and Doug were preparing a spot to sleep. Doug had found a sofa bed in a prop room and dragged it backstage. The little family probably had the most comfortable bed in the place.

"Got everything you need?" Lila asked as she offered them the bedding.

"Yes, thanks," Doug said. "We're so grateful to be here and thank y'all for taking us in like this."

"I got my princess nightgown on." Ronnie stood up from the cushions she'd laid on the floor beside the sofa bed and spun around. She was wearing a woman's white, lacy negligee that swept the floor on her small body.

"Very pretty," Lila said. "I want to thank you again for picking out this great unicorn shirt. It's very cool."

"I still think you should wear one of the ball dresses. You could look like a princess, too." Ronnie referred to the chiffon prom dresses hanging on a rack in the dressing room awaiting their scene in the zombie play.

"Yeah, well, I don't think those would be too good for hiking in," Lila said.

She glanced at the Patton family, their combined weight making the sofa bed sag deeply. Gloria was feeding the baby. Finally animated, the kid waved an arm and snuffled loudly as he nursed. Doug had an arm around his wife and Lila's heart melted a little. It was nice to see an intact family. She prayed hers was. Her throat tightened as she thought about her parents.

"Well, if you guys have everything you need. I guess I'll say goodnight." She made a hasty exit before she cried in front of Ronnie and got the little girl started again. It was a pleasure to have her happy—or at least content in the moment.

Lila returned to the dressing room to find everyone mostly settled for the night. Sondra sat cross-legged on Lila's bedroll, talking to

Ari, who lay on his back with an arm over his eyes. When she saw Lila, she waved her over.

"I saved you a spot here." Sondra patted the sleeping bag on her other side.

Lila forced a smile. "Thanks." She eyed the new sleeping arrangement and the flat pillow Sondra had generously allotted her and decided Sondra was a complete douchebag—as if she'd had any doubt.

She lay down on the sleeping bag with no cushion beneath it, and covered up with a trench coat from the costume rack.

"Tell me more about yourself." Sondra was as chipper as if she was on speed. "Where are you from? I can tell you're not a native New Yorker."

"How?"

"You have some kind of flat accent. Midwest?"

"Ohio. I'm going to college at NYU. Was going."

"What's your major?"

"Undeclared. What about you?" Lila didn't feel like talking and guessed Sondra was the type who'd be only too happy to take the burden of conversation and run with it. She was right.

"No college for me. I've taken a few classes here and there, but mostly I'm working on my modeling career. Hands not face." She held up her bandaged hand. "God, I hope this doesn't leave a scar. You've probably seen my hands in ads before. You know Staunton Jewelers? My hand was featured in their fall catalogue. Just last week my agent landed me a choice gig as *the* hand model for Ogilvie lotion. That's nationwide exposure, not just local." Her dark eyes suddenly glistened with tears. "Of course, all that's fucked now. That's so my luck. I finally get my big break and the world goes to hell."

Lila grunted. She had no comforting words to offer.

"It'll get better though, right?" Sondra leaned forward, resting her arms on her knees. "It has to. The government will find a way to fix everything. Or that Carl guy will."

The echo of Ann's constant insistence help would come

reminded Lila of her, and of the way she'd died. She looked over at Ari. He glanced back at her from beneath the arm across his forehead.

"Things will work out," Lila said. "I'm sure you'll model again some day."

"That's what I think, too. And hey, probably the competition will be less fierce." The tears were blinked away and Sondra smiled again.

Complete douche, Lila confirmed to herself.

CHAPTER TEN

Ari fell asleep to the drone of Sondra's voice explaining how hand modeling was different from what people thought, and woke to the sound of Doug coming in to tap Joe for the last guard duty of the night.

Ari rose from his sleeping bag. "I'll take his shift. I can't sleep any more." Better to be doing something useful than lying sleepless and restless.

He walked with Doug out of the dressing room to the backstage where Gloria and Ian slept peacefully on the sofa bed. Ronnie had crawled in beside them, leaving no place for Doug to lie. The man shrugged. "Guess I'll use your bedroll for the rest of the night if that's okay."

"Sure. Anything happen outside tonight?"

"Some noise in the distance; gunfire, some explosions like grenades going off and a larger one like maybe a gas line blew up. There was a glow in the west that could be from a fire. Nothing nearby though," Doug reported.

"Busy night," Ari commented.

"I think it's going to get wilder before all this is through," Doug said, then bid Ari goodnight and went to lie down.

Ari walked across the stage, past the lunch tables of "Atomic High" according to the sign on the backdrop. He went through the dark theater, past the rows of empty seats and imagined the ghostly applause of theater-goers from years past. The chances of this little theater ever seeing another audience was slim.

He turned off his flashlight before entering the theater lobby. They'd agreed on no lights so as not to draw attention. The lobby was ghostly with only moonlight spearing through the windows. There was a faint smell of chocolate in the air from the candy counter—a welcome relief after the odor of sweaty feet and Febreze that lingered in the actors' dressing room.

Ari peered out the window and saw the glow in the distance Doug had mentioned. With no one to fight fires, how many blocks might be demolished before a fire burned out on its own? There were other dangers besides zombies in this besieged city. So far they hadn't come across any violent people, but Ari had no doubt they were out there. The longer this went on and people had to scavenge for increasingly scarce food and supplies, the more certain types would use force to keep the best for themselves. Man was an animal at heart; the strong survived and the weak were eaten.

The door behind him opened and Ari looked toward it. Lila, wearing a man's trench coat that ended nearly at her ankles, padded across the floor on bare feet. "Hi. I couldn't sleep any more either so I thought I'd join you."

"Cool."

There were low, backless benches around the lobby for patrons to sit during intermission. Ari sat on one near the window, scooting over far enough so Lila could sit beside him. As she sank down, he studied her profile, the slender bridge of her nose, her firm chin and the curve of those lips he'd almost gotten a chance to taste earlier. She was cute with her hair tousled from sleep and looked like a little girl in that oversized coat with her bare feet poking out from beneath it.

"Aren't your feet cold?"

She glanced down and wiggled her toes. "Naw. I'm always hot."

Ari grinned. He didn't fire back a teasing comment, instead, letting the double entendre breathe and watching Lila blush. In the dim light he couldn't see her cheeks blushing, but had no doubt they were from the way she shifted on the seat.

"That didn't come out quite right," she said.

"I think it came out just right," he replied, low and sexy and moved a little closer to her.

She laughed nervously. "Have you always been such a flirt?"

"When there's someone worth flirting with."

Running out of words, she leaned forward, resting her arms on her knees. Her shoulder length hair fell forward curtaining her face and hiding it from him. "So, tell me some more about Ari Brenner," she said. "What were you like as a kid?"

"Trouble, I told you. My mom worked a couple of jobs so I was on my own a lot, but even when I was young enough to have a babysitter, I'd sneak out and get into shit. My mom always liked to believe it was the kids I hung around with dragging me down. But the truth was I was kind of the ringleader."

"I can see that." She tucked her hair behind her ear and glanced over at him. "Mean little punks like you used to give brown-nosing, straight-A girls like me a hard time."

"I bet you gave them a hard time right back." He leaned forward, too, so he could see her eyes better.

"No. I just told on them. I was kind of a snitch. A real by-the-book type. I hated when things weren't fair or when someone weak got hurt."

"I wasn't a bully," Ari said abruptly, suddenly anxious for her to know he hadn't been a complete tool. "I never beat up littler kids. But me and my boys did steal things and wreck stuff just for the hell of it. By the time we were in high school, we were stealing more expensive things and wrecking other peoples' cars, which is how I ended up spending time in juvie."

"Was it bad there?" she asked. "You always read how juvenile detention only makes moderately messed up kids even worse."

He shrugged. "I have to say I was lucky. In my case it was the best thing that could've happened to me. There was a great guy there, a real mentor. And I was in a different frame of mind by the time I'd served my time. I finished high school, which was in serious doubt before that, and after bumming around for a while, I joined the army."

"Mm." Lila frowned. "Do you really think this is a good time to join that team with all the pies the U.S. has its finger in?"

"It's the perfect time. There's work to do. I want to do it. And the pay and benefits are excellent." He was annoyed but not surprised at her liberal reaction. He'd figured Lila's politics veered to the left. Not that he was some right wing zealot. He agreed with some aspects of both parties but generally believed all politicians were self-involved assholes. The army was a job, as good or bad as any, and it kind of pissed him off to hear her question his choice.

Lila must've caught his tone, because she instantly backed off. "Sorry. I tend to get worked up about foreign policy. But I guess none of that matters now. We're in a new world. I wonder if this has spread overseas."

"Maybe not, if the drug wasn't shipped out of the country. Although I suppose an infected person could be treated, recover, travel someplace by jet, die there and then reanimate. Guess it all depends on how long patients live before they relapse and how long it takes the corpses to reanimate."

Lila exhaled a long breath. "Let's not talk about this tonight. Moratorium on the subject of zombies."

She was right. Zombies weren't conducive to romance and he was much more interested in getting closer than in discussing the future right at the moment. In fact, he eased himself a little closer physically and put his arm behind Lila's back, resting his hand on the bench behind her. Next move, an arm around her waist. Usually he wasn't this slow to move on a girl who was obviously interested in him, too. But Lila was outside his usual zone and he didn't just want to grab at her.

"Now you've heard my sordid childhood story. Tell me about yourself. An A-student, Girl Scout, and 4-H, too, I'm guessing. Isn't that what kids do in Ohio, raise pigs or horses or something?"

"Now who's stereotyping? We didn't live on a farm. I've never ridden a horse. I've rarely been to a county fair for that matter. So no 4-H here."

"But I bet you joined clubs and volunteered for committees in school. You seem like the useful kind of girl who knows how to get things done. Class president maybe?"

"Vice president. And yes, I was in a few clubs."

He smiled, taking that "few" to mean "many". He would've liked to have seen what Lila looked like back then, all pigtails, braces and earnest face. She was right. He would've either ignored or teased a girl like her when he was younger. Now he admired her idealism and caring nature. She was good at keeping things calm in their little group, whether by distracting and entertaining Ronnie or by defusing tension. In a crisis, a man wanted to rely on a woman who knew how to get things done. Suddenly that was a far sexier quality than a nice rack or long legs.

"Well joining's a good thing," he said lamely, trying to express his admiration without saying it bluntly. "Maybe if I'd played more sports or been in some clubs, I would've gotten into less trouble back then. But live and learn."

"I've changed a lot since high school." Lila straightened her back and a shaft of moonlight etched her face in white and black. "Not so much of a joiner these days. I think a lot of it was tied up with trying to please my parents, or to be some kind of model citizen rather than figuring out what I believed in myself. Maybe that's why I'm so interested in philosophy and comparative religion courses. They've opened my mind to bigger thoughts than I ever dared to entertain back then."

And that, in a nutshell, was why Lila was unlike any girl he'd been with before and why he was a little nervous around her. She was damn deep. She considered things beyond the day to day, and was concerned with more than how she looked, what she owned or wanted to own. It made him realize he'd been wading in a very shallow dating pool up until now.

"I've never met anyone like you before." The words slipped out of his mouth before he could stop them, the truth although it sounded like an unoriginal pick-up line.

She could've come back with some smart ass comment, and they could've kept up the banter for the next couple of hours while the black of night turned to gray, but instead Lila turned toward him and leaned in. She cupped the side of his face and pressed her lips to his. It was only a small kiss, nothing heavy or deep, but somehow it rocked him to his core. His stomach clenched and his lips burned as if he'd never been kissed before. And his cock went stiff as a board.

Ari recovered fast and went into make-out mode, slipping a hand around her waist and curving the other at the back of her neck, feeling her warmth against both palms. He kissed her harder, deeper, pulled her body against his. By the time he let her go, they were both gasping for breath. He rested his forehead against hers and just breathed for a moment, his heart thumping against his breastbone. "Whew, that was…"

"I know."

"But I'm supposed to be keeping watch." He knew if they went on like this, pretty soon they'd be throwing down on the lobby floor with neither of them paying any attention to the world outside at all. "I should, uh, do that."

"You're right. Absolutely," she panted.

Reluctantly he released her body. Lila took her warm hand from his cheek, leaving it cold. She sat back on her side of the bench, leaving a little space between them, and looked out the window. "This probably isn't a good idea anyway. We're in the midst of a crisis. Who needs the distraction?"

"Mm-hm," he agreed, even as he imagined lunging at her again, dragging her off the narrow bench onto the floor and doing so much more than kissing. He rose and went to the window, turning his mind away from Lila and back to the task at hand. Nothing moved on the street and the orange glow of fire in the west seemed to have faded a little.

"Do you want anything to drink?" she asked. "I could go make you a cup of coffee or something. You didn't eat much dinner either."

"No, I'm fine. Thanks." A movement in one of the upstairs windows across the street caught his attention and his gaze shot up there. "Did you see that?"

"What?"

"Up there. Something moving."

"I thought I saw the curtain move when I was watching earlier in the day." She rose to join him by the window. "Think someone's over there?"

Before he could answer, a head and shoulders crashed through the window they were staring at before the body was dragged inside the building. Shattered glass rained down on the sidewalk below. A scream shattered the silence and then dead quiet followed.

Both of them stepped quickly back from their own window.

"Jesus!" Ari breathed. "What the hell?" But he knew what had happened. A survivor in that building had been attacked and run toward the window. He pictured a zombie or two springing on them, the person falling through the glass before being hauled away. The message hit home hard. The revenants were everywhere out there, roaming the city, infiltrating the buildings in search of more food. None of Ari's group was safe and they had a long way to go to reach the river. His raging hormones were doused like someone had turned an ice cold fire hose on him. He had to be more diligent. This was no time to be fucking around, literally or figuratively, with a girl.

"I think I'd like that coffee now," he said.

CHAPTER ELEVEN

The next day was bad from the beginning. For one thing, Ari had a headache and his nerves were jittery from drinking way too many cups of coffee during his watch. The Pattons' baby kept crying and he was afraid the noise would draw zombies. Everyone seemed to be in a foul mood, picking at and arguing with each other about minor things. He felt too irritable himself to soothe any egos and was glad when Lila stepped in between Derrick and Carl to mediate and escalating argument.

"Listen, guys. There'll be plenty of time later to figure out why patching in the hard drive isn't working. It's no one's fault. No one's questioning anyone's abilities. We know the data is on there and getting it someplace safe is what's important. So let's pack up and get on our way."

"Ari." Sondra was right by his elbow, looking up at him with pleading eyes. "Did you think about what I said yesterday? I don't think I'm being unreasonable. Humboldts is on the way to where we're going so we might as well stop there as anywhere else—get the baby some diapers and things."

He resisted the urge to shove her away. "We'll stop wherever's convenient and safe. Drop it." He couldn't believe how whacked Sondra was to be at all concerned about choosing a particular department store. Had she not noticed the zombies around her? Or was this her crazy means of coping? Focus on a stupid detail and pretend everything is normal like an ostrich with its head in the sand.

The day went from bad to worse when Doug Patton got the runs from something he'd eaten and spent nearly an hour in the restroom, delaying their start.

At last they got underway, walked a few blocks without incident, and then Ian decided to get fussy. Gloria did her best to calm the baby, but his crying escalated. Perhaps the kid could sense the tension in the air or maybe he was just being a normal baby. No amount of shushing would quiet him and Ari was terrified his piercing yells would attract zombies like ringing a dinner bell.

Since they were near Humboldt's, Sondra got her way. The building was locked so Ari broke into the store. A marauding horde of zombies charged up the street as he ushered the last of the group inside the building. He slipped through the door himself and watched for a moment to make certain they hadn't been spotted, but the creatures raged past. How many more near misses before they got caught and at last, and could they even fight with people like Mrs. Patton and the children along? At some point he might have to make a hard decision and cut the weak ones loose in order to keep the rest of them safe. Getting Carl to freedom was his main mission. The sacrifice of a few for the good of the entire world was never a pleasant thing to consider but sometimes it was necessary.

Inside the store, Deb and Joe went on a quick sweep of the ground floor while he led the rest of the group to the furniture department. They dropped onto chairs and couches, exhausted more from anxiety than from walking a few city blocks. It was no Sunday stroll out there.

"I'm going to get some things for the baby." Doug Patton started to head off.

"Wait a minute," Ari called. "We don't know if the store's secure and you're not even armed."

"I'll go with him," Lila volunteered, hefting the rifle which she'd yet to use. It wasn't that Ari didn't trust she would if necessary, but he didn't feel comfortable having people disperse to all departments of this huge store on individual errands.

"Wait until the others come back with a report," he ordered.

Derrick grumbled something under his breath about dictators, but Doug obediently sat back down.

Ian cried and Ari cringed inside. What would it take to quiet that kid? He found out a moment later when Gloria draped a blanket over her shoulder and nursed the baby.

"I'm hungry," Ronnie whined.

"Have some more Fritos." Derrick tossed a bag at her.

"I don't want any more. I want *real* food."

"We're all hungry. Just shut up about it," her brother said. "Grow up a little."

Ronnie was right. They couldn't keep eating snack foods. They needed better nutrition to keep up their strength. Another stop at a grocery store or restaurant would be necessary before the day was through.

Joe returned from scanning the east side of the store. "I didn't see or hear anything. But there are two floors above this. It's too big to scan it all. I don't feel comfortable here."

Me either, Ari thought. The sooner they got what they needed and got on their way, the better.

"I brought company." Deb approached from the other direction along with a group of about ten people.

Ari's stomach dropped. He should be glad to see more survivors, but the larger their number became, the more danger for everyone. Where two or three could move fast and hide well, bigger groups were slower and more obvious. Nevertheless, he held out his hand and greeted the leader of the group, a woman in her thirties. "How you doing? I'm Ari."

"Hunter." She briefly related their story. The group of survivors was mostly Humbolts employees, seven women and three men who'd hidden in a storeroom until the first wave of zombies had passed. They'd come out of hiding, barred the doors, cleaned up the place and were living on an upper level from with access to several fire escapes if need be.

"Until now it's been pretty quiet. We patrol and watch from the windows, but none of those things has tried to get in the building yet. Thanks for breaking our door, by the way." She fixed Ari with a hard stare.

"Sorry. We needed supplies and shelter." He indicated Gloria and Ian. "We've got a baby with us."

"Where are you headed?"

"The waterfront. We're going to get a boat." He didn't ask if they wanted to come along and hoped she didn't suggest it. If anything, he'd like to leave the Pattons here.

Hunter ordered a couple of her people to secure the door and invited everyone up to the second floor. "Do you have food with you? We'll trade whatever you need for more food and water."

It was ridiculous of her to claim the entire contents of the store as theirs to bargain with, but Ari let it go. No point in starting an argument. Besides, the Humboldt crew was armed with guns from their sporting goods department. He couldn't imagine it coming to a shootout. They weren't quite Lord of the Flies yet. But if these people continued to squat here instead of moving on, they'd soon become desperate for fresh supplies and likely to take them from anyone who wandered into their territory. The department store had a wide variety of useful items. Unfortunately food wasn't one of them.

"We'll share what we have," Ari said.

He and the rest of the group joined their hosts, who escorted them around the store to the various departments. Sondra seemed content to stay in women's clothing and try on one outfit after another. Maybe the act of shopping assured her the world still spun on its axis.

Soon they were supplied with everything they needed including personal care and baby items. In return, the Humboldt group took most of their provisions. Ari wasn't happy to lose the rest of their groceries, but he'd figured they'd need to stop for food today anyway.

When they were finished trading, everyone gathered near the top of the escalator. Ari stuck out his hand to shake Hunter's. "Guess we'll be moving on." He glanced at the Pattons and wondered if there was any polite way he could suggest they stay behind.

"Pam and I want to go with you," a woman named Lauren said abruptly. "We can't stay here. We'll all die before anyone comes to rescue us."

Hunter glared at her. "I told you a hundred times we're better off sitting tight. This is only the third day. Something's bound to happen soon. The government will fix this."

It seemed there were a lot more people in the "stick your thumb up your ass and wait for rescue" camp than Ari had thought.

"I'm sorry," he said to Lauren. "We can't take on any more people. It's hard enough to move with the group we've got." He looked around at their familiar faces. "In fact, if any of you would rather stay here with these people, you're welcome to."

"Nuh-uh," Hunter shook her head. "We've got all we can support right here. No one stays and no one goes."

"We do," Pam spoke up, supporting Lauren. "We want to get the hell out of here. Hunter, you can't keep us here. Why would you want to? You said yourself we're running out of food." She pointed at Ari. "And *he* can't stop us from going with them."

As the argument escalated, Ari sought advice by pondering W.W.V.D.—What would Vogt do? His sergeant wouldn't have put up with insubordination that was for sure, but this wasn't the army and these people weren't soldiers. He offered a suggestion. "Maybe we can trade, keep the numbers even. If a few of our members stayed and a few of yours wanted to join us..."

"You mean my family," Doug Patton interrupted. "You can't leave us behind. We won't be abandoned."

"I'm not talking about abandoning anyone. Only if you wanted to stay."

"Why would we? We're not crazy."

"Doug." Gloria set her new diaper bag on the floor and reached out to take her husband's arm. "Maybe it would be best for Ian. If we wait here with these people—"

"We'll end up dead. No, honey. I know you're scared, but we've got to keep going," the big man beseeched his wife. "We've got to think of the future. There isn't one here."

Great. At this rate Doug was going to talk the whole pack of Humboldt's employees into joining them. He should've been an army recruiter.

"Let's stay calm and keep our goal in mind," Ari cautioned. "The most important mission is getting Carl and the data to safety. Maybe it's time to split up and have just a few of us strike out for the marina." At last, he'd put out there what he'd been thinking, and now he held his breath, awaiting reactions. There was an immediate clamor of voices protesting the suggestion.

"Who would you leave behind, Ari?" Lila asked softly, looking up at him with questioning eyes. "The children, Mrs. Scheider, me? Anyone who slows you down?"

"No, of course not." Goddamn, why did this have to be so tough? "But the baby keeps crying, putting all of us in danger. I'm trying to consider what's best for the mission."

"Enough!" Deb snapped. "No one's staying and no one's coming with us. We got what we needed and now we're moving on. Just our group. End of story. Come on, Julie."

She headed toward the frozen escalator and that's when the bad day suddenly got much, much worse. There was the sound of shattering glass from below.

"Attack!" the watchman on the ground floor shouted. "They've broken in. They're coming!" A burst of gunfire followed his words.

Hunter ran to look over the balcony railing at the mezzanine below and Ari followed her. If the number of zombies was small, perhaps they could kill rather than run from them. But one glance showed the undead swarming through the ground floor.

Ari's heart stopped. "We've got to get everyone out of here."

He and Hunter ran back to the others. Many were already heading to the fire exits. There were two—one on either side of the store, and all of these people had to make it through the doors and down the stairs to the alley. Locating their camp on the second floor may have seemed like a good idea in theory, but in reality it might prove disastrous.

The nearer exit was already jammed with the Humboldts employees so Ari grabbed Ronnie by the hand and ran toward the exit at the other side of the store. They dashed through house wares and hardware toward the red glow of the exit sign, shining like a beacon in the dark. When they reached the door, he passed Ronnie off to Mrs. Scheider. "Get her out of here."

Deb already had the door open. She, Julie and Carl headed down the stairs. The rest of their group was still somewhere in the store. Ari went to find them and passed Derrick pulling Gloria Patton by the hand. She carried Ian in one arm and looked back over her shoulder, screaming for her husband as Derrick tugged her along.

"Come on, lady," Derrick urged. "Just run."

"I'll find the others," Ari promised as he went in the opposite direction.

The zombies were pouring up the stairs to the second floor now like frantic shoppers on the day after Thanksgiving rushing for the best deals. Bargain priced human cuisine. Some of the creatures were riddled with bullets from the watchman's rifle, but he'd missed their vital spot so they kept coming. There were at least a dozen monsters and most were focused on the people queued and struggling to get through the exit.

Ari stopped and shot into the running horde of zombies. Aiming for their heads, he cut a swath across the group, the gunfire ringing in his ears as pretty as a choir anthem. Some dropped like stones and others tripped over them. Soon the creatures were tangled together, their momentum slowed.

Easy as bowling. The cocky thought darted through his mind a second before he was tackled from behind by one of the silent predators. The zombie's weight bore him to the floor. Ari dropped his rifle and reached for the skinning knife at his belt while twisting to face his attacker. He wouldn't die this way—bitten in the back of the neck and never seeing the thing that had killed him.

Ari rolled and jabbed upward with his knife simultaneously. The blade stabbed through the revenant's chest before hitting bone and wedging there. He fought against the weight of the creature pinning him to the floor. Pushing it off him, he wrenched out his knife.

The zombie was a woman—had been a woman. Only a bag of rotten flesh now. She fell back when he pushed her off him, but immediately rallied and started toward him again, ignoring the gaping hole above her breast.

Ari leaped to his feet and rushed toward her, slicing at her face and cutting across the eyes. When she continued to stagger blindly toward him, he grabbed her hair, pulled her head down and hacked at the back of her neck. His knife cleaved cleanly through vertebrae, severing the neural connection. She went lifeless and Ari dropped the body, which sagged to the floor. *They aren't that hard to kill. There are just too damn many of them.*

He whirled around, taking stock of the situation. The zombies had descended on the knot of fleeing Humboldts' people at the door, but the survivors weren't going down without a fight. Ari saw Lauren, the woman who'd wanted to go with them, using an acetylene torch to hold off a zombie. She set fire to its clothes and the fire quickly burned upward to catch the zombie woman's long hair. In seconds, her head was flaming like a birthday candle, but even then the creature kept after Lauren. Ari saw this with a glance before continuing to search for his own people.

Two zombies had someone pinned to the floor and were tearing into him like lions on a zebra. Ari's stomach lurched. The large figure in the green polo shirt and jeans was Doug Patton. His instinct was to drive the predators off Doug, but it was far too late for that. At this point, it was better to let them finish feasting, hopefully leaving nothing of Doug behind to rise again.

Joe appeared from around the corner of a display case. He ran toward Ari and grabbed his arm as he went past. "Come on."

"Lila's still in here."

Joe pulled on him. "You can't look for her. We've got to go."

Ari shook him off. "You go. Take the others someplace safe. I'll catch up."

Lila. Despite everything he'd said about the mission coming first, he couldn't leave her behind. She might be alive, hiding somewhere, needing his help. He had to find her.

CHAPTER TWELVE

Lila gripped Sondra's hand as if it was a life preserver and she was floating near the Titanic. Bodies buffeted them this way and that, people clawing and fighting to get to the door. An elbow cracked into Lila's ribs, pain spearing through her. A woman fell back against her, nearly knocking her off her feet, but she continued to cling to Sondra.

When everyone had started running, Lila had been swept along with them. She'd seen Sondra, standing with a deer in the headlights look in her eyes, and seized the woman's hand. Soon they were caught in the pile-up at the exit door. Immediately, Lila realized this was a dead end. People were panicking, pushing each other to get out first before spilling through the door like clowns exiting a tiny car.

The zombies would see this large, struggling group and attack them first. Maybe the few who had made it down the fire escape would get away, or maybe they'd be chased down. Either way, she and Sondra weren't going to make it through that door. Lila wanted to be free of the struggling crowd, but she was trapped by bodies.

A deafening round of rifle fire added to the mayhem of screaming, yelling people. Lila caught a glimpse of the undead coming toward them and surrounding the leader, Hunter like a horde of ants crawling over a dropped Popsicle. Lila jerked on Sondra's wrist, at last pulling her free from the melee and over to a rack of men's jackets. They dropped down behind it to hide.

"My ankle," Sondra moaned. "I think it's broken."

"Sh." Lila peered past a black sleeve, inhaling the rich scent of leather. She thought the smell would remind her of this moment for the rest of her life—the heart-stopping terror, the inability to move. Although, maybe the rest of her life would only be the next few minutes.

She didn't have her rifle. She'd set it down just before all hell broke loose. All she had on her was the big hunting knife Ari had given her. Lila let go of Sondra's hand and drew the knife. The heft of it in her hand was comforting. She wouldn't hesitate to use it. Non-violence could take a flying fuck. But she'd rather get out of here without having to confront a zombie if possible.

"Follow me," she whispered and ran in a low crouch from the rack of jackets to a display of packaged dress shirts with Sondra limping behind her.

Lila peered around the edge of the display case. About twenty zombies blocked the way to the rest of the store. She and Sondra were effectively trapped near one wall of the building. The monsters were ripping through the group at the door. The people fought back, shooting into the swarming zombies, but at such close quarters, they sometimes hit each other. Others were engaged in hand to hand combat, slicing at their attackers with knives. But a single-minded, unwavering will to eat drove the zombies and their sheer numbers overpowered the humans.

All of this happened in mere moments and now the bulk of the zombie crowd was focused on either eating or pursuing their prey out the door. The way was clear. It was possible she and Sondra could sneak past behind them. Lila turned to Sondra. "We've got to run for it. Now."

"I can't. My ankle."

"Run or I'll leave you here to die." Without waiting for an answer, Lila grasped Sondra by the wrist and pulled her to her feet. Together they ran from men's wear toward house wares.

There Ari stood with his back against a display of crock pots, hacking with the hatchet he'd picked up in sporting goods at three zombies surrounding him. He swung with a whirling arc, but the blade missed them all.

All Lila could think was that she had to help him. She let go of Sondra's hand at last and ran toward him. She raised her knife and brought it down with a chopping slice across the back of one of the zombies. But with her unskilled aim she missed the target of his neck and buried the blade in the thing's back. Before she could pull it out again, the zombie whirled toward her. The buried knife was ripped from her grasp and she was left weaponless.

The dead creature surged toward her. It was the first time she'd seen one so close. He was only a middle aged man with thinning hair and glasses. Yes, the creature still wore glasses. But he snapped at her like a mad dog. Lila danced back out of reach of his snatching hands.

A gunshot snapped from behind her and she swore she felt the bullet whoosh past her before slamming into the zombie's face, shattering a lens of its glasses. And then Sondra was tugging Lila's arm, yelling, "Run. Run!" with a pistol dangling from her hand.

The two women raced past the disoriented zombie before it could recover just as Ari felled his second opponent. Gasping for breath, he stood over the two unmoving zombies. He looked up and his gaze met Lila's for a moment, then he stooped and hauled his hatchet out of the back of a zombie's neck. He ran with Lila and Sondra toward the other exit. They didn't look back to see if they were chased. They simply ran, flat out, dodging display racks of tools and automotive supplies.

Ari nearly tore the door of its hinges and ushered them through. Lila pelted down the rickety metal fire escape. She glanced back to see Sondra stumble and Ari catch her and help her down the stairs. Coming through the door behind them was the zombie with Lila's knife sticking from his back. Lila faced forward and ran faster, skipping the last few steps and landing on the pavement with both feet. She scanned the alley from one end to the other. The way was clear. She ran in the opposite direction from the other fire escape, which would be around the corner. A quick glance back assured her Ari and Sondra were still there. She wasn't sure where to go, but went in the direction she thought the others would take, rounding the corner of the building and heading toward the street. These alleyways were too narrow and dangerous with little chance of escape.

Lila paused at the corner to check out the street. Ari and Sondra caught up with her and she was happy to let Ari take the lead.

"How's your ankle?" she asked Sondra.

"Hurts," she whimpered.

"It's probably only sprained or you wouldn't be able to run on it. We'll stop someplace soon." Lila put her arm around Sondra's waist and supported her as they followed Ari down the street, moving swiftly from one bit of cover to another.

"Hey! Over here." Derrick's voice came from across the street and he emerged from the shadow beneath an awning to wave at them.

They crossed the deserted street, dodging around the fenders of abandoned cars. Derrick waited for them, pressed flat against the side of the building.

"You made it. Where's Doug?"

Ari shook his head.

"Damn, that's too bad." Derrick frowned. "I told her he'd be okay."

Lila wanted to prop Sondra against the wall and take a breather, but there was no time for a break. They followed Derrick as he led them to the rest of the group, down yet another alley and into a Tastee-Freeze that had been deserted since long before the zombie attack. A hole was smashed in the glass door, allowing access to the lock.

They filed inside. The furnishings were vintage '60s soda fountain with a long counter and metal stools bolted to the floor. A clock with hands frozen at two fifty-eight hung on the wall, as well as faded posters announcing various ice cream confections. Someone had spray painted "suck on this" below the poster of a happy child with chocolate covered frozen banana. The ice cream display case was grimy with dirt and also colorfully painted with graffiti.

Derrick led them behind the counter to a back room, which was larger than the serving area. Apparently the owner of the Freeze had once lived a one room apartment back here.

Gloria Patton sat on the edge of the bed, her face bright red and eyes puffy although she was no longer crying. Julie was beside her, bouncing Ian on her knees and singing quietly to him. Ronnie pressed close to her side, watching blank-eyed with no smile on her face.

Mrs. Scheider sat on the floor, leaning against the wall with her eyes closed, while Carl, Joe and Deb stood in the center of the room arguing. They all looked up when Derrick and the others entered.

"You made it!" Deb threw her arms around Lila and hugged her, crushing her bruised ribs. Lila grunted in pain, but hugged her back.

"I told you they'd come," Derrick said. Lila could tell from his tone there'd been some discussion about whether he should go back and wait for them.

"Doug?" Gloria jumped up from the bed, her eyes searching Ari's face.

"I'm sorry," he said. There was nothing else to add, no explanation that needed to be given under the circumstances.

Gloria let out a keening wail, and Joe hurried to shush her, holding her and pressing her face against his chest. "Sh, Mrs. Patton. Please be quiet."

They'd lost one. It could have been much worse, but that was of no comfort to Gloria. Lila collapsed onto the ground, leaning against the opposite wall from Mrs. Scheider. She thought of the people they'd met today and wondered how many had made it out alive. What were they doing now? Where had they run to?

She stopped thinking about it. There was no point. Besides, she was too exhausted and jittery to focus on anything. Bits of thought scattered through her mind like kaleidoscope colors, but she couldn't put them together into any coherent pattern. Mostly she thought of what it had felt like to drive a knife into human flesh and then stare right into the face of death.

She looked at Sondra. Ari had helped her to the bed and Julie took a look at her injured ankle while Ronnie held the baby. Sondra winced and whined and made a big deal about how much pain she was in. Lila still sort of detested her but the woman had saved her life.

"You shot that thing," Lila said. "Thank you."

Sondra smiled at her. "I just squeezed the trigger. I've never shot a gun before in my life. Lucky I didn't accidentally shoot you instead." And then she was off, telling everyone every detail of their escape and how she'd saved Lila's life.

Julie wrapped Sondra's ankle with tape from the first aid kit and Deb passed out the last of the water bottles, admonishing everyone to drink lightly until they could get more.

They'd lost almost all of the merchandise they'd acquired at Humboldt's and the sport shop. Backpacks, sleeping bags, even Ian's diaper bag had been abandoned as they ran for their lives. So the entire stop had been for nothing. They'd gained little and lost a life.

Ari leaned against the wall then slid down to sit beside Lila. He leaned close and whispered, "Are you all right?"

She nodded. "You?"

"Sure." He rested his head against the wall and closed his eyes like Mrs. Scheider.

Lila wanted to curl up on the floor and put her head in his lap. Instead, she leaned next to him, shoulder to shoulder. Her eyes fell shut and the drone of conversation washed over her. Being alive had never been sweeter than at this precise moment, after the near loss of it. They were safe, for now, and that was enough.

CHAPTER THIRTEEN

Their trip to the marina began to take on the quality of an epic quest. A few short miles—it should've been accomplished in a day, even on foot. Two at most. But Sondra's twisted ankle and Mrs. Patton's nearly catatonic state following the loss of her husband forced them to postpone the start of their journey for another full day. They squatted in the deserted Tastee-Freez, while Ari and Joe went and brought back food for them.

That night they didn't dare to have any light. With no bedding, they lay in complete darkness on the linoleum and waited restlessly for morning. The theater where they'd spent the previous night seemed like a plush palace in comparison. The only good thing as far as Lila was concerned was that she lay next to Ari, his body curved around hers, his arm slung over her. She didn't mind being on the hard floor so much with his body heating her back and the beat of his heart lulling her to sleep.

The next day there was nothing to do but sit and wait for Sondra to heal and listen to her babble. Everyone made attempts to offer their sympathy to Gloria, but she was beyond their words. No one could reach her or connect with her. At last, impatient Deb snapped at her. "Look, you got a kid here. Pull yourself together. Feed him. Take care of him. Live because of him. You can mourn later."

Lila cringed at her harsh tone but evidently it was what Gloria needed to hear. The blank look left her eyes as she focused on Deb's face, then she took her infant son from the other woman and held him to her breast.

A dull afternoon of waiting, playing cards, taking naps, coloring pictures with Ronnie, putting together a meal of canned food and cleaning up after it with limited water, was followed by another night. Once more Ari took the spot beside Lila. If the others noticed how close together they slept or that they were curled together when they woke in the morning, no one said anything about it.

The next day Sondra could limp around the room. Dr. Joe pronounced her well enough to travel as long as they didn't go too far that day.

Lila was ready to move on. She couldn't have taken another day of idly waiting. They might be risking their lives out there, but they were in just as much danger here in the Tastee Freez.

They headed out, walking in their diamond shape with Ari on point, Deb and Derrick flanking him on either side, Joe and Lila bringing up the rear and the others protected in the center. Lila was nervous, acutely aware of her position and the need to almost literally have eyes in the back of her head. Zombies might attack from behind at any time and her neck was sore from swiveling it to constantly look over her shoulder.

"We need rearview mirrors," Joe commented as they marched along.

Lila eyed the empty cars they passed and wondered how hard it would be to rip one off.

Today, the fifth day into the crisis, the air reeked so badly from rotting corpses it was hard to breathe. All of them wore handkerchiefs or other strips of material over their noses and mouths as if that would help. Lila wondered if a person could get sick merely from the overpowering odor. Weren't organisms present in the stench of decay? Just as she would begin to think she was adjusting to the awful smell, they'd pass another site of a zombie attack and the rank odor would break over her in a fresh wave.

They walked along a side street and were several blocks from the Tastee Freez when Lila checked behind them and saw a little girl. She was skipping in the middle of the street, a child of about Ronnie's age with a doll in her arms. Only when she lifted the doll to her face to kiss it did Lila decipher what she was actually seeing. The child wasn't skipping she was shambling and thing Lila had taken for a doll was a severed arm the girl chewed on. Lila gave a low whistle, their signal for a zombie sighting, and everyone's heads swiveled almost simultaneously to look behind them.

The creature was some distance away and hadn't spotted them yet. Ari motioned them forward and the group hurried around the next corner.

Lila's heart pounded, her nerves fried by a fresh jolt of adrenaline like a double espresso to the system. She grew even more diligent about scanning the empty streets around them. With everything so quiet, it was too easy to be lulled into believing they were safe and could walk unnoticed all the way to the Hudson River. But the truth was every step was as treacherous as quicksand and their enemy could erupt from anywhere at any moment.

"You hear that?" Joe asked and shaded his eyes to look up at the sky.

The distant sound of a helicopter—maybe more than one—was the sweetest music Lila had ever heard. She stared into the cloudy sky, but saw nothing. Too many tall buildings blocking the way. But the chopper noises were followed by the sound of gunfire echoing from the skyscraper mountains

They all stopped, straining to see or hear more. Something was happening in the distance. At last, something was being done to help.

"Maybe that Hunter woman and Ann were right," Joe muttered so only Lila could hear. "Maybe it really is safer to find a place and hole up until everything is sorted out."

"Come on," Ari called. "Keep moving."

"My ankle," Sondra said. "I've got to rest soon."

Lila stifled her irritation. It wasn't Sondra's fault she'd been injured, and maybe her ankle really did hurt as much as she claimed. It had certainly been swollen yesterday. But the woman was such a drama queen Lila couldn't help but feel she enjoyed being the center of attention.

"There's a diner up there." Deb pointed. "Maybe we can find some food that's not spoiled."

The greasy spoon joint was open for business and smelled like the bowels of hell. They entered carefully, listening for sounds of other survivors or the roving undead, but the place was still except for buzzing flies. The floor was tacky with blood. Red was smeared on the walls, the booths, the counter, remnants of customers mingling with abandoned plates of the lunch special, which a hand-written sign announced was tuna salad and minestrone soup.

Lila's eyes watered from the stench. She wanted to turn around and go right back outside, but Ian was fussing, working himself up to a good, hard cry. They didn't need that noise drawing attention.

Gloria found a booth in the back that wasn't gore spattered and sat down to feed her son. She moved like the undead herself, a blank-eyed automaton going through the motions of living. Sondra and Ronnie sat across from her. Ari kept watch while the rest of them went to the kitchen to scavenge for food.

Derrick and Carl investigated the dry goods pantry, bringing out boxes of cereal, crackers, chips and cans of soup and pudding. Julie opened one of the industrial sized soup cans which Deb put in a pan to heat. The stove was gas so she could light the burner with her Bic. Lila realized she hadn't seen Deb smoke a cigarette the past couple of days. Either she'd run out or was choosing the most stressful time possible to give up the habit.

After Julie opened a gallon can of tapioca, Lila scooped it into bowls. Joe produced a package of bacon from the freezer, which he claimed hadn't completely defrosted yet. He laid strips on a griddle over another burner then got bread from a rack on the wall.

"Don't dare spread that mayonnaise on it. No doubt it's spoiled,"

Mrs. Scheider warned as he unscrewed the lid of a jar.

"I'm not an idiot. I didn't get it from the fridge. It's freshly opened," Joe said.

Even the grown-ups are getting short-tempered, Lila thought with amusement. The rising scent of frying bacon tantalized her nose and had her saliva glands working overtime. It almost covered the horrible odor of decay all around them. Deb prepared a pot of coffee and it started to percolate on the back burner.

The familiar breakfast smells of bacon and coffee eased Lila's taut nerves and gave her comfort. But the very moment she relaxed, the sound of shattering glass came from the front of the building. Sondra and Gloria's screams resounded through the air followed by gunfire.

"Shit! You guys, go." Derrick grabbed his rifle and rushed to the front to help.

The others ran for the back exit. Deb grabbed Carl by the arm and dragged him along with her. Lila was torn between escaping with them and going to help Ari. But he'd given them all instructions to "run, Forest, run" if they were attacked. While she hesitated, her moment to decide was past as zombies swarmed around the lunch counter. Lila threw the cast iron frying pan of bacon at the closest one then ran out the kitchen door into the alley.

Joe, Carl and Deb were pushing a dumpster in front of the door to block it. Lila barely made it out in time before they heaved the heavy metal container in front of it. Bodies banged against the door from inside. The loud, horrible thumps made the door rattle in its frame, but the dumpster held firm.

"Come on." Deb led the way up the alley.

"But the others." Lila protested.

"We can only hope they made it out the front. We'll meet them at the building on the corner like we said we'd do if we got separated."

Lila knew she was right, but it didn't make leaving the others behind feel any better. She trotted to keep up with the group, but her heart and mind were with Ari in the diner. It didn't seem possible he and Derrick would manage to fight off the zombies and get everyone safely out.

On the way to the office building they'd chosen as a meeting point, they saw a running group of people in the distance followed by a posse of revenants. Flattening their bodies against the nearest wall, they held still and waited for the commotion to die down before resuming their run. They burst into the building's lobby. Joe and Deb did a quick sweep of the ground floor, which was mostly a maze of cubicles. Julie, Carl and Lila waited near the front, watching anxiously for the rest of their group.

When Lila sighted them, her throat tightened. Ari carried Ronnie, her arms and legs wrapped tight around him as if she was a little monkey. Sondra limped beside Derrick, holding onto his arm, and Gloria with Ian in her arms brought up the rear.

"Wait. Where's Mrs. Scheider?" Julie said. "She was in back with us."

"She went to use the restroom just before... Shit!" Carl exclaimed.

"No." Lila looked around the lobby as if the woman would magically appear. "I'm sure she was with us." But no amount of wishing would make it true. Mrs. Scheider was missing.

Ari and the others burst through the door just as Deb and Joe returned to give the all clear status on the ground floor of the building.

"We left Mrs. Scheider," Lila announced.

"Damn it!" Derrick's face was a mask of blood, the whites of his eyes stark against it. "We fought off about a dozen zombies and got everyone out without a scratch, and you guys ditched Mrs. Scheider?"

"It was an accident. We didn't mean to leave her behind. We didn't notice she was missing until we got here. But she was in the restroom, so she might be alive."

Ari unfastened Ronnie's arms from around his neck and set her on the floor. "I'll go back and see if I can find her."

"Wait," Deb said. "She's gone and it's terrible but we can't risk losing you. What happened to 'it's all about the mission'?"

"I'm afraid Deb's right," Joe added. "It's not likely Patricia made it out alive."

Lila had nearly forgotten Mrs. Scheider's first name. Hearing Joe say it filled her with a fresh pang of guilt and sorrow.

"No one went back for my husband. No one saved him!" Silent Gloria was suddenly vocal, her eyes blazing and her face twisted in a scowl.

Ari turned to her. "It was too late for him, but it might not be for Mrs. Scheider. I'll only do a recon. If it's too dangerous, I won't go in." Before anyone could argue, he left, slipping out the door and running down the street much faster than he could with all of them slowing him down. Maybe he'd been right before and he should take the data, Carl and only a couple of other useful people like Deb or Derrick and head for the marina. They could probably make it there in an afternoon, take a boat and be on the mainland by evening. The rest of the world might be overrun with zombies, too, but it couldn't possibly be as dangerous as being trapped on an island with them.

Lila sank to the floor, but her leg jiggled nervously as she waited for Ari's return. She listened while Sondra related the story of their escape, how the zombies had stormed the diner, crashing right through the large, plate glass windows; how Sondra had grabbed Ronnie and Gloria and led them outside through the broken window while Ari and Derrick held off the zombies; and how they'd dodged and hid to shake some of the monsters which pursued them.

"Shut up, Sondra," Derrick cut across her chatter. "Just shut up for a while." He sat on the floor, holding Ronnie on his lap and rocking her. She was pressed against his chest, her thumb in her mouth and the stuffed unicorn clenched in her other hand. Her eyes were wide open and staring.

Lila wrapped her arms around her legs and rested her head on her knees. Seconds slipped past like droplets of blood, clotted and sticky. Ari wasn't coming back. ... He was. ... He'd have Mrs. Scheider with him, safe. … Both of them were dead and they were waiting here for ghosts—or maybe zombies.

"They're here," Joe announced. "He's got her." He opened the door and Ari came in, carrying Mrs. Scheider in his arms. There was blood everywhere, her face, her arms, and his, too. Ari staggered and Joe helped him lower the woman to the floor.

Joe stripped away her blouse and checked her wounds. With no running water and their supply of bottled water running low, he used it sparingly, rinsing away the blood from her neck and shoulder. Deb knelt beside him, holding a flashlight trained on the wounds, while Julie dampened fresh cloths and offered them to him.

Lila did the same for Ari, wetting a T-shirt and offering it to him to clean up with. "Are you hurt?"

He shook his head. "It's her blood—and some of theirs. The things were gone when I got back there. She had run into the pantry and barricaded the door, but not before they bit her. Luckily she was still conscious and heard my voice, because she passed out almost immediately after I found her."

"If their blood mixed with hers, she must be infected," Deb said.

"I don't know," Carl answered. "I don't know if the mutated blood could enter her bloodstream. If she's not the same blood type, I couldn't imagine that happening."

"I can't imagine any of this happening, but it is," Joe said sourly as he continued to swab the bites on Mrs. Scheider's shoulders and upper back.

The old woman stirred, blinked, and opened her eyes. She looked around at them all hovering over her.

Julie offered her water, holding a bottle to her mouth and cupping the back of her head. "How do you feel?"

Mrs. Scheider swallowed. "How do you think I feel?"

"Like you've been bit by zombies." Derrick matched her dry tone.

"We're so sorry we left you. We thought you were with us."

Julie smoothed her hand over the woman's gray hair, the salon style now flat and limp.

Mrs. Scheider tried to sit up and winced at the pain.

Joe pushed her back down. "Just lie still and rest while I bandage you." He took the strips of cloth Gloria had torn from a shirt and began to bind her wounds.

Lila knelt beside Ari, wet another rag and sponged at the blood he'd missed along his hair line. She cupped his face and wiped away the traces of gore, but knew they were there whether they showed or not. The memories of what he'd seen and done—what all of them had—could not be erased so easily.

When she'd finished wiping his face clean, she paused for a moment, his face still cupped in her hand. She studied the dark outer ring of his iris and the velvety brown within and the way his pupils dilated as he looked back at her. Tension crackled between them. A kiss floated on the air waiting to be snatched. Then Lila let go, took her hand from his warm skin and sank back onto her heels. "There. That's better."

But it wasn't. Better would have been leaning in and giving him a long, deep kiss.

The near miss in the diner along with Mrs. Scheider's injuries and Sondra's swollen ankle put a stop to their travels for the day. They'd only made it a hand full of blocks from the Tastee-Freez. No one, not even Ari, had the stomach to venture back out to find food so they ate the last of their power bars and shared some sports drinks.

"I sure would've liked some of that bacon," Derrick murmured.

Lila agreed with him, but tried to remember they were lucky to have any food. She thought of her mother's voice telling her to clean her plate. "Think of the starving children in third world countries." She slowly chewed and swallowed her half of a power bar and prayed her mother and father were still alive and safe.

They moved out of the lobby to set up camp in office cubicles so generic they were utterly forgettable. Temporary walls, cheap furniture and pathetic attempts by their owners to personalize the cubicles were all the impression Lila had of the place. Sleeping on industrial grade carpet with no cushions or covers the group passed another night, huddled together in darkness.

By morning, Sondra's ankle was much better, but Mrs. Scheider was pale, weak and unconscious again. Joe felt her pulse and listened to her labored breathing. "I don't know what's wrong with her besides this bite. Perhaps she's just had too much strain on her heart. She needs to be in a hospital getting fluids and oxygen."

"She should rest another day. We all should," Gloria said.

It doesn't look like she has another day in her, Lila thought.

Ari stood, looking down at the woman for a few moments. Lila could almost see him weighing his options. The need to keep moving was obvious, as was the fact that Mrs. Scheider was not likely to recover. But he didn't want to simply pronounce her dead and abandon her, leaving her struggling for breath.

"I'm going up a few floors to take a look at the city and get some perspective," he said.

His double meaning wasn't lost on Lila. She would've liked to go along with him, but sensed he needed time alone to consider his decision. She watched him disappear through the door to the stairs then went to help Julie and Deb scavenge food in the offices and break room.

All they could find in the desks was snack foods and a couple of apples. By the time they'd brought their loot to the conference room and everyone was seated around the table to eat, Mrs. Scheider was much worse and Derrick went to get Ari.

Although her stomach was grumbling, Lila couldn't stand the thought of eating. She didn't know how they could either with Mrs. Scheider lying there wheezing. They should've laid her in a different room, but it was too late to move her now.

Lila knelt beside Joe, dipped a cloth in water and held it to the old woman's dry lips. She wished she had ice chips to feed her and remembered doing that for her grandmother when she was in the hospital on her deathbed. She held Mrs. Scheider's frail hand, closed her eyes and prayed for her to leave the world peacefully—and not reanimate. The thought of having one's corpse tottering around trying to eat people was horrible.

After a few minutes, Lila rose and went to get herself a drink. But after Ari arrived and knelt beside Mrs. Scheider, she went over to him. "Hey, you're back." His shoulder felt strong and warm beneath her hand and when he looked up, her stomach gave a little flip.

"I see you found brunch for everyone."

She babbled on about food for a few seconds, but wasn't really listening to herself. She was caught by the pain in his eyes, the knowledge that he would be the one to behead Mrs. Scheider if she rose again.

Lila volunteered to clear the room. She went to the conference table and told the others the end was near—conscious of the irony of her word choice. Everyone filed past Mrs. Scheider as if she was already a corpse and they were paying their last respects.

When the room was empty, Lila returned to crouch beside Ari. "Do you need me to help?"

"No. I'll handle it." He gave her instructions about making sure the perimeter was secure and she left to follow through on his orders. But she couldn't stop thinking about what he was facing, especially when Joe came out of the conference room to announce Mrs. Scheider had died.

All of them reacted with the same numb acceptance. They'd experienced too much death to react very emotionally to the loss of yet another of their number.

"She was a great lady." Deb offered a eulogy. "Strong, smart and with a sharp sense of humor. I really liked her."

"She was the coolest old lady I ever met," Derrick added.

That summed up what Lila felt as well. She stared at the conference room door which Joe had closed behind him. Everyone knew why and what would probably happen next inside that room.

Lila's felt sick at the thought of Ari in there all alone, dealing with this as he had with so many other things the rest of them couldn't handle. It wasn't right or fair. She walked toward the closed door.

"Where are you going?" Julie asked.

"I'm going to help him." *Or at the very least, be with him when he has to do it.*

Inside the room, Ari sat on his heels beside Mrs. Scheider's still body, his hatchet across his knees and his hand rubbing absently up and down the wooden handle. He looked up when Lila entered. "What's happened?" He started to rise.

"Nothing. I just wanted to… I could help you." Lila would have liked to offer to do the job for him. She wished she were brave enough to lift that ax and make the vital cut, but she knew in her heart she didn't have the emotional strength to do it. Not to someone she'd known and cared about. "Or maybe I can't help you, but I can at least wait with you. Ari, you don't have to do this alone."

He was silent a moment, still looking at her, and then he nodded. "That would be nice, if you'd wait with me."

Pulse racing, Lila hunkered beside him on the floor to keep watch over the dead woman. All of them had discussed earlier the option of cutting off her head simply to be on the safe side, but decided it would be good to find out if she'd been infected and how long after death the body reactivated. Perhaps they would sit with Mrs. Scheider for hours and nothing would happen. Maybe she was simply dead.

After several minutes had slipped past, Lila asked, "How long do you think?"

Ari shrugged. "That one in the subway seemed to rise right away. But Carl seems to think the delay can vary from minutes to days, which would explain why some of the zombies looked like they came from a funeral home instead of a morgue."

"But when bodies are embalmed all the blood is replaced with formaldehyde. Where does that leave Carl's theory about the mutated blood cells causing some kind of reaction? And why would it take different lengths of time for the reanimation to occur? For that matter, why would a bite be enough to infect someone?"

He looked at her from beneath his brows. "I've got no answers. I'm just along for the roller coaster ride." Mrs. Scheider's fingers twitched and his attention focused on them. "And here comes the next hill so hold on."

Lila's stomach plunged. She remembered how much she hated amusement park rides.

Ari rose and reached out to take her hand and draw her to her feet. He continued to hold her hand as he gazed into her eyes. "You don't have to see this. You can leave now."

She shook her head. "No. I'll stay. I don't want you to have to be alone."

He hefted the ax in his hand and Lila's gaze was drawn to the sharp edge. She swallowed bile that rose in her throat. Ari gave her a little push toward the conference table. "Go over there, then, and wait."

Behind him the corpse stirred, her elbows bracing against the gray carpet as she started to push up from the floor.

Lila did as Ari bid her, gripping the back of one of the metal-frame chairs and staring at a framed print of splashy colors and shapes on one wall. What would Ann, the art curator, have thought of the piece? She clenched the chair and flinched at the sound of Ari's small grunt as he swung the ax and metal cleaving flesh and bone.

There was a pause before he said. "Okay. It's done."

Lila turned from the table and walked back toward Ari, standing with the hatchet hanging from one hand by his side. He'd wiped the blade clean but there were spatters on his hand and forearm. Lila avoided looking at the decapitated corpse. She grasped Ari's arm and pulled him away from the body.

"You've done all you can. It's not like we can bury her. I'll find something to cover her body with and we'll leave her here."

She pulled Ari into her embrace, locking her arms around his back and hugging him tight. He hesitated only a moment before dropping the ax on the floor and wrapping his arms around her, too. They held each other for seconds or maybe hours. Lila felt the heat and strength of his body and the way it trembled against hers. Silently, she offered what comfort she could.

At last they reluctantly separated. Ari stooped and kissed her briefly, a warm brush of lips and touch of her cheek before he turned away. He stooped to pick up the ax while she went to tell the others Mrs. Scheider was truly dead now.

She found a suit jacket in one of the offices and took it back to the conference room to drape over the dead woman. She tried to do it without looking too closely, glimpses of white hair and a blood-stained blouse were all she took in as she laid the coat over her. Lila said a prayer, wishing Mrs. Scheider well as she continued her journey to another state of being.

When she returned to the others, they were discussing moving on since it was still quite early in the day. A contingent composed mostly of Gloria and Sondra wanted to rest another day, but the others were ready to go.

"We've got to get out of this city," Deb said. "Even if we only make it a few more blocks today before we have to stop for the night, we've gained a little more ground."

"We should think about finding a car and driving. The streets may be gridlocked, but maybe on the sidewalks," Carl suggested

They'd already addressed the issue before, but Ari patiently explained his reasoning again. "Getting a car or two isn't a problem, but I doubt we'd make it far before hitting an impasse and meanwhile the noise would draw zombies to us. Going on foot is the best way to travel."

"Let's go then." Lila picked up her backpack and slung it over her shoulders. It could be difficult to get everybody moving and leading by example was usually the best way to motivate them. "We have a few hours of daylight left."

It was getting more difficult every time to mentally gear up to go back outside. She understood Gloria's whimpering and Sondra's whining, but couldn't afford any sympathy for them. "Come on. I'll carry Ian for a while, Gloria." She held out her arms to take the baby. Gloria looked doubtful but passed him to her. He was a heavy little thing and immediately began squirming in her arms.

"Here. Give him Bright." Ronnie offered her plush unicorn with the air of a brave soldier offering her canteen to a dying mate. Lila knew what a sacrifice it was for her.

"Thank you, Ronnie. That's very generous of you." Lila took the stuffed toy and gave it to the baby, who gripped it for all of two seconds before dropping it again. "But maybe you'd better carry Bright for him. I don't know if Ian can hold onto him."

She propped the chunky baby against her shoulder and patted his back, calming him down. By now the rest of the group had gathered their things and they headed out into zombie city once more.

After their dramatic and draining day and the loss of another one of their party, the group was exhausted and edgy. For Lila, a sense of inescapable doom draped her like a smothering mantle. She usually considered herself an optimistic person, but for the first time she seriously doubted they'd make it through this crisis alive—not a single one of them.

They walked for a number of blocks without incident, moving as quickly as they could given their large number. Lila's arms ached from carrying Ian, who felt heavier with each step she took as he fell asleep against her shoulder. Finally she passed him off to Julie to carry, trading the child for a rifle.

Ari called a halt as the deep gold of the late afternoon sun cast dark shadows from the tall buildings around them. They needed to find shelter before it was too dark to see.

"We'll try here." He led them into a Good Night's Rest hotel. The lobby was pristine, not as much as a piece of flesh or a finger marring the front counter or the sitting area.

"So far, so good," Carl muttered.

Fanning out, they checked the ground floor and left the upper levels unexplored. Instead they barricaded each of the doors to the stairways to ensure if there was something up above, it couldn't come down. The rooms were all locked. Tapping and calling at the doors didn't summon any survivors from within. Lila imagined that in the middle of the afternoon on a weekday, the motel had probably been pretty empty to start with. Everyone met back in the lobby where Derrick and Joe had locked and barricaded the front doors.

"Guess we have free run of the place," Deb announced. "Let's get a keg and throw a party."

"There are mini-bars in the rooms," Sondra pointed out, not quite registering the sarcasm. "We could collect a bunch and have a drink by the pool."

Pool. The very word conjured heavenly images of bright summer days and cool water washing over her skin. Lila thought the only more beautiful words right now would be "hot shower".

They got key cards from the registration desk and chose a block of rooms right by the pool and the breakfast room. The milk in the mini fridge had gone bad, but there were stale yet edible bagels and muffins and boxes of dried cereal. Apples, tangerines and brown-skinned bananas added fresh fruit to their meal.

"My God, I never thought I'd love Raisin Bran," Julie crunched a handful of dry cereal.

Juice boxes made fine mixers for the little bottles of rum and vodka they liberated from the mini-bars in a few of the rooms. Sondra played bar tender and mixed drinks for everyone.

Lila took muffins, fruit and juice to Joe and Ari, who were guarding the front. They kept the indoor lights off as nighttime spread over the city.

"I'll take your place for a while," she told Joe. "The others are going to clean up in the pool after they're done eating. Go ahead. I'll take a turn later." She tried to convince herself she didn't make the offer with any ulterior motive—like spending some time alone with Ari keeping watch, and later in the pool. An image of them having a swim in the intimate dark long after the others had gone to their rooms floated in her mind. Was it wrong to want that in the midst of death and destruction? Maybe. Did she care? Hell, no. If they weren't going to make it out of this alive, she at least wanted one good memory to see her through at the end.

"You sure?" Joe asked.

"Oh yeah. Go take it easy. I think Sondra's got a juice box cocktail with your name on it."

After Joe was gone, she took his seat by the window. Her leg bumped against Ari's as she slid into the chair beside him. That slight, accidental touch set off a crazy hormone attack. She felt their embrace from earlier imprinted on her body, remembered the last few mornings when she'd woken pressed against him, and relived the few kisses they'd shared. None of that was enough. She wanted more now.

"Anything interesting out there tonight?" she asked.

"Nothing but a few rats scavenging and that's about as interesting as I want it to get."

They lapsed into silence for a bit, while Ari polished off the food she'd brought him, but it was a comfortable silence, the kind old friends shared rather than the awkward pauses of a first date.

"What day is this? Friday?" she asked. "If it was a normal Friday night, what would you be doing?"

"Mm, I don't know what's a 'normal' Friday night anymore. If you'd asked me that back in high school or the summer after, I guess the answer would have been partying with friends, getting too drunk, hitting on girls, maybe going home with one. While I was in basic, we didn't get leave most Fridays, so we'd play poker or pool on the base in our free time. Since I've been home again," he paused. "Well, it's only been about a month, but everything feels different. I thought I'd go back to old routine, hanging with my boys, but I don't know, I've felt kind of out of it. Like, I want something different now, you know?"

"I get that," Lila said. "The summer after my freshman year of college, I was so looking forward to going home to Ohio and seeing my friends again, but it wasn't the same there anymore. *I* wasn't the same."

"What'd you do?"

"Worked at my uncle's car dealership and waited for a new school year to start. I'm not saying I didn't have some good times with my old friends, or enjoy some parties, but my heart wasn't in it and I was just marking time. When I got off the plane in New York at the end of summer, I felt like I was coming home at last."

They talked a little more about what their plans and dreams had been before everything fell apart. They talked about movies, music, stand-up comics, favorite foods, family squabbles, anything except zombies for once.

When Deb and Julie came to relieve them from their duty, Julie's auburn hair was still damp from her swim and hung lank around her face. Deb's braids had shed the water like sealskin and remained in beautiful, wild profusion. The women's hands were clasped together as they approached across the lobby. Lila thought how comforting it would be to be together with your loved one while going through this crisis—but frightening too, seeing her in danger and wanting to protect her at all costs. Deb and Julie were lucky to have each other.

"The water's cold but it feels great," Julie announced. "And everyone else is pretty much finished so you should have it all to yourselves." She smiled and winked at Lila.

Lila felt her cheeks grow warm and willed herself to stop blushing. There was no shame in having a fling, or whatever she was having with Ari. But she hated everyone knowing and talking about it. It was like being in middle school and having rumors flying through the class before a couple had even finished the note-passing stage of their courtship.

The pool room was as dim as the rest of the building and the pool itself was an ominous, flat, black sheet. Lila imagined frightening things under that dark surface waiting to grab and pull under anyone foolish enough to dare to enter the water. She shook off her paranoia.

A few of the others were still in the room. Derrick was helping Ronnie dry her hair, while Gloria put a fresh diaper on Ian. Sondra stood looking at the hot tub and combing her straight, black hair. She brightened and smiled when she saw them—saw Ari, Lila corrected herself. Sondra hadn't been too subtle in her attempts to get close to him over the past few days, asking him specifically to look at her ankle, leaning on him or offering him coffee and coy looks.

"Hey guys. The water's nice." Sondra took off the towel wrapped around her body to reveal a trim waist and blood red bra and panties that hugged her curves. "Maybe I'll take another dip with you."

Gloria snapped Ian's onesie and lifted him in her arms. "Sondra, don't be dense. Leave them alone." She gave Lila a pointed look. "Sondra will be rooming with me."

Good God, even Mrs. Patton knew about their flirtation. Lila was embarrassed but grateful to Gloria for helping her out. She felt more of a connection with the quiet, mourning woman than she had since meeting her as Gloria gave her a brief smile before ushering the others from the room. Sondra pouted but went with her leaving Lila and Ari alone in the empty, echoing pool room with not even the hum of a pump to disturb the quiet.

Ari took off his shoes and socks and tested the water with one foot. "Well…I guess people have, uh, some expectations about us."

"Guess so." Lila played with the hem of her tank top, not quite ready to pull it off in front of him. "Wonder where they got those ideas."

He smiled. "Are they wrong?"

She shrugged and played it loose. "Time will tell." Flirting was not her thing. She felt silly indulging in this kind of banter, but she could hardly come straight out with "Yeah, I fully expect to sleep with you tonight and screw your brains out."

Then Ari stripped his shirt off and tossed it aside and Lila's heart stopped for a second. Damn, his body was fine, muscles upon muscles that made her appreciate what the U.S. Army could do to a man other than turn him into a killing machine. Without hesitation he undid his fly and took off his pants leaving him clad in a close-fitting pair of boxer briefs.

Lila swallowed. Enough girlish wavering about showing a little skin. She took off her shoes, her top and shimmied out of her jeans. Her bra and underpants were mismatched and modest, unlike Sondra's scanty set. Every naked bit of her flesh burned as if she had a fever as Ari swept a glance up and down her body. She hadn't felt this way around Doyle in longer than she could remember. Maybe it was because Ari was practically a stranger, someone new and sexy and very different from the guys she'd dated in the past. Maybe it was the situation they were in or maybe it was simply him. But Lila was so hot she thought she'd spontaneously combust and she felt dizzy. If he grabbed her and tossed her down right there on the tile floor beside the pool, she'd have had her legs around his back faster than Jesus Christ turned water into wine.

But instead of turning toward her, Ari dove into the pool, cutting cleanly through the water and swimming with steady strokes toward the shallow end. Lila followed his example, dousing her overheated libido in the chilly water. It was a wonder steam didn't rise.

Taking a lap and a half back and forth across the pool, cleared her head and calmed her down. She emerged, dripping, in the shallow end and sat on the steps to watch Ari swim a few more laps.

At last he surfaced. Crouching in the shallow water by her feet, he looked up at her. "So, you never answered the question you asked me. What would *you* be doing on a normal Friday night?"

"This," she said. "Sneaking into a hotel pool and swimming."

"You and your boyfriend did a lot of that?"

"Absolutely." She smiled then sobered a little, reflecting on Doyle, their relationship, and where he might be now. "No. Doyle and I weren't what you'd call an exciting couple but we were content. Happy even, I think. For a while. There just wasn't anything keeping us together anymore."

"I'm sorry." Ari moved closer, climbing out of the water to sit beside her on the steps. "I know you're worried about him."

"We're all worried about someone." She shrugged. "But let's not think of that right now."

He took hold of her wrist, his thumb stroking over the pulse point. "No. Let's think about... getting you back in the water." He suddenly lunged backward into the pool and pulled her with him. They grappled and splashed and laughed as she fought him off. He pulled her into his arms and dragged her over into deeper water. She clung to him to keep from going under.

And then he was kissing her, his lips cool and wet from the water, but warm underneath. Her mouth opened to the pressure and her tongue darted out to swirl around his. She gripped his slippery wet shoulders and held on, skin sliding over skin. The water might be cool but heat pulsed between her legs with every beat of her heart.

Suspended in the water but supported by Ari's arms, Lila felt safer and lighter than she had in days. The bobbed there, kissing and holding one another until he miss-stepped and they both plunged under and rose, sputtering.

Coughing and laughing, he rasped, "Are we done swimming now?"

"I think so." Lila backstroked into shallower water, and he followed.

They climbed out of the pool and found a couple of thin hotel towels on one of the deck chairs. Wrapped in the rough fabric, Lila scooped her clothes and shoes from the floor. She glanced at Ari also gathering his clothes. When he straightened, the damp towel around his waist molded against his groin, giving a nice view of the bulge she'd felt pressing against her in the pool. The gooseflesh popping out on her arms had little to do with being chilled from swimming.

Ari walked over to her and her breathing went shallow. She licked her lips, prepared for more kissing, but he merely slipped an arm around her waist and guided her from the room.

Passing the lobby, Lila glanced toward the front windows where Deb and Julie kept watch. The two women leaned toward each other, talking earnestly. She thought about what Deb had told her about their commitment ceremony and their plan to adopt. There might be a lot of orphaned children needing homes by the time this situation was resolved—assuming it ever was.

Ari went to the room Deb had assigned him and unlocked the door for Lila to enter. This time her shiver was nerves more than lust. There'd been too many new rooms containing too many horrible surprises for her to feel comfortable entering a dark bedroom.

Ari went to the window to make sure the drapes were completely closed before turning on his flashlight to guide her way. The room was stuffy and smelled faintly of cigarettes even though they were in the non-smoking area.

"Sorry there are no candles to make it a little more romantic." He glanced ruefully around the standard bland motel room.

"After the places we've slept the last few nights, this is heaven," Lila assured him as she went over to one of the two queen-sized beds and pulled back the covers. Her heart was tripping along in a much more pleasant way than when zombies were chasing her. She was a little nervous, but an excited, happy kind of nervous.

She dropped her wet towel to the floor and combed her fingers through her damp hair, trying to smooth it out a little. It was tangled mess, but it felt so good to be at least a little cleaner.

"Leave it. You look fine." Ari's husky voice sent a renewed flush of heat through her. He cast aside his towel and walked toward her, all lean muscle and naked skin, the gray briefs leaving little to the imagination. He pulled her to him with enough force to startle a gasp from her.

Lila's arms went around him. She slid her hands up his smooth, warm back and curved one hand around the back of his shorn head. Had she scoffed at his military crew cut when she'd first seen him on the subway train? The soft stubble of hair felt sexy as hell scraping her palm, the hard skull underneath, solid. She tipped her head back and her eyes fell closed as his breath brushed her lips, and then his mouth sealed over hers drawing her into a deep, exploring kiss.

For long minutes, they kissed, hands roaming, desperate to feel every part of each other. He unfastened her bra and she took it off. His mouth descended on her breasts, sending waves of shimmering heat through her. Then he bore her down to the bed, pinning her beneath him. She loved the feel of his weight on top of her. It made her feel secure, safe, grounded in reality at last.

He broke off their kiss at last, gasping for air. "I've wanted this for so long."

"Me, too," she panted. Not that "so long" had been very long. As real time was measured, they'd only known each other a few days, but it seemed like years. Nothing like a monumental crisis to break down barriers and bring people close real fast. Which was kind of a sad commentary on how people interacted with each on a daily basis, always maintaining their distance.

Ari rocked a little, pressing his hardness into her. Lila lifted her ass and pulled at her underwear, trying to get free of it. Awkward and laughing, they struggled out of the last of their clothes then crawled, shivering under the covers, seeking one another's warmth.

"A real bed. My God, this feels good, and so do you," he flirted.

"Mm. Maybe we should just curl up and fall asleep."

"Uh, I don't think so."

"No," she agreed, and grabbed his ass, pulling him to her once more and wrapping her legs around him. "Like my mom always said, 'You'll have plenty of time to sleep when you're dead.'"

CHAPTER FOURTEEN

Ari's body quivered, the muscles in his arms and back shaking, but not in the "my God, I just decapitated a woman I know" kind of way. He was exhausted in a good way, all the tension drained out of him. He fell back onto the bed beside Lila and stared up at the smoke detector on the ceiling. "That was…"

"Not bad," she completed.

He grinned at the understatement, shot a sideways look at her smug smile and began to laugh. Damn, he'd forgotten what laughter felt like.

She laughed, too, and snuggled up against his side, all soft curves and warm skin. He loved the way she felt and the contented sound of her breathing. He really liked her wit and sense of humor and the way he could count on her to stay calm in a crisis. There was no woman he'd rather be with right now, including sexy Sondra, who'd let her interest in him be known numerous times. That empty-headed wench had nothing on Lila.

After everything that had happened that day, he should've been tired, but he was feeling too much of an endorphin rush to fall asleep immediately. He rose from the bed. "Want something? Water, lukewarm soda, room temperature tea?"

"If there's any bottled water left, that'd be great." She yawned and stretched, raising her arms above her head and making her chest move in interesting ways that distracted him for a few moments.

"Um, right. Water." He reached in his backpack and pulled out a half full bottle, all he had left. He took a small sip and gave the rest to Lila.

"Thanks."

He noticed she only drank a little, too, carefully conserving what was left before capping the bottle and setting it on the nightstand.

"I should be sleepy, but I'm not. Let's see what's on." She picked up the TV remote and pointed it toward the dead television. "Ah, Gilligan's Island. The world ends and Gilligan's still broadcasting somewhere out there in the cosmos. Gives me a real sense of continuity."

Ari smiled and slipped into bed beside her, propping up a pillow behind his back.

Lila scooted over so her head rested on his chest and continued to stare at the blank face of the television. "Ginger or Maryann?"

"If I say both, you'll think I'm a dog, so Maryann, of course," he replied and pressed his lips to the top of her head. "Professor or Gilligan? Or Skipper?"

"Maryann," she replied without missing a beat. "I'd join Deb and Julie's team if I had to live on that island. It's so obvious men made this show. There are no male hotties for women viewers to ogle."

"I've seen this episode. They try to make a raft made out of bamboo and cocoanuts. Give me that." Ari seized the remote from her and pretended to change the channel. "That's better."

"W.W.F.? Nascar? Basketball? I can't quite see. The reception's terrible."

"Sports. Is that all you think I'm about?" he asked. "This is the History Channel. Tombs of the Pharaohs."

"Mm. Interesting. But I've had enough of dead bodies and dying civilizations lately. Turn it to something lighter. Maybe just cartoons."

"Classic or modern? We've got Bugs on one channel and Adult Swim on Cartoon Network."

"If it's the one where Bugs sings opera and carries Yosemite Sam up to Valhalla, leave it there for a while." She fell silent, rubbing her hand in idle circles on his bare stomach, making it twitch. Pretty soon Ari forgot about watching pretend TV in favor of more interesting entertainment. He reached for Lila again and found he had more energy left than he'd thought.

⌘ ⌘ ⌘ ⌘

Ari woke to a pounding on the door. He jerked upright, knocking Lila's arm off him. "What?"

"Hey, wake up," Derrick's muffled voice came through the door. "We've got visitors. Living ones."

"Okay. I'll be right there." He scrambled out of bed to get dressed, hating the feel of the stiff, blood-stained shirt, but he had nothing clean to wear. He glanced at Lila, who'd also sprung up and was searching for her underwear. A pang of sharp regret stabbed through him that their breathing space had been so brief. He wished they could've at least stayed undisturbed till morning. Hell, he wished they could've had a full week of doing nothing but lying around in this bed, watching make believe TV, and having sex and bonbons.

He laced his shoe then rose and looked at Lila, zipping her jeans. Newcomers brought all sorts of changes. These might be their last few moments alone together. Who knew what the next day would bring. He went over to her and drew her close, cupping her cheek in one hand and giving her a kiss that might be for goodbye. When he pulled away, he said, "I'm glad we..."

"Me, too. Very glad." Her hand was cool and soft on the side of his face for a second and then he had to step away.

"I'm going to get going. Don't feel like you have to hurry." Ari took a deep breath before opening the door.

Derrick waited for him in the hall. He jerked his thumb toward the lobby. "They're waiting with Joe. Two guys. They saw light in here and came to check it out."

So much for being careful. But it only took one small, moving light, maybe no bigger than the tip of one of Deb's cigarettes, and a single pair of eyes to see it to signal there were living people in the motel.

"Why're you up? I thought it was Joe's watch?" he said.

Derrick shrugged. "It's almost morning anyway, and I couldn't sleep any more. I'm too hungry." He nodded toward the door Ari had closed behind him. "So, Lila. Did you tap that?"

"Shut up, you little perv. None of your business." He strode ahead of Derrick to the lobby where Joe stood talking to the two men, who looked to be in their late twenties or early thirties. They were fit and athletic, the kind of guys Ari needed to help strengthen his group. He wouldn't mind traveling with them, unless they had an agenda of their own.

They looked up as he approached. Joe's habitually gloomy face was more cheerful than Ari had ever seen it. "Ari, this is Walter Marsh and Taishawn Streeter."

"Hi." Marsh was a stocky, boulder of a man, who looked like he could bench press Gloria Patton and then some. "Saw your lights. Thought we'd come over and say 'howdy'. You should really tell your people to keep blackout at night. Even a little light can be dangerous."

Ari's hackles rose at the man's condescending tone, but he didn't bother to explain he'd already given that order. Instead, he nodded and shook Marsh's hand and then Streeter's. "I'm Ari Brenner."

"Taishawn. How you doin'?" If Marsh looked like a weight lifter or wrestler, his buddy had the appearance of a long distance runner. Streeter was a tall, long-limbed black man with hair shaved even closer than Ari's. "Your man Joe here says you got a whole party you're trying to move all the way to the river."

Ari nodded. "Ten of us altogether."

"Eleven counting the baby," Derrick added helpfully.

"Shit. That's a big group. Lucky you made it this many days."

"We lost a few on the way," Ari said, thinking of Ann's quivering white tennis shoe and Mrs. Scheider's last painful breath. "But we're doing okay."

"That's tough," Marsh folded his arms and nodded. "We had a bigger group when we started out, too. We were at Colossus, working out when things started happening."

"Did you guys already know each other?" Joe asked.

"Not really. Just casual acquaintance at the gym."

"You buddy up fast when shit like this hits," Streeter said. "Marsh here's got a plan. He can fly helicopters. We're on our way to the Sanilac building. They've got a corporate helipad on the roof. You could come with us."

"That's a great idea!" Derrick said.

"I think we're closer to the marina," Ari pointed out. He knew the office building the men were talking about and tried to calculate the number of blocks there, as well as the difficulty of climbing all the way to the top. It was hard to know whether the marina or the office building posed more dangers.

The two strangers looked past Ari so he knew Lila had come to join them before he heard her greeting them and introducing herself.

"Nice to meet you." Marsh held out his hand to shake Lila's.

For a brief moment, Ari wanted to pull her away from him. He didn't want to share his people or information with these strangers. He didn't want to fall in with their plan and have things change. But that was crazy. They offered a viable solution, just a different course from the one he'd been on.

"A helicopter," Lila said after Marsh explained his plan. "Would it be big enough to hold all of us?"

He nodded. "Sure. I've seen the copter come and go from the Sanilac building. It's a Bell 222. It'll carry ten including the pilot."

"Uh, we already have ten people. With the two of you that makes twelve," Ari said.

"It's more about weight than numbers. You said you had a couple of kids? They can sit on someone's lap. We'll make it work." Marsh paused. "That is, if you want to go along."

Before Ari could answer, they were interrupted by more early risers drawn by the sound of their voices. Sleep-rumpled and yawning, Deb and Julie wandered out to the lobby.

"Shall I wake the rest of them so they can be a part of this discussion?" Lila asked Ari.

He'd just as soon make the decision without Carl, Gloria or Sondra's input, but they were a part of this. Besides, there was no point in wasting time, repeating everything for their benefit after they finally rose. "Sure. Go get 'em."

While they waited, they gathered in the sitting area in the lobby. Deb and Julie introduced themselves and Julie went to get refreshments for their guests.

"We've been running on fumes," Marsh said. "But I'm sure you've had an even harder time feeding this many people. Snack foods only take the edge off. I'd give anything for a hot, cooked meal."

"Why haven't you guys left town by now?" Joe asked. "It's been days since this started."

"We were trapped for a while," Streeter said. "Near the hospital there were hordes of the damn things coming in waves. Then the army comes in, ground troops and helicopters shooting the shit out of anything that moved. We couldn't go anywhere. Just had to hole up and wait for the worse of it to be over."

"Where'd you hide?" Deb leaned against the check-in counter, arms folded. Ari felt her mistrust as if it was a reflection of his own. It made him see his own doubt for what it was, an alpha personality threatened by another alpha entering his territory. He should be grateful these guys were willing to take them along, happy to pass some of the burden to other strong leaders.

"After we escaped from the gym, we ended up at a school near the hospital. But with things they way they were outside, we were stranded there for a while," Marsh said. "I remembered seeing a chopper land on the Sanilac the day the shit hit. We decided to head there."

"What about the children? Julie returned with sodas for the men.

Streeter shook his head, his gaze downcast. "They didn't make it."

"None of them? You couldn't take any of them with you?"

"It was an elementary school. These were little kids. They couldn't outrun the zombies. It was safer for them to stay there. There was school faculty with them."

Julie dropped the subject. There was enough blame to go around. They'd all left people behind.

Ari checked the street outside, where early morning gray illuminated a car with its fender crumpled against a light pole, and the windshield ruptured by the driver's body. A crow picked at the woman's face. Ari scanned the block as far as he could see in either direction. It was deserted.

As he turned away from the window, he came to a decision. They needed the extra protection Marsh and Streeter could offer and the idea of flying with a trained pilot was better than his half-assed plan to hotwire a boat. Of course, the rest of the group would air their opinions, but he knew which side he'd weigh in on.

Lila returned with the others. Sondra, dressed for bed in an oversized T-shirt with nothing on her bare legs, turned on all her charm around the two new men. She really was a shameless flirt, the kind of girl who didn't know how to dial it down no matter what the circumstances. Gloria stayed only long enough to be introduced and then returned to her room to take care of Ian. Lila hadn't wakened Ronnie.

"This is Carl," Ari introduced the scientist, who shook hands with Marsh and Streeter.

"Pleased to meet you. Lila says you got a plan to get out."

Marsh explained for the third time about the helipad and his ability to pilot a copter.

"That seems like the way to go," Carl said as he took a seat on the couch beside Sondra and Taishawn. "And it looks like you're well armed." He indicated the rifles the two men had set aside.

"You know you can't just shoot 'em though, right? You have to cut their heads off to kill them," Derrick said. "I was the one who figured that out."

"We've taken down a few," Streeter assured him, "haven't we, man?"

"A few." Marsh leaned back in the armchair across from the couch, looking as relaxed as if this was his own living room. "What was Joe saying about you having some kind of cure?"

"Not yet." Carl leaned forward, eager to share. "But I have an idea, a modification of the formula that could alter the effects of the original antidote." He launched into an explanation of the cure for A7 and why he thought it had caused this drastic result. "But the solution wasn't totally flawed. I think with slight changes I could create not only a real cure for the A7 virus, but also counteract the effects of the current antidote."

He would've gone on to explain in more detail than any of them could hope to grasp the specifics of what he intended, but Derrick interrupted. "The information is on a hard drive I got from Carl's computer at Quantus. We were attacked while we were there and I killed one of the zombies."

Ari rolled his eyes. Derrick seemed intent on impressing the newcomers with his accomplishments as if they were Daddy come home.

Marsh gave a low whistle. "It sounds like you hold the key to saving the world," he said to Carl. "We've got to get you off this island and some place safe."

No shit. What do you think I've been trying to do? Ari couldn't help his irritation at Marsh's manner, as if they'd been doing nothing but cooling their heels by the hotel pool until he came along to take charge of things. But once again he suppressed his emotions. This was no time to let personal feelings color his judgment. So his ego was a little bruised. The damn world was at stake here.

"We have a choice," he addressed the group, cutting across the chatter. "Continue on our way to the marina or try to fly out of here with these guys. The Sanilac building is about the same distance as the river, but in the opposite direction. Once we get there we'll have to climb all the way to the roof and there's no guarantee the helicopter will even be there."

"You don't sound convinced." Streeter stared at him. "Well, you haven't seen the waterfront yet. It's crawling with flesh-eaters, picking off anyone who tries to get to a boat."

"I'm only trying to present all possibilities," Ari said. "Everyone should have a complete picture of both options before they decide."

"I want to fly," Derrick said. "So does Ronnie."

"I'm in." Sondra leaned close to Streeter. "These guys seem to know what they're doing."

One by one, the others agreed, some more enthusiastically than others. But even Lila, after pausing to glance at Ari, was on board with the new plan. Even as Ari cast his vote in favor, too, he felt ridiculously abandoned.

Marsh looked outside where the light had turned from gray to pink. "We should get started. With luck, we can be flying out of this shit storm by noon."

Maybe to face another shit storm on the mainland. They'd gone days without hearing from the outside world, and Ari dreaded what they would find there.

As Marsh started giving orders, Ari felt his own authority slipping away. And even though this was what he'd longed for since the beginning, someone else to step up and take control, his sense of desertion grew as people addressed their questions to Marsh or even Streeter instead of him. Damn, he really was pathetic.

As he gathered things from his room, Lila came to get hers, too. She closed the door behind her and went to him, knocking his backpack from his hands and putting them on her hips instead. She slid hers around the back of his neck and pulled him down for a kiss.

Minutes later when they finally drew apart, she murmured,

"How are you doing? What do you really think about these guys? Dicks, right?"

He shrugged. "I don't know. They haven't done or said anything wrong. I just don't... mesh well with either of them."

"I know. But do you think we can trust them?"

Ari paused to consider. "They haven't tried to take anything from us. They're inviting us to travel with them when they could move faster alone. I can't see any reason not to trust them, although Marsh might be wrong about that chopper and we could go a long way out of our way for nothing."

Lila nodded. "That's what I thought, but I still feel like we have to give it a try. A helicopter would give us so much more flexibility. We could land anywhere it seems safe. With a boat there's a chance of not finding a harbor that isn't overrun with zombies. But I still don't like Marsh much. He seems really arrogant."

He felt the same way, but if they were going to follow Marsh now, they had to wholeheartedly recognize him as the leader. Ari turned and stooped to pick up his bag. "Well, whether he's a dick or not, Marsh is the man in charge now so all we can do is follow his lead."

CHAPTER FIFTEEN

"Shut that kid up or I swear I'll gag him," Streeter glared at Gloria over his shoulder.

"We need to stop for a while," the plump woman replied, breathless from trotting along at the long-legged pace Taishawn set. "Ian needs to be fed and changed."

"We can't stop every two minutes. We gotta keep moving."

"Hey," Lila interrupted. "You guys aren't traveling alone now. You had to know a group with children in it might slow you down." She really didn't like these guys and with every step regretted her choice to join them more.

"We'll call a halt in another few blocks," Marsh declared. "Meanwhile, muffle the baby and keep walking."

"Here, Gloria, let me try." Julie took the little one in her arms and his wails amped up. She jiggled him and crooned softly but couldn't get him to quiet down.

"I don't think we have a choice, Marsh," Ari said. "We're going to have to take a break."

"Fine. We'll get some food as long as we're stopping."

Their new leader directed them to a convenience store. Ari went inside to check out the interior and returned more blood-spattered than when he'd gone in. He announced it was now clear. He'd taken care of a lone revenant snacking on old body parts. "The thing was pretty weak and easy to kill. I think you're right about them needing fresh meat to survive," he said to Carl.

The group went inside to ransack the store, while Ari, Streeter and Marsh kept watch. Lila had to admit it felt safer having them there. Not that some of the rest of them couldn't handle the job, but these men seemed at ease with their weapons and a bit more lethal in their bearing.

Gloria changed Ian's diaper and sat with him in a corner to nurse. Lila brought her something to drink and petted the top of Ian's soft head. "Everything better now, buddy? You got what you wanted?"

His mother looked up at Lila. "Those men are going to cut us loose. I can feel it. Don't let them do it. Promise me, you'll stick up for me."

Lila crouched beside her, frowning. "No. I'm sure they wouldn't. Besides, none of us would let them."

"Oh wouldn't they?" Mrs. Patton spoke bitterly, shooting a hard look at the rest of their company moving around the store. "They'd gladly be rid of the trouble Ian and I cause, his crying and my dead weight, but they could salve their consciences by laying the blame on the new guys."

"That's not true. Stop thinking like that." The woman was growing paranoid. Coupled with her misery over the loss of her husband it was an ugly combination.

"We'll see," Gloria muttered, moving Ian to her shoulder to burp him.

Soon they were on their way again, moving quickly in the shadows of the tall buildings. Lila walked with Ronnie, holding her hand and cajoling her to be strong and walk just a little further. They were within sight of their destination, when a cadre of the undead burst from the bar they were passing.

A jumble of sensations hit Lila all at once: the door banging open, the creatures' running feet, Sondra's piercing scream, Ronnie's little fingers gripping her hand, shouts, shots, the sharp odor of gunpowder. Lila scooped Ronnie off the ground to carry her, but the child was too heavy to run with and Lila couldn't defend herself with the girl in her arms. She glanced over her shoulder to find Joe intercepting one of the zombies, hacking at it with his hunting knife, then she faced forward and concentrated on hurrying as fast as she could

After firing an initial salvo of bullets into their attackers, Marsh and Streeter didn't stop to help anyone. They raced toward the Sanilac building, leaving the slower members of the herd to the wolves.

Lila caught a glimpse of Ari fighting hand to hand with a zombie that had gotten a grip on Gloria. Lila wished she could help, but her arms were full of Ronnie. She had her own mission. Her feet thudded on the pavement, heavy from the extra weight of her burden. Far ahead, Marsh and Streeter were already entering the door of the building with Sondra racing right behind them, her ankle remarkably, completely healed.

Derrick ran up beside Lila and reached out for his sister. Lila passed her off like a baton in a relay without slowing her pace. Ronnie wrapped her arms around her brother and he darted away with her.

Lila whirled around, drawing the handgun she carried, and assessed the deteriorating situation. Ari still grappled with the zombie that had attacked Gloria, while Gloria staggered away. Joe was down on the ground beneath two zombies, his arms and legs flailing as he tried to fight them off.

Carl, too, fought for his life against one of the creatures, a young boy, who'd latched onto his arm with ferocious teeth that threatened to tear through his jacket sleeve. Deb slashed at the back of the boy's neck with her knife. Just as Lila went to help, Deb hit the spot and the zombie went limp. Carl threw him off with a grunt, the boy's body landing in a crumpled heap on the ground. He picked up the precious bag containing the hard drive and ran with it.

Julie had taken Ian from Gloria, and was encouraging the stout woman to run faster. Deb and Carl joined them. Deb urged all of them toward the building then turned to shoot at several zombies on their tail.

Lila went to help Joe. She moved behind the two creatures which were crouched over him, ripping at him like a pair of hungry dogs with a steak, completely oblivious to her approach. She shot first one then the other directly in the back of the neck. Both zombies fell still. Lila dragged their corpses off of Joe, straining at the effort of hauling their limp weight. But one look at the doctor's mangled body told her it was too late. At least one of the things had gone for his throat and torn a huge chunk out of it. Joe's blue eyes were staring, fogged over, dead. She could see it without checking his pulse, but she checked anyway. And then, without hesitation, Lila shot him directly through his throat to make certain he wouldn't rise again.

"Come on." Ari was beside her, tugging on her arm, dragging her with him as he ran. She looked up and saw the others had nearly reached the building. Only she and Ari were left...with a few zombies chasing them. She forced her leaden legs to move faster, every breath like knives in her chest.

Deb had gotten the others inside before turning to fire at their pursuers until her clip was empty. The shots echoed in the canyon between the buildings. She held the door open for Lila and Ari and they bolted through it. Derrick locked the door behind them.

Streeter and Marsh moved a desk in front of the door as a barricade. They wrestled it into place while the creatures outside continued to beat against the glass like desperate birds trying to escape a house.

Lila bent over, hands on her knees, gasping for breath. Nausea overtook her and she wretched and spat bile onto the floor.

Beside her, Ari recovered much quicker. He straightened and strode toward Marsh and Streeter. "What the fuck? You left us out there!"

"Back off." Streeter stepped toward Ari, challenging him with a glare and threatening him with his height. "Back the hell off. We all ran."

"Yeah, but you ran first. You didn't fight or help anyone."

"Survival of the fittest. If someone can't keep up, they go down."

Ari's fists were clenched, his body quivering with tension. Lila was sure he was about to throw a punch. "We never should've come with you."

Marsh moved in beside Streeter. "The same thing might've happened if you'd gone your own way. You still would've been on your own."

"Bullshit," Deb exploded. "The difference is we wouldn't have been expecting your help. You only brought us along to use as cannon fodder, like you probably did with those school kids."

Lila was as enraged as the others, but the growing altercation wasn't helping anyone and meanwhile, zombies were still pounding on the glass, trying to get in. She moved to insert herself into the argument, holding up her hands and shouting, "Hey! Let's all calm down. This isn't the time to fight. There are those things out there," she pointed at the door, "and for all we know, more inside the building. So get it together and save your arguments for later."

Everyone still bristled like angry cats poised to attack, but her words got them moving. Marsh and Streeter fortified the door with more office furniture. Ari, Deb and Derrick swept the immediate area to make sure they weren't barricading themselves in with more of the undead.

Julie held Ronnie, who cried hysterically, hiccupping sobs that shook her body. Carl checked to see that the hard drive was undamaged. Sondra found a water cooler and carried cups of water to Marsh and Streeter.

Lila moved in a dreamlike haze to Gloria to make sure she was unharmed. She wrapped an arm around the woman's shoulders and hugged her. "We're almost there. Only a few hundred stairs between us and freedom."

Gloria stared at her. "There is no way out. You know that. The world out there is just as bad. There's no place to go."

Lila clenched her jaw, suppressing the urge to shake her. "But we have to believe in something. We have to set some kind of course and follow it, or give up and die. Hope is the only thing that will keep us sane right now."

Gloria laughed harshly. "Too late."

Lila took her arm away, done soothing and supporting. "If you can't pull it together for yourself, do it for your son. He deserves a mother who at least pretends to believe in a future."

She rose and went to put a fresh clip in her weapon, trying not to think about how it had felt to fire the gun and see the two zombies' necks explode in a shower of blood and flesh. What bothered her wasn't that she'd done it, but how satisfied, almost gleeful, she'd felt ending their existences. She'd wanted to shoot them until her clip was empty. That wasn't the person she wanted to be, taking joy in destruction.

And she *really* didn't want to think about Joe right now. There'd be time enough later to process her feelings about that shooting, and maybe even a little time to think about last night with Ari and what it had meant to her. But right now was the time for action.

"Okay, guys," she addressed the others. "We've got a long haul ahead of us. Let's gear up and be ready for it, 'cause clearly these guys," she gestured at Streeter and Marsh, "aren't going to wait for anyone to keep up."

The advance team returned to declare the area, zombie-free. Everyone jettisoned most of the contents of their backpacks to make them as light as possible and they started for the stairs.

Lila prayed with all her heart for a helicopter to be waiting on the roof of the building when they arrived.

CHAPTER SIXTEEN

Ari was in better shape than he'd been in his whole life. He was used to running miles with a heavy weight on his back, scaling walls and climbing obstacles. But even so, his calves ached after a half dozen floors. He could only imagine how difficult this climb was for some of the others like Gloria Patton.

He dropped back to help the stragglers along. Surprisingly, little Ronnie wasn't one of them. She seemed intent on reaching her helicopter ride and darted up the stairs like a girl on a mission—her tears turned off for the time being.

Meanwhile, Gloria, red-faced and panting, brought up the rear, along with Lila, who was carrying Ian, and Carl.

The scientist cursed a steady stream under his breath as he gripped the handrail and laboriously climbed the steps. "I've been meaning to join a damn gym," he said. "I spend way too much time sitting on my butt. Guess this is a good argument for taking better care of your health."

Lila laughed. "If we'd known zombies were coming, I think we all would've kept fitter. Not to mention taking combat training."

"I've got to rest," Gloria wheezed as she leaned against the wall on the next landing.

The footsteps of the rest of the group clattered up the stairs ahead of them. "Hey," Ari called, "Take a break."

"No," Marsh's voice echoed down the stairwell. That was it. No explanation or embellishment. Just "no".

Ari agreed with Deb. The only reason these guys had brought them along was to throw them under the bus if they were attacked—a distraction to give Marsh and Streeter time to get away. And he also thought she was right about the men using the school kids as fodder to aid their escape. Something about the way Streeter had said "They didn't make it" before switching his story to say they'd left them with faculty at the school.

But they were committed to this route now. Only another dozen or so floors and they'd be at the top of the building. Ari didn't like Marsh, but doubted the man would make such a climb if he wasn't almost a hundred percent sure he'd find a helicopter on the roof as he expected.

Gloria slid down the wall to sit with her head lowered as she breathed in and out.

Ari crouched beside her. "You feel like you're going to faint?"

Lila passed the baby to Carl, who awkwardly accepted the struggling bundle. Ian, who was already fussing, began to cry in earnest, his wails ringing through the stairwell.

Lila knelt on Mrs. Patton's other side and offered her a nearly empty bottle of water. "Don't give up. You can do this."

The flushed woman looked at her and nodded. "I will. I heard what you said earlier and I'm not giving up. I just need a breather."

Ari glanced back and forth between them, understanding they were resuming an earlier conversation. He left them to it and went over to Carl. "How about you? Are you going to be all right? Wouldn't want to lose our ace in the hole."

Carl waved him away, jiggling the baby awkwardly. "I'm good."

Gloria climbed to her feet, leaning on Lila, grasped the banister and started up the next flight of stairs, a look of grim determination on her face.

Lila and Ari exchanged a silent look. Ari was glad the woman was finally motivated, but worried about having her collapse. Gloria looked about a floor or two away from a heart attack.

"I'll carry the kid now." Ari took Ian from Carl. He hadn't held the baby yet and was surprised to find the little guy felt like he weighed more than Ronnie. While the girl was all spindly arms and legs like a spider monkey, Ian was solid flesh. "Kid, you're going to be a linebacker some day," Ari told him.

Distracted from crying for a moment, Ian stared at him with big, googly eyes, reached for Ari's dog tags and stuck them in his mouth. Happy to have the baby occupied, Ari hefted him onto one hip and resumed the climb.

Step after step, floor by floor, they made their way to the top of the building. By the time they reached the last landing, everyone was drenched in sweat and the rest of the group had already disappeared through the door leading to the roof.

Carl opened the door and the sunlight nearly blinded them. Ari shielded his eyes as he emerged from the dark stairwell. Across the roof, the corporate helicopter was parked on its pad as Marsh had promised. His heart soared as if he was already flying away, but it quickly landed with a thud as he realized the copter didn't look big enough to carry them all. He passed the baby to Lila and strode toward the group clustered near the helicopter.

Marsh and Streeter stood shoulder to shoulder, their weapons in their hands, not pointed at anyone, not yet, but a sinister threat all the same. Sondra was by Streeter's side, one of her famous modeling hands resting on his hip, claiming her allegiance.

"What's up?" Ari tried to sound casual, as if he and Streeter hadn't been ready to tear each others' throats out down in the lobby.

"I was wrong. It's a six-seater, not eight." Marsh was blunt.

"But we can fit everyone in," Deb said. "People can double up on the seats."

"I told you before. It's about weight. The machine can't carry this much weight and fly. A few of you will have to stay behind." He looked at Gloria.

"Unbolt a few seats and take them out. That'll knock off some pounds," Carl suggested.

"We don't have the tools or time for that." Marsh stared at Ari, challenging him with his gaze. "Since I'm the pilot, I'll decide who goes and who stays. After we get someplace safe, we can send help for the others."

Ari doubted that would happen. Marsh couldn't make such a promise, not unless he intended to fly back himself, which he wouldn't do. Looking into Marsh's eyes, Ari also knew the man had been aware how many this helicopter would carry and had lied about it seating ten.

He swallowed his anger and kept his tone cool. "Who do you plan to take with you?"

Marsh had the grace to hesitate before he replied. "Those with the greatest chance of survival."

"Survival of the fittest," Streeter echoed. "I told you, the slow and the weak got no place in this world now."

Sondra gripped his arm, sticking to him like a burr. "You'll take me, right?" She looked up at Streeter, eyes anxious, breasts pressing against his arm, reminding him of what she had to offer.

He looked down at her and grinned. "Told you I would, sweetheart. You got a ride. Might have to earn it later, but you're on."

"Carl, of course," Marsh said. "He's worth gold."

That left two seats.

"I'll take the lesbian. She's tough." Marsh nodded toward Deb. "And you, Ari. You've got strength and skills. The rest of them couldn't have come this far without you. You deserve a ride out."

For one heartbeat, Ari imagined himself in that chopper, rising from the rooftop and flying away, tearing off the clinging vines that dragged him down, becoming himself again—alone, self-sufficient, no needy people asking him what to do next. Then reason slammed shut like a cage door, the bars solid and real. He had no choice. Of course, he wouldn't abandon them—not any of them.

"Great offer, but no," he said. "I'll give my seat to Gloria and Ian."

"You son of a bitch!" Deb shouted at Marsh. "You knew this. Even before we climbed all the way up here you knew we couldn't all go, you bastard. Do you think I'd leave my girl behind?"

Marsh shrugged. "Not really. It's your choice. I'll take Derrick then. He's a scrapper."

"Only if my sister goes," Derrick said. "She can sit on my lap."

"Sorry, kid. You're skinny and so is she, but with this one's weight," Marsh nodded at Gloria, "that's too many pounds. Can't do it. It's not safe."

"Then take Ronnie," Derrick said.

"Derrick, you can have my spot," Carl offered. "You shouldn't be separated from your sister. You're all she's got."

Marsh shook his head. "Nu-uh. You're too important to leave behind."

Ari hated to agree with him on anything, but he was right. Carl must be taken someplace he could work on a cure. Too bad Marsh and Streeter hadn't remembered that when they'd abandoned him on the street.

"Sondra?" Lila said. "Won't you give Derrick your seat? Or you, Mr. Streeter. It's the right thing to do."

Sondra looked down, unable to meet Lila's eyes, but Taishawn stared back at her. "Don't try to guilt me. This is the way it works. Better get the fairytale ideas out of your head and accept the truth—the world's a hard place."

"Forget it, Lila. They're assholes. They're not going to budge," Derrick said, then turned to Gloria. "Take care of Ronnie. Promise me."

"I will." She nodded. "I promise to look after her as if she was my own."

"Derrick?" Ronnie's voice rose and she grabbed her brother's arm.

He squatted to face her, took hold of her shoulders and looked into her eyes. "It's all right, Ronnie. Mrs. Patton will look after you and help you try to find mom or dad. I'll look for them, too, and probably we'll be together again soon."

"No! No, Derrick. I don't want to go. I want to stay with you."

"It's not safe here. You know what it's like. These guys are going to take you some place better. You should go with them." Derrick's voice was rough and thick. He suddenly seized Ronnie and gave her a hard hug. "Be good. See ya later."

Ari's throat was choked, too. He clenched his jaw hard. "Jesus, Marsh," he snapped. "The boy doesn't weight that much. Just let them double up. Let him on the damn helicopter."

"Can't do it. I'm not risking all of us crashing." Marsh had already turned away, heading toward the cockpit.

Ari took a step after him, ready to fight for Derrick, but Streeter brought his gun down off his shoulder and leveled it at him. "It wouldn't bother me at all to shoot you."

Ari knew he wasn't lying. There was a glitter in the man's eyes. Taishawn Streeter may not been just a regular guy working out at the gym a few days ago, but he'd turned quickly into a hard-ass, selfish prick without remorse or mercy in his nature. Streeter continued to keep his weapon trained on him while the others took their seats on the helicopter.

"I'm sorry," Carl said to Julie. "This is so wrong."

"You've got to do it. Go. Find a way to fix this," Julie gave him a quick hug. "Take care of yourself."

Gloria took Ian from Lila and murmured her thanks before addressing Ari. "Thank you. I know you tried to help Doug but there was nothing you could do. I needed to blame someone for his death so I accused you of leaving him behind, but I know it wasn't your fault. I'm sorry. And I want to thank you from the bottom of my heart for giving Ian and me a chance."

Ari nodded.

"Hurry up, lady, if you're getting on," Streeter prodded.

Gloria went toward the copter. Sondra had already boarded without a word of goodbye, thanks or good luck to any of them. She stared out the window on the opposite side of the helicopter, refusing to look back.

The engine growled to life and the rotors whirred, whipping the air around them. Lila held her windblown hair back from her face.

Derrick buckled Ronnie into one of the seats. Ronnie threw her arms around her brother's neck and clung to him until he pulled away and stepped out of the chopper. Then she gripped the little stuffed unicorn Ann had given her. Her face was twisted into a gargoyle's frown and tears spilling down her bright red cheeks.

Derrick moved away from the helicopter. Lila went over to put an arm around him. At last Streeter lowered his weapon, ducked his head to avoid the rotors and ran for the chopper. He boosted himself inside and closed the door.

Through the window, Ari could make out Marsh's head bent over the controls. A few seconds later, the helicopter rose into the air. Ari squinted as the wind blew grit into his eyes and when he opened them again, the copter was already a block away, flying low across the tops of the buildings. The sound of the blades cutting through the air faded. The sunlight reflected off the metallic body of the copter, blinding Ari for a moment, and then the bird veered southwest, disappearing behind a cliff of granite and glass.

"That's it." Lila had come over to stand beside him.

He glanced down at her. "Guess so."

"So we start for the marina again."

"Yep." He glanced at Derrick, who'd gone to the far edge of the roof for some privacy, and at Deb & Julie, who clung together in a fierce hug. Then Ari looked back at Lila, her beautiful eyes and grim mouth.

"We'll make it." She reached for his hand and squeezed it. "We will."

He nodded, too tired to say anything. He wished she'd stop trying to be encouraging. He didn't want a cheerleader right now.

Lila seemed to sense that and stopped talking. She let go of his hand, slid her hands around his waist and rested her head against his chest. He embraced her solid warmth, rested his cheek against her hair and closed his eyes.

Breathe. Just breathe. He remembered Lila telling him in the tunnel when he'd begun to panic about which direction to take. He followed her advice now and his accelerating heartbeats slowed. He drew strength and comfort from her like a vampire sucking blood, but the difference was, he gave it back and when they finally broke apart, both were replenished.

Deb and Julie came over with Derrick trailing behind them. His face was splotchy, his eyes red, but his voice was firm when he spoke. "Now what, captain?"

"How do all of you feel?" Ari asked. "We have a lot of daylight left so we could start for the waterfront. Or we could stay here for the night and regroup."

"Stay here," Julie voted. "And I mean right here on the roof. I don't think I could face those stairs again."

"I bet there are executive offices on the top floors. They might have a kitchenette where we could get food," Deb suggested.

"I don't want to go back inside yet," Derrick said abruptly. "Can't we just sit here a little while?"

Ari took stock of Derrick's pale face and drained expression. "Sure. We can do that."

He sat on the asphalt, leaning against the wall near the door, legs bent and arms wrapped around his shins, and the rest of them sat in a row beside him—five survivors perched like birds on a wire, silent, resting.

They remained that way until the sun was too hot to stay on the roof then Deb rose and held out her hand to Julie. The rest of them hauled their tired bodies upright and followed her inside.

The stairway that he'd climbed with rising hope in his heart Ari now descended in a leaden haze. He second-guessed every decision he'd made along the way, decisions that had led to losing Ann, Doug and

Joe. He wished they'd never met Marsh and Streeter, wished he'd never chosen to follow them. Even though Carl and the data were probably on their way to safety, Ari couldn't help but feel he'd failed by not delivering the scientist personally. What if something went wrong? Would Marsh leave Carl and the others to fend for themselves as he'd done once already?

When they reached the top floor of the building, Lila bumped shoulders with Ari as they walked down the corridor behind Deb and Julie. "Hey. Stop it. I can read you like a book. You're blaming yourself for stuff that's not your fault. Don't."

He shrugged, not denying her words, but not ready to admit to them either.

"If anyone should feel bad it should be Julie and me." A hint of laughter shimmered in Lila's voice. "At least you three rated enough to be asked along. Julie and I are apparently so useless Marsh didn't even consider taking us. Nice to know how we rate."

Julie snorted with laughter. Lila grinned, and a chuckle bubbled up in Ari's chest. Lila's comment wasn't that funny. It certainly didn't earn a belly laugh, but suddenly he was laughing uncontrollably. Deb joined in, too; the four of them with tears in their eyes, wheezing for breath, collapsing on the floor and letting their tension wash away on a wave of hilarity.

"It's not funny." Derrick's sober voice brought Ari under control. He looked at the boy standing in the middle of their sprawled bodies, glaring down at them. "Nothing about this is funny."

"Oh, sweetie, I know. That's why we're laughing. It's too horrible to do anything else." Lila climbed to her feet and reached for him, but he jerked away.

"I'm going to look for food." Derrick strode away, readying his rifle before throwing open the door of one of the offices.

Ari went to back him up. He would've been shocked if there were zombies all the way up here after so many days with no fresh food source, but you couldn't be too careful. He followed Derrick into a lavish suite of rooms. Some lucky corporate type had had an eagle-eye view of the city with windows spanning an entire wall. A glossy desk dominated one room, but there was also a sitting area and kitchenette as Deb had guessed.

Derrick poked through the fridge, searching for anything edible. Ari set down his rifle and came up beside him. "Hey, man. I'm sorry about the meltdown. I know you're hurting about losing Ronnie."

Derrick didn't respond, just kept pulling things out of the fridge.

"You were brave to put her on that helicopter. It was the best thing you could've done for her."

The boy slammed the items he'd scavenged onto the counter and whirled to face Ari. "Was it? Do you think Gloria is really going to take care of her? If things get bad, she'll be busy with her own kid. She's not going to think about Ronnie first." His voice cracked. "And even if they're okay, Ronnie will always think I was trying to get rid of her. We fought all the time. I was mean to her. I never wanted her around. She's going to remember me as the big brother who hated her."

"No she won't," Ari said.

"I'm never gonna see her again." His voice was broken and so was his face—cracked wide so Ari could see all the emotion Derrick had fought to keep hidden.

His heart ached for the kid, but Ari couldn't bring himself to spout comforting lies like the women would have. "I don't know. They might have refugee camps and you might find her there." God, he was hopeless at this. Was he supposed to hug Derrick now?

"I'm sorry, man," he added helplessly.

Derrick nodded once, a sharp jerk of his head, then turned back to sorting through the food on the counter. Ari gave him time to collect himself and went off to search through the cupboards. He came up with a jar of olives—for martinis, he supposed, and crackers. The bar was well-stocked, however. He grabbed a bottle of vodka and one of gin. Might as well make use of those olives.

The three women joined them after searching the other offices and brought a few more items for their meal. Julie cut the mold off some cheese and sliced it to go on the crackers. Apples, mottled brown bananas and more power bars completed the meal. It seemed American office workers were fueled by power bars.

Ari mixed vodka and a splash of vermouth, stirred not shaken. Since there was no ice and the drinks were room temperature, it hardly mattered. He floated an olive in the martini glass he got from the bar and drank it in a few gulps. The alcohol burned down his throat and set up a nice warm fire in his stomach before spreading through his blood stream. He filled his glass again and guzzled, appreciating the relaxing buzz that soon filled his brain.

Armed with drinks and their meager meal, the five of them sat in a circle on the plush carpet.

Ari found he was ravenous after climbing all those stairs. He'd hardly been aware of the ache of hunger in the pit of his stomach, but one bite of cheese and cracker woke his appetite. He could have easily devoured all the food himself. Instead, he poured another martini. Why the hell not?

Julie raised her glass, her pale blue eyes a little uncertain. "I don't know if this is a time for toasting but I'd like to propose one to all those we lost."

Personally, Ari didn't want to think about them right now. He'd done his best to shove every trace of them from his mind, but he lifted his glass anyway and took another drink.

Pretty soon the haze in his brain fogged his eyesight. He listened to Deb and Julie's low and high voices rising and falling in counterpoint to one another. He looked at Lila, leaning toward Derrick and talking earnestly. Her hair was wind-whipped and wild around her shoulders and falling over her eyes.

Ari thought of how she'd looked last night, lying in bed with her hair spread over the pillow, her face contorted in ecstasy. He wanted to see her like that again. Abruptly he was as hard as stone and aching to hold her. If he grabbed her hand and pulled her from the room, would it be rude? Did he care? He was pretty far past caring what anyone thought about anything and their time together was too short to waste.

Just then, Lila looked over at him. Their gazes locked, silent messages telegraphed like lightning between them, and she smiled, a mischievous grin that made him even harder.

She turned back to Derrick. "Why don't you lie down and get some sleep. That's what you need right now."

The boy drained the last of his drink, and Lila took the empty glass from him. "Another one of these isn't going to help you feel better, I promise. You'll just wake with a headache."

Derrick didn't argue. Maybe he felt like having someone tell him what to do next. When Lila rose and offered her hand, he took it. She pulled him to his feet and led him to the beige leather couch. He took off his shoes and lay down. Lila spread a jacket over him and stroked his hair before leaving him.

She walked toward Ari, gazing at him with a look hot enough to sear his skin. He stood, a little unsteadily after three—or was it four?—drinks, and took her hand. Hers was cool and dry, his a little sweaty.

Julie and Deb looked up simultaneously, brown eyes and blue studying them.

"We're going across the hall," Lila said.

"Cool," Deb replied, smiling. "We'll keep watch."

Ari and Lila left the room, walked a little way down the hallway and entered another fancy office. "So this is where all the bailout money goes," he said, looking around at the décor. His gaze lighted on another comfortable couch and stopped there. "Crap. I don't have any more condoms."

"Want to bet Mr. Corporate Exec has some?" Lila went to the restroom and came back with a box. "Really, do these people do any actual work?"

Ari pulled her hard against him, interrupting her with a kiss, fierce and hot. It wasn't just a matter of want. He needed her right at this moment with the desperation of a man who'd been slogging through the desert and encountered an oasis. He fell into her, arms open and drank her up.

Lila seemed just as eager for him, her hands all over, stripping him bare and rediscovering his skin underneath. Within seconds they were both naked and grappling each other to the floor like wrestlers. He pinned her beneath him, covering her with kisses, throat, chest, breasts and lower. A few minutes down between her legs and she arched up with a shudder and a moan. When Ari glanced at her face, tears tracked from the corners of her eyes down her temples and caught in her hair.

He crawled up to lie beside her, pressing against her, wanting entry, but concerned about the tears. "What?"

She wiped her nose and shook her head. "It's nothing. It's just been a really hard day and I needed this release." She pushed him onto his back and straddled him. "And so do you."

He lost himself in her then, groaning and rising into her heat and wetness, every thrust an affirmation of life. He gripped her waist, anchoring himself to her and closed his eyes as waves of pleasure broke over him.

Far too quickly, it was over. He wished he could promise her other times when they would spend hours building up slowly and making it last. But these might be the only precious moments they could spend together and their urge had been like a speeding train destined to collide.

Lila collapsed on top of him and he wrapped his arms around her heaving body, warm and moist against his.

"You're sure you're okay," he asked. "Today was…"

"Hell." She completed his thought. She had a knack for that. Her voice was muffled against his skin, puffs of breath tickling his neck. "I'm trying to put it out of my head. All of it. But I keep reliving Joe and those things I had to put down. I know they weren't human any longer. I know that. But it's still hard."

"Mm," he murmured, nuzzling the top of her head. He had nothing more useful to offer, no words that could take away from the horror, so he simply kissed her and hugged her hard enough to drive the breath from her body.

"I think," she said after a few silent minutes, "the only way to deal with all this is to stop feeling at all, put up a wall and don't let anything through it."

Ari rubbed her back, considering. "But then you could end up like Marsh or Streeter, so hard and selfish you use other people as human shields. We have to keep some humanity or we're no better than the zombies."

Lila lifted her head, propped her arms on his chest and looked into his eyes. "That's insightful."

"I have my moments. I'm not all about action, you know."

She smiled. "I do know, and that's why I like you so much."

"I like you, too." *A lot more than I ever would have expected.*

She slid off him to cuddle next to his side, one arm flung over his stomach and her head resting on his shoulder. More quiet moments passed and Ari felt himself drifting toward sleep.

He roused himself and shook Lila awake. "We should go back with the others. It's safer if we're all together."

She yawned and reached for her clothes. "Besides, Julie and Deb might want some time alone."

Ari hadn't thought of that. He felt sorry for Derrick, the odd man out. The rest of them had someone special to cling to. The boy was all alone now that his sister was gone. Ari promised himself to keep Derrick close throughout this ordeal. He and Lila would be a pseudo family Derrick could count on.

They dressed and returned to the office down the hall. The city spread out below them, a landscape of stark light and shadow. The trek here, the climb and its aftermath had taken most of the day and now evening drew close once more. Ari gazed at the view and imagined how it would have looked at night with lights glowing in hundreds of windows. Instead, when darkness fell, the city would be plunged into blackness once more, like a dark jungle where ravenous beasts roamed.

He was suddenly almost too exhausted to keep his eyes open. But he had to keep alert on watch, even if it meant chewing coffee beans from the blend in the cupboard by the espresso machine. Derrick joined him at the window. "Go ahead and get some sleep. I've had a nap. I'll take first shift."

Ari glanced at the deep shadows under his eyes. "You sure? You still look pretty tired."

The boy nodded. "I couldn't sleep any more. But you look wrecked. You should crash."

"Thanks." He clapped Derrick on the shoulder and went over to where the women were making up pallets for the night. They'd gathered couch cushions from the other offices that occupied the top floor, but there was little to cover up with. Most of their supplies had been abandoned on the ground floor before they began their climb to the roof.

"Go ahead and take the couch," Deb said.

Ari glanced at the furniture then back at the nest on the floor they were creating. He didn't want to lie alone on the couch even if it might be more comfortable. Without a word, he dragged the cushions from the couch and stretched out beside Lila.

Ari stared at the ceiling as the last of the light drained from the room and then closed his eyes against the pervading blackness. He felt Lila's hand curl around his, their fingers entwined, a barrier against hopelessness and fear. At last, he relaxed and slept.

CHAPTER SEVENTEEN

Streeter hadn't lied. The waterfront was swarming with zombies. The band of survivors had stopped several blocks away from the marina to check out the situation. They were on the second floor of a building, above what appeared to be a family-owned deli, peering out the windows at the 79th Street Boat Basin; close enough to smell the river, hear the cries of the circling gulls and see the undead attacking those who attempted to reach the boats.

Lila watched zombies rove and feed for only a few moments before handing the binoculars back to Ari. Her empty stomach rolled at the thought of running a gauntlet past all those creatures. "How are we going to get through?"

"Very carefully," he said dryly, taking the glasses from her and putting them to his eyes.

"Maybe a distraction," Derrick suggested. "Pick which boat we're heading for then draw them away from it with an explosion or something."

Ari lowered the binocs and nodded. "That's not bad. It might buy a little time, but whatever boat we go for is going to have to start—probably without keys. Like I said, I've hotwired cars a time or two, but never a boat. I'm not positive it'll work the same."

"I grew up on the water," Julie said. "Our family spent every summer on Christie Lake. I know boats and how to pull-start an engine if the electric starter breaks."

"That's fantastic!" Ari's relief was evident. Lila knew he'd been sweating his ability to get a boat running.

"But pull-starting only works on smaller engines," Julie

continued. "You have to take the cover off and disconnect the wiring harness before you can do it. If we go for a bigger boat, it's more like a car and we'd have to hotwire the starter. An older boat would be better. Because newer engines are computerized, they might be trickier."

"How would you do it?" Ari asked.

"Pull off the key switch. The wires are located behind it. You have to be careful to connect the right ones. Every manufacturer has different color codes. Connect the positive and negative and touch to the starter wire."

"Did you boost a boat before, baby?" Deb said. "I didn't know you were so gangsta."

Julie smiled. "My high school boyfriend took me out on his family's boat a lot. Once we got stranded when the engine wouldn't turn over and I watched him jump it that way."

"Why didn't you tell me this before?" Ari asked.

"You seemed to know what you were doing. I didn't realize you were bluffing."

"Well, look at you. Not so useless after all," Lila commented, carrying on her and Julie's running joke about their relative value to the group. They'd teased each other all the way to the waterfront—every time one of them had evaded or outrun a zombie. The journey had been dangerous but they'd managed to avoid any more hand-to-hand death matches with the creatures. They could move a lot faster and more stealthily with only five of them. But Lila guessed they weren't going to make it to a boat so easily.

Julie shot Lila a look and chalked up an imaginary tally mark in the air before turning her attention to the marina. She took Ari's binoculars and scanned the moored boats. "You see the Bayliner, that one in the slip next to the sleek Monterey Cruiser? That's what we should go for. It looks like an early 90's model so nothing computerized. Won't be too fast, but we don't need speed. We just need something trustworthy we can start."

"All right." Ari paused and closed his eyes for a moment,

rubbing his forehead. "So we need a distraction or two. We can make some Molotovs easily enough with bottles from the deli and siphoning gas from the cars. Also we could set a car on fire, put a weight on the accelerator and head it toward the marina."

Lila wondered if the zombies would be attracted by loud explosions and fire or if they only responded to the smell of blood and the sight of fresh victims.

"Hey," she said, "what if we could draw them with chum, like in *Jaws*. Smells seem to attract the creatures and, of course, running people. We could drench a mannequin in gore and attach it to the front of that moving car." She tossed off the first idea to dart through her mind.

"And put explosives in the car so when they come near it blows up in their goddamn faces," Derrick added excitedly.

It would certainly be a distraction.

"I appreciate your enthusiasm," Ari said, "but we don't have any explosives or a way to detonate long distance. I don't know how to rig a car bomb with the materials we have so I think we should keep it simple."

Lila felt like she'd been downing No Doze with Mountain Dew she was so wired. They were nearly to their goal but the zombies were an impenetrable wall blocking their way. She followed the others down to the deli where they opened and emptied bottles of soda, setting the bottles upside down to dry completely before they put gasoline in them.

Ari showed them how to twist strips of rag to act as a fuse. "These things are dangerous as hell," he warned. "They'll easily go off right in your hand, so when you light one, you'd better be ready to throw it immediately."

While the bottles dried, Ari and Derrick went to siphon gas into five gallon buckets that had once held pickles according to their labels. Deb and Julie were in charge of finding a mannequin to act as bait. They'd discussed tying a human corpse to the front of the car to add to the olfactory factor, but a mannequin would be more erect and manageable and probably look more alive than a boneless corpse. Besides, most bodies that weren't completely decimated were out there walking around.

Lila stayed in the deli to make chum stew. She tied a handkerchief over her nose and mouth as she poked through the freezer full of spoiling meat. "Never thought I'd wish for fresh blood," she muttered, as she took out chops and bacon and all the ground beef she could find. She had her doubts about the idea of ground up animal meat drawing them. But having the mannequin move was the key. She hoped their enemy wasn't smart enough to tell the difference between living and dead as long as their quarry was moving.

The women returned with a long-limbed mannequin—copper colored, faceless and wearing a Dolce and Gabana knockoff.

"Sorry," Deb apologized. "They didn't have any with realistic features, and we weren't about to go shopping for one."

"It'll work, if it's the movement and scent that attracts them," Lila said.

Derrick and Ari returned, arm muscles straining from the weight of the buckets they carried. And even now, facing an uncertain future and possible death, Lila felt a sharp tug of desire at the sight of Derrick's corded biceps and forearms and his fists gripping the bucket handles. She remembered how those hands had felt on her body last night, and more importantly, the emotions being with him had aroused in her—warmth, connection, a deep bond.

Please God, help us through this, she prayed. *I'm not ready to die. Please give us more time together first.* Years would be great, but she'd settle for days the way things were now.

With a deli full of food at their disposal, some of which was edible, none of them had any appetite as they prepared for their bait and switch maneuver. Maybe the smell of the rotten meat had something to do with that.

Lila and Julie carefully poured gasoline into the bottles, filling them halfway, inserting the alcohol-soaked fabric twists and fastening the caps on with duct tape.

Outside, Ari chose a car and the other three prepared it by fastening the dummy to the grill and putting gasoline soaked rags in the seats. They wanted it to burn not explode—at least not until the vehicle had driven closer to the marina.

Lila coated the dummy with bait. She plastered gobs of stinking meat on the stylish mannequin, quite enjoying ruining the faux designer dress. She threw the rest of the smelly chum in the back seat of the car, while Ari added some human blood to the figurine. Lila winced at the application of guts and goo that had once been part of a living person. How quickly they'd all become immune to the horror. She reflected on the one good insight to come from this event. It was now easy for her to see that a body was merely a meat puppet, quite separate from the spark of life, the soul, inhabiting it. She'd believed that before, but now felt she actually *knew* it deep inside.

After preparing the car, they went back inside the deli for a final conference.

"Not all of them are going to run and check this thing out," Ari warned. "We have to be prepared to fight. Check your weapons and make sure you have more clips ready."

They went over everything, making certain they had working lighters and reviewing the timing for using the bombs and the route they would take to reach the boat. When there was nothing else to discuss, no more preparations to be made, and the moment to act was upon them, everyone fell silent.

"I just want to say, it's been a pleasure knowing all of you," Julie began.

But Ari cut her off. "Don't. No speeches or goodbyes. We're going to do this thing and then drive away on that boat. That's it. So let's go." He picked up his backpack and strode from the room without a glance at Lila.

The sight of his back turned on her as he walked away hurt a little, but she totally understood his point. There was no room for doubt right now. They had to convince themselves they'd succeed. Sentiment, however heartfelt, would only detract from their focus.

Lila scooped her own bag from the ground, the incendiary bottles clicking together. She was nervous about lighting one of them and tried not to picture the thing blowing up in her face.

The marina was a massive grid of slips with moored boats ranging from two-man runabouts to fully equipped yachts. The larger, more expensive boats were docked in a high rent section of the marina, while the one they'd chosen was in the "cheap seats" closer to land along with other mid-priced craft. The plan was to attract the zombies to the far side of the marina and hopefully slip past them unnoticed. Ari was responsible for getting the car going on its course. Lila and Deb would throw the homemade bombs, and Derrick and Julie would run for the boat and get it started.

"How's your pitching arm?" Deb asked, hefting one of the bottles in her hand.

"Norwalk Girls' Softball for eight years," Lila said. "Unfortunately, I wasn't a pitcher. But today I'm so hopped up I think I'll be able to throw about a mile."

They trotted to a truck and crouched behind it, waiting for Ari's signal. It came in the form of a car engine turning over. He would steer the car as close as he dared, then bail.

Lila peeked around the edge of the truck to watch both zombies and seagulls swooping and devouring interesting tidbits from the docks or the decks of boats. It seemed the zombies preferred fresh game but would scavenge on dead meat when necessary. Again, Lila wondered what happened to them when all forms of sustenance ran out. Would their nervous systems continue to activate their bodies or without fuel would they eventually run down like windup toys?

She glanced at the car coming slowly up the street, driving around abandoned vehicles and over smaller obstacles. The mannequin strapped to the hood didn't look much like a real person but perhaps enough to fool zombies. Lila's gaze swung back to the revenants. Some responded to the sound of the car engine, heads snapping up from their food and swiveling toward the noise. When the vehicle came into view, several began to run toward it. Soon nearly every zombie within her sight rushed to join them. The creatures seemed to have a herd mentality.

The car passed out of Lila's view behind a building. She pictured Ari lighting the rags, putting the brick on the gas pedal, jumping from the car, rolling across the pavement and scrambling to his feet. This was a critical moment. Some of the zombies would see and chase him. She and Deb must distract them with the bombs, giving him time to get away.

"Go!" Deb ordered Derrick and Julie, but the pair was already on the move, racing from this first hideout point to the next. They'd visually mapped their way all the way to the boat. Deb lit and hurled the first of her bombs. It sailed over the stalled vehicles to land with a crash on the pavement. The shatter of glass was followed immediately by a small yellow fireball that lit the area.

Lila's hand was moist against the slick surface of a glass bottle. She clicked her lighter twice before flame bloomed. With trembling hand, she set the flame against the wick. The fabric caught immediately and began burning its way toward the bottle. She drew back her arm and launched the bomb with all her might, aiming for the huge target of an abandoned Hummer. She wished it was as easy as in the movies, where simply hitting a vehicle magically made it explode, but in real life it wasn't that easy to make a gas tank ignite. The bottle crashed against the Hummer and blew up.

As she pulled another bottle from her pack, Lila checked on Derrick and Julie. They were yards away, crouching behind a kiosk to rest before starting the next leg of their run. The way to the boat was rapidly clearing as the zombies migrated away. But they would return just as quickly if any of them sighted Derrick and Julie. Lila lit another fuse and threw another bomb, back behind them this time. It hit a wall and exploded with a satisfying crash.

Deb threw another, too, then tugged on Lila's arm. "We should go now."

They'd discussed this ahead of time. Ari would circle in the other direction to meet them on the docks, but Lila had a horrible feeling they were leaving him behind as she raced after Deb toward a bait and tackle shop. The bottles in her bag clinked together and she feared they'd break, dousing her backpack and clothes in gasoline.

She and Deb reached the wall of the shop and pressed flat against it, panting. The new hiding place afforded her a better view of the entire marina and also the flaming car with the gore-streaked mannequin strapped to the front like a sick hunting trophy. With its weighted accelerator, the car was gaining speed despite bumping over obstacles. It careened down the street toward the docks. Ari had aimed it for a stretch free of other vehicles, but the sedan soon veered off course and crashed into a building.

From all directions, zombies raced toward the burning car. The first undead reached the mannequin and pawed at it. Finding it wasn't human, their interest evaporated. Instead they opened the car doors and rummaged inside, checking out the rest of the meat Lila had thrown there. At least one's hair caught on fire, but he continued to burrow among the burning rags for tidbits.

Others raced past the car, heading for something else. Lila guessed they'd spotted Ari. She lit another Molotov cocktail and hurled it with all her strength into the midst of the running zombies. When the glass broke, the fire hit the gas vapor and the thing exploded. The fireball caught the hair and clothing of some of the zombies and set them alight. They raced on as if unaware of their flaming bodies.

"We need another distraction," Deb said after she'd thrown two more bombs in different directions.

"A big explosion," Lila agreed and a cartoon light bulb went off in her head. The idea was so simple one of them should've thought of it before. "Why not a car? Put a wick into the gas tank and set it on fire just like the bottles."

"Then run like hell. Sounds good. Let's do it." Deb took immediate action, finding a vehicle with a gas tank cover that didn't require a key to open it. She pulled the fuses from the rest of her bottles and tied them together. Lila tied a weight on the end of the strand and threaded the wick down into the gas tank. When she thought it had reached fuel, she held the wick to the side and loosely fastened the cap back on, then exchanged a look with Deb.

Deb flipped open her lighter.

A quick glance told Lila that Derrick and Julie had almost made the boat. There were still no zombies in their immediate vicinity. The distraction tactics had worked so far. She turned her attention back to Deb in time to see the fuse catch fire and start sizzling down its length toward the car.

The women ran, darting behind the building and across open ground to the next spot they'd chosen for cover. They crouched and waited for a thunderous explosion. Nothing happened. Maybe the wick had burned out or the enclosed space had stifled the flame before it could ignite gas fumes.

Lila turned her attention to the docks, only yards away now. Derrick and Julie had boarded the boat and were crouched beside the dashboard. Lila could just see the tops of their heads. They were well hidden. Safe. She grabbed Deb's arm, holding her back and whispered, "Maybe we should wait a few moments and give them a chance to do their work. If we're spotted running, we might attention to them before they're ready to go. Besides, Ari needs to catch up."

Deb nodded and hunkered back down to wait. A second later an explosion shook the ground, trembling through their bodies. The bang was followed by a whooshing noise, a yellow glow in the air, and a warm rush of air as the blast spread outward from its epicenter. Shrapnel rained down from above like pellets of hail peppering Lila's body. She ducked her head, pulling herself into a small ball.

Good thing we were sheltered by this building, she thought. She looked at Deb to congratulate her on the success of their bombing. Deb was hunched over like she was...and there was a piece of jagged metal protruding from her back near her shoulder.

For a moment, Lila stared at the offensive object, trying to make sense of it.

Deb raised her head, her expression confused "What?" She reached over her shoulder.

"Don't!" Lila stopped her with a hand on her wrist. "You've got something embedded in your back, but maybe we shouldn't pull it out." She envisioned a gush of blood, a punctured lung, and Deb wheezing for her last breath right here on the ground.

The other woman's eyes widened, and she winced as shock wore off and pain set in. "Ow, fuck! It hurts. Do something. Get it out." She turned her back so Lila could operate.

The metal had torn through Deb's jacket and shirt. Lila gently tore the fabric away so she could see how bad it was. The shard was deeply embedded in the flesh to the right of Deb's shoulder blade. Could it be piercing her lung? Lila had no idea how much of the chest lungs occupied.

"Just pull it." Deb begged. "It can't stay in there. We've got to run for the boat

Lila reached out a trembling hand to take hold of the long shard of shrapnel. She moved it a little and blood oozed from the wound. She needed something to bandage the wound with and searched in her backpack for more of the fabric they'd used to make the fuses. There wasn't any, so she took one of the alcohol-drenched wicks and pulled it from its bottle of gasoline.

"Okay, I'm going to pull it out on the count of three and stuff this rag in the wound. It'll sting so bite down on something if you think you're going to cry out."

Lila took a deep breath and let it out slowly. She held the cloth that reeked of gas close to the wound and took hold of the metal with her other hand. "One. Two. Three..."

CHAPTER EIGHTEEN

It was a lot more difficult than Ari had estimated to set the brick weight on the pedal and dive from the moving vehicle before it picked up too much speed. He landed on the sidewalk with a jolt that sent a sharp pain through his shoulder and drove the breath from his body. But there was no time to recover. The zombies would be on him like flies on meat. He rolled to defuse the impact and pushed up from the sidewalk, staggering to his feet.

A glance at the car told him it was already careening off course, heading toward the wall of a building. But the same glance also informed him the zombies were running toward it—and toward him. Behind him, he heard the crash and pop of the bottle bombs going off. Lila and Deb were hard at work trying to create a distraction for him.

He ducked into the first open doorway he could find, a fish market that advertised the fresh catch of the day in the window. Unfortunately, the fish in the unrefrigerated display cases were days past fresh now. The store reeked almost worse than the odor of decaying bodies pervading the city. Ari ran through the shop and out the back door. His plan was to run a parallel course to the one the rest of the group was taking. When he reached the marina, he'd cut across to the boat. If all their diversionary tactics worked, the revenants' attention would be focused further inland, away from the docks.

There was an alley behind the fish shop and the rest of the row of buildings. He followed the narrow passage, jogging steadily, but holding back some speed in case he needed to sprint later. He paused at the corner of the last building in the row and peered around the corner. His view of the waterfront was limited by the angle, but the docks definitely looked emptier than they had earlier.

Pressing his body close to the wall, he eased around the edge and started toward the front of the building. Now he could see hordes of the undead streaming toward the car he'd abandoned. Whether it was the movement or the mannequin that had caught their attention, they were eager to check it out. Even from a distance, he could smell the burning oil rags, which he'd set fire to before he'd abandoned the car. They had burst easily into flame and he hoped they'd somehow make the entire car explode in the zombies' faces like Derrick had wished.

Ari couldn't see the rest of his group from where he was and prayed they were making their way to the boat as planned. Lila's eyes, squinting as she laughed, flashed in his mind and he wished he'd given her a proper goodbye with a good, long kiss, instead of being such a hard ass.

Suddenly, a bottle arched through the air, the glass catching the sunlight and his attention. The bottle shattered on the ground and a satisfying fireball rose from it. He mentally cheered Lila or Deb as some of the zombies ran to investigate the new distraction.

Ari retreated from the corner of the building, back in the direction from which he'd come. He needed a moment to plot out the rest of his course, cover to cover, all the way to the boat. The sunlight shone on the gray waves as he looked beyond the marina to open water. Soon they'd be out there, heading down the Hudson to freedom—or whatever passed for freedom these days. Visions of refugee camps and soldiers destroying zombies danced in his mind like sugar plums, but the mainland might not offer any more safety than what they'd found here in the city.

A flicker of movement in the corner of Ari's gaze snapped his head to the left. A zombie as silent and deadly as a stalking mountain lion was slinking toward him. Its eyes were flat and dead, but its mouth gaped wide and hungry. Blood stained the man's face and clothing, a coverall that made Ari think of Hector for a moment. An appliqué that read "Crowder's Carpet Cleaning" was stitched on the pocket. These details etched themselves in his mind as he drew his knife and launched himself at the zombie. He couldn't shoot it without drawing the notice of the others so it would have to be hand-to-hand until one of them was dead. Or deader.

Ari slashed through the air, but the zombie raised an arm that deflected his blade. The knife cut through the navy coverall and into his upraised arm before the hilt was ripped from Ari's hand.

The creature clutched at him, but Ari spun away, avoiding him by inches. He knew zombies' hands were as vice-like as a pit bull's jaws once they clamped down. He didn't even want to think about what their teeth would feel like tearing through his flesh.

Ari ran toward the alley with the zombie on his heels. He preferred to kill rather than try to outrun it, but first he had to get his knife back. The hilt still protruded from the monster's upper arm, the blade deeply embedded like a carving knife standing in a Thanksgiving turkey.

On the ground in the mouth of the alley was an empty liquor bottle. Ari remembered Sergeant Vogt's advice about urban combat. "If you're disarmed, you might have to use whatever's at hand to fight with. Being creative can save your life."

He bent to retrieve the bottle, holding it by the neck and smashing off the bottom against the wall. In seconds, the zombie was on him, weaponless but plenty lethal with its unnatural strength and gnashing teeth. Ari slashed at the thing's eyes but missed, slicing jaggedly down its cheek instead.

Repairman Zombie grabbed Ari and drew him into a tight embrace. Ari wrapped his arms around the creature as if to return a friendly hug, and plucked his knife from the zombie's arm. But having the knife in his hand didn't make it easy to cut the back of the monster's neck. He was too close, the zombie's reeking, rotted-meat breath blowing into his face, the empty eyes staring dead-on into his.

Ari sawed at the side of the creature's neck with the broken bottle with one hand, then stabbed the knife into its upper spine with the other. He missed the spine and the thing clawed at Ari's back and snapped at his face. Ari reared back to avoid its gnashing teeth, but the arms around his back were like steel bands binding him to the rotting corpse.

At a loss for how to fight the super-strength creature, he fell back on the simplest tactic he knew to get out of a clinch from his old street fighting days, a head butt. Ari slammed his forehead into the thing's nose. Pain sparkled like fireworks behind his closed eyelids, but the move served its purpose, snapping the zombie's head back. Its grip loosened just enough that Ari could squirm away from that punishing grip.

However, his knife which was still buried in the thing's back. Free of the revenant's arms, Ari darted behind his opponent and pulled the blade free. It released from the zombie's flesh with a wet, sucking sound.

The zombie started to spin around to face him, but Ari plunged his knife again, this time in the tender hollow at the base of its skull. The energy cut as abruptly as a switch being turned off and the body toppled to the ground, a discarded shell once more.

Winded and panting, Ari stood over the collapsed zombie. He scanned the area for more of the revenants. For the moment, they were all at a distance, unaware of him.

He pressed flat against the wall again, taking a moment to catch his breath and plan his next move. There was a wide open stretch between his position and another hiding spot behind a Jet Ski and watercraft shop. Then he'd have to navigate across the parking lot littered with vehicles abandoned by their owners before they'd made their desperate bid for the boats. Beyond that, he would run along the waterfront to the dock where he could just see the Bayliner he was aiming for. He wondered if any of the others had made it there yet. He couldn't see them from his position.

Ari glanced to the left, not forgetting the stealth of the zombie that had attacked him. He wouldn't be surprised again. Just then an explosion sent a shock wave rolling through the air. Ari spun back in the opposite direction, searching for its source. It wasn't the sedan he'd set on fire but another vehicle close to the ice cream shop which was one of the rest stops for the group on their way to the boat.

Ari grinned. He had no doubt either Lila or Deb, maybe both, had blown up the car. He peered around the edge of the building again to witness an orange fireball, black smoke and zombies clustering around the wreckage as if they were at a bonfire roasting weenies. The way would never be clearer than right now.

He ran for the watercraft shop, legs and arms pumping, lungs burning, and when he reached it, since the way was still clear, he didn't stop. He wove his way between the haphazard cars in the parking lot. A naked zombie woman popped from behind a pickup truck right in front of him like a pornographic jack-in-the-box, her breasts bobbing and her arms missing. Ari didn't take the time to kill her, just knocked her aside with a push that bounced her off the side of the truck like a pinball.

He reached the boardwalk and his feet pounded over wooden slats instead of asphalt. The scent of the water was almost stronger than the rotten meat on which the gulls feasted and the green trimmed Bayliner was in sight.

Ari glanced inland, checking for pursuers, and his heart dropped. Lila and Deb were running for the docks, too. Deb was obviously injured and Lila had an arm around her. Zombies were on their heels.

As Ari watched, Lila pushed Deb toward the boat and Deb lurched like a zombie herself as she staggered forward. Lila whirled to face their attackers. She took a bottle from her backpack, lit the fuse and tossed the bomb in the midst of the running zombies. Glass crashed and fumes ignited sending up a small fireball. A few zombies were engulfed in the flames, their hair or clothing catching on fire, but the rest kept coming toward Lila.

Ari ran to help her. He dodged around cars until he was close then jumped up onto a hood, grabbed the rifle strapped to his back and fired into the group of zombies. At least some of the shots cleaved the spinal cord and a few zombies dropped, their bodies tripping up the others. It was enough to slow them down a little.

But a couple of faster zombies were already on Lila. A man with a gaping chest wound seized her arm. She slung her backpack into his face and tried to jerk away, but he gripped her hard. He looked like he'd been healthy and fit when he was alive and whole. Another man wearing a charcoal gray suit and a string of entrails like a necktie took hold of Lila's other arm and lifted her hand to his mouth as if he would kiss it.

Ari sighted down the rifle, aiming for the second one's head, but Lila was too close. This was no sniper's weapon; it was meant to cut a lethal swathe, and he was no sharpshooter. He jumped off the car hood and hurtled across the ground separating him from Lila. Bending low, he plowed into the suit-wearing zombie like a linebacker, driving his shoulder into the creature's gut and pushing him backward.

The dead man seemed content to switch victims and grabbed for Ari instead of Lila. Past the thing's shoulder Ari could see many more coming. In a few seconds they'd be overrun. It was impossible for his blood to carry one more drop of adrenaline than was already scorching through his system. As if he was on industrial strength steroids, for a moment Ari was convinced he was invincible. Yelling like a madman, he pulled the knife sheathed in his belt and drove it into the cadaver's throat with all the force in his body. His arm pistoned, stabbing until the dead man slumped.

Without pause, Ari tossed the corpse aside and went for the other. The body building, chest wound zombie had Lila pinned to the ground. She was beating on his back and squirming to get out from under him as he lunged for her throat.

Ari didn't try to pull him off. Trying to break that powerful grip would be futile. Instead he sawed across the back of the thing's exposed neck with his knife, cutting through gristle and bone until the man flopped to a stop, draped over Lila like an obscene blanket. Ari hauled the body off her while Lila crab scuttled backward from underneath it.

Ari held out his hand. She seized it. And they ran, barely ahead of the rest of the pack. The creatures were right behind them. That was the problem—they weren't so impossible to kill once you knew how, but there were always more and they were as persistent as cockroaches.

The boat was near now. They'd reached the docks and were pounding toward it. But if Julie and Derrick didn't have the motor running, they'd all be trapped on board.

Ari had a death grip on Lila's hand, dragging her beside him, but he suddenly stopped and thrust her ahead of him. "You go. I'll hold 'em off."

She hesitated.

"Go!" he ordered, doing his best Sergeant Vogt impression. Without waiting to see that she obeyed, Ari spun around, took the rifle from his shoulder and peppered the approaching zombies with bullets. He sprayed back and forth as if watering a lawn with lethal chemicals. Bits of pink and red gore flew through the air like confetti.

Then his clip emptied. The gun clicked and the hailstorm of bullets stopped.

"Ari. Here!"

He turned toward Lila's voice and caught the new clip she tossed to him. He jammed it into the gun and started firing again. Stupid, brave girl hadn't run, and thank God for him she hadn't.

The revenants continued to surge toward them, only a dozen, but it was a dozen too many. Ari braced his legs and fired at their heads, scalping the faux-hawk off a once pretty girl in a once white sundress, ripping through the side of an old man's face, and hitting directly into a policeman's gaping mouth, dropping him.

"Die! Just fucking die!" he bellowed as he swung the rifle back and forth.

And then he heard the blessed sound of a motor puttering to life like a choir of angels singing. He backed down the dock, still shooting.

A second later, Derrick was beside him, also firing. Together they held off the remaining zombies, only a half dozen now, but still stupidly, relentlessly coming.

"Come on," Lila called. "We're casting off."

Ari and Derrick ran for the boat. Ari skidded on a slick of goo and started to fall. His arms pinwheeled and he nearly dropped his rifle before he caught his balance and ran on. The boards shook beneath his weight. He leaped onto the deck of the Bayliner and turned to make sure Derrick was still with him.

Derrick raced down the dock with several revenants right behind him. One tackled him and then they were all on him like a pack of hyenas. Ari jumped off the boat and ran back, firing into their midst, praying he wouldn't hit Derrick by accident.

When he got too close to shoot, Ari hit at them with the stock of the gun, bashing zombies like whack-a-moles. He wished he still had his ax, but there'd been only so many weapons he could carry. Seeing Derrick's hand beneath the pile up of zombies, he grabbed hold of it and pulled him out from under them. He hauled the kid to his feet and ran with him. This time he didn't let go of Derrick's hand until they'd reached the boat. Julie was already guiding it away from the pier. They jumped over a yard of water before hitting the deck and collapsing in a heap.

"Are you all right?" Lila dropped down beside them. "Were you bitten?"

Derrick pulled his hand away from his neck so they could see the blood gushing. It looked really bad, like maybe the zombies had hit an artery.

Lila exchanged a look with Ari. "Deb's been injured, too. Shrapnel. You take care of him, while I bandage her."

Ari nodded. "Derrick, keep pressure on the wound. I'm going to find something to bandage it with."

As he headed for the cabin, he looked at the wharf receding

behind them. The undead milled around from dock to boats and back again, searching for a way to reach them. Some even jumped into the water and began to swim after them. They looked as forlorn as Ari had felt when the helicopter had risen from the rooftop leaving them behind. *Wait. You forgot us,* their brainless zombie eyes seemed to say.

Ari ducked below deck to search for a first aid kit and towels. There were dishcloths in the galley and everything else they needed stored in cupboards near the head. He returned topside and gave some of the alcohol swabs and gauze bandage to Lila. Then he returned to Derrick, who lay on the floor, slumped against one of the seats. His eyes were closed and his face was paper white. For a moment, Ari was certain he was dead. He knelt beside him and felt for his pulse and Derrick's eyes shot open. "I don't want to die. Don't let me become one of them."

"I won't. But you're not dying. We'll fix this." Ari gently lifted the boy's hand from his neck and studied his mauled neck. The blood flow had slowed as it began to coagulate. That was a good sign. If it was an artery, it would have kept on gushing until he bled out.

"This is going to sting." He swabbed the bite with the alcohol drenched cloth and Derrick flinched and hissed.

"How do you know I'm not dying?" Derrick sounded panicked. "Maybe just their bite kills. We don't really know anything about how it works."

Ari gripped his hand. "Mrs. Scheider was old and worn out. You're young and strong. I'm sure you'll be okay." He wasn't certain at all, but projected all the confidence he could muster. Derrick needed a strong dose of assurance even more than the aspirin Ari gave him to take down the swelling of the tender flesh around the bite.

Ari placed a patch of gauze over the wound and fixed it in place with adhesive tape then he checked the rest of Derrick's neck, chest and back for more bites. His shirt was ripped and there were red scratch marks down his back, and not the fun kind a guy got from his lover. Ari swabbed them with alcohol, too.

"Let's go below. Find some clean clothes and you can lie down and rest." Ari grasped Derrick's arm and pulled him to his feet then supported him as the boat pitched beneath them. The wind was churning up choppy waves in the harbor and the gray clouds on the horizon looked ominous.

Please God, haven't we been through enough? Just let the damn weather hold off for a while. Give us a few minutes to catch our breath.

In the time they'd spent together Lila had talked about her belief in karma and how the seemingly random bad or good shit that was flung at a person wasn't God's cosmic punking, but merely what a soul had earned or needed to learn from. She'd said believing that helped put things in perspective when she had a really shitty day where everything went wrong. Well, he could use some of that belief now, because he hated to think God was simply a cruel son of a bitch who enjoyed torturing people. A collective lesson for humanity to learn from was certainly preferable to a collective ass kicking for no apparent reason.

As Julie expertly guided the boat into open water, she asked Lila for an update on Deb's condition. Lila reported the gash in Deb's back wasn't as bad as it appeared. She'd pulled out the metal and staunched the wound, and was bandaging it as Ari took Derrick below.

In the cabin, Ari settled Derrick on a bunk, covering his shivering body with a blanket and checking the bandage on his neck. There was a spot of red on the gauze so the wound was still bleeding but not nearly as badly as it might have. Ari got up to leave, but Derrick grabbed his hand, stopping him.

"Wait. Don't go. I don't want to die alone."

"Cut it out. I told you, you're not dying." Ari figured his usual impatient tone would do a lot more to convince Derrick than sudden out of character kindness. "Try to get some sleep. You need it. And look, here's Deb to keep you company."

Deb came down the steps into the cabin, leaning heavily against one wall for support. Her shirt was off and her arm and shoulder were wrapped like a mummy. Her dark face was ashen, even her lips pale.

She must have bled buckets, which might have been part of what drew the zombies to her and Lila.

"How you doing?" Ari asked.

She sank down on the other bunk. "I feel like a vampire on a lucky day." At Ari's blank look she added, "Nearly staked through the heart." Then she managed a smile. "But we made it. We really made it."

For the first time, Ari let the glow of victory swell inside him. "Yes, we did."

He spread a blanket over Deb and smoothed her braids back from her face. "You did good."

Ari bumped fists with her, but then Deb grabbed his hand and pulled him down to give him a one-armed hug. "You, too. You got us here."

Ari straightened and found Lila had followed Deb downstairs to put away the first aid kit. She and Ari bumped into each other as they moved around the small cabin. Ari found a cache of water bottles in a cupboard. Lila sat beside Derrick, bending over to talk softly to him.

After offering each of the injured patients some water, Ari went up on deck to check on their progress with Julie.

"Take over the wheel," she demanded before he even opened his mouth. "I want to see Deb."

"I've never driven a boat in my life."

"But you've driven cars. It's practically the same thing. Point and steer and don't run into anything." She abandoned him before he could protest.

Julie disappeared below deck and a moment later, Lila emerged. Bloody, bedraggled and with her greasy hair lank around her face, she was absolutely beautiful. If Ari didn't have a hard grip on the boat's steering wheel and his attention riveted on the water before them, he would have gone to her and pulled her into his arms.

She came to him instead, slipped her arms around his waist and rested her head against his back. "So Derrick's finally right. You are the captain."

"For now." He leaned back slightly, the better to feel her body pressed against him. He'd almost lost her today, and was just beginning to understand what an enormous loss that would be.

They didn't speak. There would be plenty of time later for sharing war stories about what had happened while they were apart. Right now it was a relief to be silent and finally at peace. The river flowed beneath them. The city drifted by on either side of them, barely betraying the horror show it had become. But smoke billowed from up ahead signaling a fire blazing out of control with no FDNY to put it out. In a few minutes, they passed the burning neighborhood, only a couple of buildings for now, but soon, perhaps, blocks of the city.

Lila let go of him and moved to the railing to stare at the cityscape as they floated past. When she turned back to Ari, her eyes glistened. "Nothing is ever going to be the same. I've known that, but we've been so busy simply surviving, I could avoid really realizing it until now."

Ari released the wheel and reached out a hand to her. "Come here."

She walked into his arms and he held her close, resting his chin on her head as she pressed her face against his chest.

"Go ahead and cry now if you want. You've earned it." He kissed her hair and breathed in her scent, earthy and real.

Her body trembled a little in his arms, but when she lifted her face to look up at him, her cheeks were dry. She shook her head. "No tears. I'm not ready for that yet. But I appreciate the cuddle." She held him hard, her fingers clutching his shirt in back, and lifted her face for a kiss.

He was happy to give it, inclining his head to cover her lips with his. Neither of their mouths was minty fresh, but he'd never tasted anything more delicious than that kiss. He sank into it as if falling into bed after a hard day of running an obstacle course. Lila slid a hand around the back of his neck, pulling him closer as she rose up on her toes and leaned into him.

For a few moments, they were fused together, only their clothes and skin keeping them from melting into one being. At last, Lila pulled away to draw breath. She settled back on her heels and turned in the circle of his arms to face forward.

Together they looked past the prow of the boat to the gray water stretching before them. "What happens when we leave the harbor? We have to think about where to dock on the mainland. I wonder where would be safe."

"Guess we'll have to get close to shore and take a look." He glanced at the gas gauge that indicated the tank was half full and thought about what would happen if they reached a point where they had to put in to shore whether it was safe or not. Then he took another look at the far horizon. The storm clouds that had threatened seemed to be breaking up and the sun shone through, streams of pale yellow that looked like heavenly light. Hopeful—that was what the sky looked like now.

Ari squinted as he saw something flashing on the open water in front of them. The light strobed with mechanical regularity.

"Take the wheel," he ordered Lila, and went to get the backpack which he'd managed to keep with him through everything. He pulled out his binoculars and focused on the horizon. The boat coming toward them had a coast guard flag flying.

"Shit!" he dropped the glasses on the cord around his neck and they bumped against his chest. Running to the dashboard, he searched for some way to signal back. "It's a coast guard boat," he informed Lila. "Do you see a button for a signal light?"

"Get Julie," she said, and he ran to obey, hollering for her before he reached the cabin.

"What is it?" Julie emerged from below, wide-eyed and worried.

"A coast guard boat. We need to signal it."

Julie went to a storage bin near the cabin and rummaged through it before producing a flare. She unscrewed the lid and held the flare by the handle over the railing. She pulled the tag and by the time orange smoke was billowing into the air, Deb and Derrick had come on deck, too. The acrid smell of smoke filled Ari's nose and he breathed it in like it was the sweetest bouquet as it beckoned the coast guard boat closer. All of the survivors clustered together, staring at the emerging shape of the other vessel.

"They've spotted us. They're coming for us," Derrick said, and then a hoarse sob wrenched from his chest. He broke down, his body shaking as he covered his face with his hands. Deb grabbed and held him with her uninjured arm, murmuring the soothing things people said to comfort other people. "It will be all right. Everything's okay. We're safe now." The words didn't change the truth, but there was nothing else to say.

Lila hugged Derrick from the other side, sheltering the boy between her and Deb. The flare burnt out and Julie dropped the spent canister into the water before coming to join their group hug. Ari watched all of them for a moment, these people who'd become closer than family in the brief time he'd known them, and then he moved in to put his arms around Lila and Deb.

"They're almost here. Everything's going to be all right," he added his voice to the litany of hope and lies. But even as he clung to his friends, he also clung to the belief that he was speaking the truth. Maybe they *would* be all right. Maybe order would win over chaos. Maybe someone like Carl was creating a solution even now.

And maybe the world would once again become a place where strangers on a train could share a compartment and never speak to one another or become friends. There were some perks to being burned in the crucible of a zombie attack, Ari reflected as he held his family close.

ABOUT THE AUTHOR

Bonnie Dee began telling stories as a child. Whenever there was a sleepover, she was the designated ghost tale teller, guaranteed to frighten and thrill with macabre stories. She still has a story printed in second grade on yellow legal paper about a ghost, a witch and a talking cat. Writing childish stories later led to majoring in English at college. Like most English majors, she dreamed of writing a novel, but didn't have the necessary focus and follow through at that time in her life. It was only in 2000 that she began writing again and became a multi-published erotic romance author. You may see her backlist of books at http://bonniedee.com. Join her Yahoo group for updates on new releases at http://groups.yahoo.com/group/bonniedee/. Bonnie Dee is also on Facebook and Twitter.

Made in the USA
Lexington, KY
22 July 2011